Silver M

HAVE A
OF 59 G~~~~~~~~~~
OF
EROTIC DOMINATION

If you like one you will probably like the rest

A NEW TITLE EVERY MONTH
NOW INCLUDING EXTRA BONUS PAGES

Silver Moon Readers Service
c/o DS Sales Ltd.
PO Box 1100 London N21 2WQ

Silver Moon Books Inc
PO Box 1614 New York NY 10156

*Distributed to the trade throughout North America by
LPC Group, 1436 West Randolph Street, Chicago, IL 60607
(800) 826-4330*

If you like one of our books you will probably like them all!

Write for our free 20 page booklet of extracts from early books
- surely the most erotic feebie yet - and, if you wish to be on
our confidential mailing list, from forthcoming monthly titles
as they are published:-

Silver Moon Reader Services

c/o DS Sales Ltd.
PO Box 1100 London N21 2WQ

or leave details on our 24hr UK answerphone
0181 245 0985
International acces code then +44 181 245 0985

<u>New authors welcome</u>
Please send submissions to
PO Box 5663
Nottingham
NG3 6PJ

www.silvermoon.co.uk
www.silvermoonbooks.com

SLAVES FOR THE SHEIK
by
ALLAN ALDISS

AUTHOR'S NOTE

Several years ago, a European magazine published several articles, complete with photographs, describing a harem of pretty young blond European women, belonging to a wealthy Sheik. They were mainly Dutch or Austrian.

The article, apparently quite genuine, was written by a well known Arab lady journalist who had managed to trick her way inside the harem. She had been able to talk briefly to some of the the women, including an attractive mother and teenage daughter. She also been able, secretly, to photograph them in their harem clothes together with the stern looking, black eunuch who was in charge of them.

The photographs showed them relaxing in the harem under his supervision and being proudly paraded by him, a long whippy cane in his hand, in front of a screen in the wall, behind which their hidden Master was sitting.

To her surprise the young European women all came from very respectable backgrounds. They were now virtually slaves, kept in the harem, and used by their Master, against their will and allowed no contact with the outside world.

How, she wondered, had these well educated young women ended up in this harem?

How indeed! This story provides some possible answers.

Readers should, however, remember that in the Middle East the position of women, and the way they are treated, has traditionally been, and still is, very different from that of Western women. What may seem shocking and cruel to Western eyes, may be viewed very differently there. There, men are enjoined that 'Women have been put into the world for the enjoyment of men, go ye therefore and enjoy them'

SLAVES FOR THE SHEIK

CONTENTS

1 - 1 A DISCREET INSPECTION

The handsome and energetic young Sheik Ali bin Faisal al Tufaya was looking very pleased.

The renovation of his new luxurious palace in North Africa, with its high security harem, had been completed. His concubines and their supervising black eunuchs had been flown in from his old palace in Shadek, in Arabia.

Yes, everything would soon be ready for him to start his Great Plan : the gradual replacement of his Arab concubines with carefully chosen, and discreetly entrapped, well educated, upper class English women.

Smiling, he looked down into the harem from behind a screen in a beautifully carved balcony.

Below him a dozen beautiful young olivia skinned women were relaxing around a prettily curved, oval shaped pool. Surrounding the pool were high marble pillars behind which was a shiny marble floored colonnade.

In the centre of the pool a fountain was playing and some of the girls were running in and out of its falling jets, laughing like excited little girls as they did so. They were naked except for a coloured ribbon tied to their gleaming metal collars.

He smiled as he saw that whilst some of the girls were swimming round the pool, several others were standing up in the shallow end and calling out childishly as they excitedly threw a large rubber ball to each other - a game that was encouraged by the carefully watching Zalu, his chief black eunuch. Like swimming, it helped to firm up their bare breasts.

He smiled again at the sight of his tattooed crest neatly emblazoned across their bellies, and below it, equally neatly tattooed onto their smooth and hairless mounds, was their registered number as an indentured servant.

How satisfactory it would be to see the soft white bellies and mounds of his future English concubines similarly marked.

Reclining on the smooth, shiny pink, marble colonnade around the pool lay several other young women, chatting to each other excitedly, like children on an outing.

These ones were still dressed - all identically and scantily clad in wide silken, transparent, harem pantaloons of different colours that were cut away in front to display their childlike, smooth and hairless beauty lips and mounds - and, above these, his prettily coloured crest.

Over their shoulders they wore stiff embroidered boleros, of the same colour as their pantaloons, which left their painted nipples bare. On their heads were little embroidered caps also of the same colour, as were their pointed Turkish slippers.

The Sheik smiled as he saw that each girl was thus either dressed entirely in a different colour or, if naked in the pool, had a different coloured ribbon tied to her collar. Each girl was called by her colour - a clever idea of Zalu's, to save the Master from having to bother to remember his women's individual names. Sheik Ali looked approvingly at the large and carefully polished brass rings that hung from most of their noses, round their mouths and down to their chins. This was the sign of having, dutifully and humbly, several times received his seed in each of their three orifices, whilst giving him proper pleasure. Only then could a girl be accepted as an Approved Junior Concubine, the first step up the harem hierarchy.

The large rings gave them an appropriately slave-like, and indeed an almost animal-like, appearance. Normally one might have assumed a girl would be horrified at being so degradingly ringed. However, here in the unnatural atmosphere of the harem, it was a much prized sign of having won their handsome young Master's approval.

The rings were a sign of proven subservience, a feeling that was enhanced for each girl by her chromium plated collar. These were made of a flexible interlocking mesh, like that of a metal watch strap, and were locked at the back of the neck. They came high up under their chins, giving the necks a swan-like appearance.

The Sheik's crest and the girls' registered number as an

indentured servant were engraved on the sides of the ring, and at the back and front was a ring for attaching a lead. All this played an important role in making the women feel that they were each his private property.

The Sheik laughed again, however, as he saw the miniature battery holder on the back of each collar, which enabled the collars also to play another quite different, and yet very important, role in the harem.

He looked at the gold and silver bands that decorated the women's long dark hair that hung down their olivia skinned backs. How much more delightful it would be, he sighed, when much of the hair was blond - and the skin was a pure white, carefully kept that way by Zalu never allowing it to be exposed to the sun or the elements. Ah well, that time would soon be coming... Air conditioning in summer, and central heating in winter, would enable a steady warm temperature to be maintained throughout the year. This was just as well, for when not swimming and playing naked in the pool, the women were still kept scantily and provocatively dressed.

The young women, both in the pool and lying at its side, kept coquettishly, and yet nervously, flashing their dark eyes up at the screen behind which he was sitting - uncertain as to whether their handsome young Master was there, watching them. They had nearly all been acquired for him by Zalu and none of them knew their Master's full name, though, not surprisingly, numerous inaccurate rumours about his identity would circulate round the harem - much to his amusement.

For them he was just the Master, their rich and powerful Master who protected them from the cares and worries of the outside world - a world from which they were now isolated, for no distracting outside television, radios, or newspapers were allowed in the harem. Their whole world was centred solely on their Master.

Their only glimpse of this outside world would, the young Sheik knew, be through the bars of the cage on the roof of the harem, when they were taken up there by the black eunuchs, each evening, for their daily airing. However, even then all that they could see, over the high walls that surrounded the harem garden, was a distant view of an empty sea, and of mountains and desert.

They would also be able to see down into the well kept harem garden but not into the walled park that surrounded the palace, and certainly not the gardeners or any visitors. The black eunuchs made sure that the women did not even get a distant sight of anything male, only taking the women up onto the roof after they had carefully checked that nothing male was about - not even a dog!

Shouting: 'Keep eyes down! A man! A man!' and cracking their whips, they would hustle the disappointed women down off the roof if there was ever the slightest risk of them getting an inadvertent, if only momentary, glimpse of another man.

Indeed, none of the women had seen another man since they entered their Master's harem. Zalu had even taken special precautions that they did see any during their closely supervised flight from Shadek to what for them was still an unknown place.

Zalu also made sure that they never saw photographs of other men - especially pop stars, or film stars, over whom they might moon or fantasise. Their fantasies had to centre on their Master and no one else!

Neither had they heard a another man's voice other their Master's and the high pitched cries of the black eunuchs. The only recordings allowed in the harem were of women.

The Sheik liked Zalu to keep his women's minds like those of little girls, even though they had the bodies of lovely women - and traditionally the harem system had, of course, always encouraged this. Zalu made sure that they only read children's picture books and magazines. Similarly the only videos they were allowed to see were innocent cartoons at which they would laugh like happy little girls.

Soon. the young Sheik reflected, the eyes glancing hesitatingly up at the screen would be blue, green or grey. He smiled at the thought of well educated Englishwomen, used to freedom and independence, soon also being subjected this strict and degrading regime. Sheik Ali noticed that the women in the pool

11

kept nervously glancing at two hugely fat pot bellied black eunuchs, who were walking up and down the sides of the pool, carefully watching the women in their charge. They were wearing huge white Turkish style trousers, red waistcoats and distinctive white hats made of silk like a brimless top hat, but wider at the top than at the bottom, like a flower pot.

Tucked into the silk cummerbunds round their voluminous waists were short handled whips, each with a long curled-up leather leash - the sort used to crack when training animals.

One of them was holding a long carriage whip with which he could reach the women even in the centre of the pool.

The other held a large man size landing net on a long pole. Just as in a fish restaurant a man might chose his dinner from amongst the fish swimming in a tank, so here in the harem, the Master might choose a woman whose hanging breasts and hairless beauty lips had been caught, as she swam, by the hidden underwater television cameras and displayed on two large screens to the watching Master.

He might them for instance, press a button marked 'Scarlet' and this second black eunuch, glancing at his electronic pager, would use his long net to catch and land the chosen girl. The net was also, of course, used to bring in, for punishment, any girl detected misbehaving, either with herself or with another girl, by the watching black eunuchs or by the secret underwater television cameras.

Indeed Sheik Ali, kept glancing down at the television monitors that were connected to the hidden cameras at the bottom of the pool. They showed the same scene as he was looking down at, but from underneath: the young women's long legs; their exposed and hairless beauty lips; their remarkably full breasts, and prominent, and often ringed nipples, which hung down prettily as they swam; their pouting little bellies, each decoratively tattooed with his crest and a harem number; and their beauty lips each decorated with a line of golden rings.

Through the rings were threaded leather laces, like the laces of a shoe, keeping each girl's beauty lips tightly compressed and preventing her from touching her throbbing beauty bud. A tiny padlock, the keys to which were held by the black eunuchs, prevented the laces from being loosened. Each girl was responsible for keeping her laces well polished.

The cameras also showed the girls' hands constantly reaching down to their own, or their companions' frustrated beauty buds, but then darting back in despair at not being able to touch them and in fear of being seen by the watching black eunuchs.

The young Sheik smiled as he saw that in two cases the crest and numbers seemed prettily distended - signs of a forced motherhood that had been carefully arranged by Zalu.

He smiled again as he saw how the girls' breasts were firmer and swelling up for their future new role as two of his milkmaids. Zalu had already had their nipples elongated and was 'steaming them up', just as heifers were specially fed when they were first in calf, to ensure a good yield during their first lactations.

He also nodded approvingly as he saw that in both cases a shiny chain mail maternity, or breeding, belt had been locked round the girls' waists and down over their beauty lips, making it impossible for them to harm the little black progeny growing inside them.

Of course, the girls natural maternal instincts often ensured that they came to accept being in an expectant state, especially as, every day, they were brought to parade their growing bellies proudly before their half beloved and half hated Master. Nevertheless, precautions had to be taken lest they be tempted to interfere with what had been planned for them.

Sheik Ali's manhood stirred as he took in the erotic scenes below the water's edge shown on the television monitors - and as he looked down, through the wooden screen, at the equally erotic scene above the water's edge.

Oh yes, he thought, as he wondered which girls to have brought to his bed for his siesta, how much more exciting it would be when the choice would be between haughty, but now well disciplined, blond English women, each secretly crying out for her lost husband, lover or boy friend. Beyond the pool, on one

13

side, were large sliding glass doors, covered in strong iron bars, though which could be seen a pretty garden.

Little gravel paths, well roofed against the sun, wound their way round the little garden. Here Zalu could send the women to get some fresh air and exercise in the cool of the early evening, as an alternative to the cage on the roof. They would, of course, still be under the ceaselessly watching eyes of discreetly placed television cameras, and of a black eunuch in a raised rostrum. With the sun almost setting, there would also be no risk of the even the most delicate of white skins getting even a hint of an unwanted tan.

Beyond the garden rose a wall, smooth sided and some some forty feet high, with an electrified fence running along the top. Although this was nominally to keep prying eyes from seeing the Sheik's women, it also served to keep the women in.

As well as Zalu and his assistant black eunuchs, Sheik Ali had brought his own devoted guards from Shadek to man the palace gates and to watch the high walls, a task made much easier by the strategically placed television cameras.

Yes, indeed, everything was now ready for him to start implementing his Great Plan. Both his yacht and his jet plane would be playing an essential part in his role as a modern Barbary Corsair, capturing innocent Christian women for his harem.

But there was one big difference. Whereas the Barbary Corsairs had mainly carried off relatively uneducated women from the southern European coasts and islands of the Mediterranean, he would be carrying off well educated, and often upper class, Englishwomen.

The preparations had been long and complex. He reviewed them in his mind one last time...

1 - 2 THE TWINS CALLED CRIMSON

Sheik Ali trained the underwater camera past the sight of long legs, of tightly laced-up beauty and of tattooed bellies to focus on the two girls with prettily swollen tummies.

In some ways these young girls were the forerunners of the Sheiks's new concept of a harem of Englishwomen for, although they were, nominally, merely despised Christian Arab girls from the Lebanon, they were in fact half English.

The bodies of the two young girls were strangely alike and they were loosely chained together by the neck. Their collars were both marked with ribbons of the same colour: crimson.

They were indeed identical twins and Zalu had persuaded his young Master that it would be interesting and amusing for him to make both girls answer to the same harem name of 'Crimson' and to keep them both chained together.

"It would be, Your Highness," Zalu had said, "as if they were one girl, but with two bodies for you to enjoy."

They had to eat together, sleep together, perform their natural functions together under the eye of a watchful eunuch and be trained by them to perform together in their Master's bed.

Zalu had even used his special pills, that delayed or brought on a woman's coming into season, to ensure that their monthly cycles were kept exactly in step.

Their father had been a rich Lebanese businessman and their mother English. They were being educated at an English school in Beirut - until it was bombed during the civil war.

The same raids had killed their parents and near relations, and destroyed their father's business, leaving them suddenly destitute.

They had fallen, unwittingly, into the hands of a certain white slaver, called Achmud, who ran what was outwardly a refugee camp for young women. He had invited Zalu to come, in the guise of a doctor, to inspect the interesting new goods he now had on offer, and in particular to verify their virginity.

Twins are regarded as a highly erotic commodity in a harem and one that is much sought after. Not surprisingly, therefore, Zalu had reported by phone very favourably, to his young Master, about the immediate acquisition of such a rare item: a pair of very pretty twin Christian girls.

The Sheik had authorised him to purchase them - unknown to the girls themselves.

Indeed, thinking that they were being rescued from the horrors of war-torn Beirut, the twins had been only too eager to sign what in fact were Articles of Indenture for an indefinite period. Slavery might now have been officially abolished in Arabia but, unknown to them, these Articles effectively made them as much the Sheik's slaves as the slave girls bought by his ancestors for their harems in the slave market.

Eagerly the twins had boarded the Sheik's waiting private jet, where congratulatory, but drugged, glasses of Champagne had awaited them.

Horrified, they woke up to find themselves safely ensconced in the harem of the Sheik, chained together by the neck and with the Sheik's crest of two green crossed scimitars, with a black star above where they crossed, already neatly tattooed onto their soft white bellies together with, in Arabic numerals, registered numbers as indentured servants.

They were lucky they learned that in this harem this number, and their owner's crest, was only tattooed onto their bellies and not branded on as was still the custom in many harems. Either way the effect was to make a girl feel that she now belonged utterly to her Master, just like his branded camels or horses.

However the girls had been shocked when Zalu told them that there was a second reason for this custom: it put up the value of a girl should her Master later decide to sell her off or to give her away to a grateful henchman.

They had also been shocked to find that their mounds and beauty lips had been completely depilated and even more when they saw the neat line of rings in each beauty lips and the polished laces that, with the little padlock that hung down between their legs, kept the lips tightly closed.

"You not now able to play with yourselves or each other," Zalu had told them with a grim smile. "You now kept only for Master."

Like the other women in the harem they did not even know where they were nor the identity of their young Master. They soon learned, however, that they must always call him 'Your Highness' and speak about him as 'The Master', or they'd get a thrashing from Zalu - six strokes on each of their bare bottoms! The Sheik laughed to himself as he remembered taking the virginity of each of these delightful young half English concubines.

He had been delighted when he found that Zalu had arranged for them to be chained down on his bedside, on their backs with their tattooed bellies nicely raised, the laces over their beauty lips eased, and the lips themselves discreetly oiled for ease of penetration.

They had been gagged lest their angry screams of protest might put their Master off his stroke. Zalu had even had their hands fastened to the bed posts above their heads to prevent them from scratching their Master, whilst their parted ankles were strapped down to prevent them from kicking.

Held helpless, they had had to submit to the lust of their virile young Master, one after the other, their eyes on stalks above their gags.

Oh, how they had hated him!

It was a scene that had been often repeated, for no Christian girl could be allowed any freedom in her Master's bed.

At first they had dreaded being chosen by heir Master, but then, as so often occurs in the artificial and isolated atmosphere of a harem, nature had taken its course.

Denied the sight of another man, other than their Master and the black eunuchs, and kept totally frustrated by the tight laces threaded through the rings in their beauty lips, they had found themselves, like the other women in the harem, slowly falling more and more in love with their half hated. but handsome, young Master.

Zalu had smiled approvingly as he noticed how the Crimson twins soon began to compete eagerly with the other women to catch the eye of their good-looking young Master - as they realised that he was their only source of sexual pleasure and relief. The Sheik now nodded approvingly as he saw that, driven on by an occasional crack of the long carriage whip of one of the fat black eunuchs standing on the side of the pool, the two girls were swimming up and down the pool. Swimming was a good exercise for reluctant young mothers-to-be in, what the black eunuchs called, 'a highly ripe condition'.

He laughed to himself as he remembered how the twins, now kept chained together by the neck and answering to their new joint name of Crimson, had wept bitterly as they realised that there was no escape from their fate as two of the Sheik's concubines.

The twins found themselves under the strict control and constant intimate supervision of Zalu and of his team of other black eunuchs.

Now, treated like children, kept unaware of what was going on in the outside world by the omnipresent black eunuchs, only allowed to see children's videos or read children's magazines and books, the harem with its jealousies and fears was their entire world. With no access even to calendars, never mind newspapers, radio or TV, they had little idea of the passing of time or just how long they had been incarcerated in the harem.

The twins realised that this also allowed the grinning black eunuchs to keep their anxious mothers-to-be ignorant of when they were due to deliver their progeny for their Master. This they were told was none of their business and any attempt to take a peek at Zalu's breeding diary promptly earned a thrashing.

Indeed, they they were taught by the black eunuchs that from now on, whether expectant or not, their only purpose in life was to give pleasure to their Master - with the threat of Zalu's cane constantly hanging over them if they failed to do so.

The young Sheik again laughed to himself at the memory of how appalled the twins had been to learn that part of this pleasure was the sight of a few swollen bellies and breasts in milk.

Yes, they had been terrified when the black eunuchs had teased them, saying that soon their Master would order them to experience an enforced motherhood.

"No, no," they had prettily cried.

Shocked, they also saw the black eunuchs' supervision even extended to intimate daily inspections of their unhappy companions who were Expecting a Happy Event. as the eunuchs cru-

18

elly called motherhood.

They watched with mounting fear as the black eunuchs checked the little growing mulatto progeny every day on their special ultra sound scanner, and saw that their cruel overseers had all the latest gadgetry for what they openly called successful slave breeding.

How even more arousing it would be, he thought, to subject haughty young Englishwomen to the threat of an enforced motherhood - and then carry it out!

After a few months in the harem, Zalu had judged that the time had come for them to undergo the pangs of a forced maternity for their Master's pleasure. He liked a girl to start breeding young and the Sheik would find the sight of twins, each bearing the twin progeny of the same black sire and due to foal on the same day, all highly erotic.

Moreover the Sheik would also be delighted later to have the twins join the ranks of his milkmaids.

After receiving the enthusiastic approval of the Sheik, Zalu had, unknown to them, taken them off their contraceptive pills, that were intended to prevent them conceiving by the Sheik. Instead he had put them onto a course of fertility pills so that they would achieve a multiple artificial conception and so make sure that nature ensured a greater milk supply.

Then, on the right day, he had loosened the laces that kept their beauty lips closed. Under the guise of giving them one of the regular douches that he gave to all the embarrassed women under his control, he had then simultaneously inseminated the unsuspecting twins with the same Negro seed - to produce useful mulatto progeny to work on their Master's estates.

He had then carefully drawn the laces taut and closed the little padlock. But, as we have seen, as a further precaution against them interfering with the little unwanted progeny now growing inside them, he had also locked them into triangular shaped breeding belts.

Later he had used his ultrasound scanner to check that they were both carrying twin boy progeny for their Master, failing which they would have been made to start again. The chain mail pouch part of their breeding belts prevented a girl from thrusting an inquisitive little finger. or even a potentially dangerous knitting needle, up inside herself. Nevertheless, it did allow the passage of her liquid wastes.

The pouch was held firmly in place over each girl's beauty lips, and under her swelling bell, by five strong rubber straps.

Two of these went up round the waist to meet in the small of the back where they were held together by a small padlock.

Two were attached to a ring at the bottom end of the triangular belt, down between the legs. Each of these then went up along the crease of each buttock and up to the hip, where it was fastened to one of the rubber straps running back from the front corners of the pouch. Thus the girl's rear orifice was left uncovered.

However, the fifth strap, in the form of a strong rubber thong, did cover it. It was also attached to the ring at the bottom end of the triangular chain mail pouch, but it was led, tautly, up between the cheeks of the buttocks to be held in place by the same little padlock in the small of the girl's back.

This rear thong covered the rear orifice but could be temporarily released by a black eunuch to enable a girl to pass her solid wastes under his supervision.

Thus when passing her wastes, whether liquid or solid, the embarrassed girl would have to half squat over a little brass bowl, a quarter filled with rose water, held by the black eunuch. With her hands clasped behind her neck and her tongue thrust out to prevent her from talking, she would have to wait for the order to perform, her eyes anxiously fixed on the black eunuch's dog whip.

Not until the black eunuch had, in the Turkish fashion, washed the blushing girl clean, and had refastened the thong between her buttocks, was the girl allowed to release her hands.

In the case of a girl locked into a breeding belt, making her keep her hands clasped behind her neck, also made sure that she did not take advantage of the partial release of the belt.

Whether a girl was expectant or not, it was all a humiliating routine - and one in which a small mistake such as not performing instantly on command, or performing without an order to do so, would earn a girl a thrashing.

Strict control over natural functions was, of course, a traditional way that black eunuchs used to impose, humiliatingly, their authority over the women in their charge.

Again, the Sheik told himself, it would be very amusing to watch, hidden behind a lattice screen, a proud young English woman, perhaps a respectable married woman or a career girl, being subjected to such degrading treatment. The Sheik had been delighted when Zalu had reported that, although they did not yet know it, both twins were now expectant, and could not understand why they were now locked into what the black eunuchs teasingly called maternity belts.

He found it even more amusing when both had their first morning sickness - something that Zalu had told them was simply a minor tummy problem.

Finally had come the day when they first felt their progeny kicking inside them. Anxiously they had asked Zalu what was happening to them, only to be given ten strokes each of the cane for Inquisitiveness.

Slowly they had realised the truth, but were mystified as to how it could have happened, for the black eunuchs were assiduous in washing out a girl after she had been selected for the Master's bed.

Both girls had been appalled when Zalu had, at last, told them that they were carrying future black labourers for their Master's estates.

The Sheik remembered how, with another girl kneeling at his feet with her head under his robe as she pleasured him, he had laughed and laughed as he watched the twins, now effectively his property, both desperately scratching in vain at their breeding belts as they sought in vain to get rid of their unwanted progeny.

It would be even more amusing if the girl frantically scratching at her belt was a formerly free and independent English woman. The Sheik grinned as he remembered how the Crimson twins, their forced maternity now well advanced, had been taken by his black eunuchs to an isolated corner of the airport at Shadek. There, they had been carefully put on board his private jet, together with the other concubines he was taking to his new palace in North Africa.

Under their thick, long, black shrouds they had been gagged and handcuffed. Also, before leaving, Zalu had had their registered numbers, as indentured servants, which were already tattooed on their bellies, now also tattooed on the inside of their wrists, as required by North African law.

They had not been told where they were being taken and the frosted glass windows prevented them from catching a glimpse of the land below.

On arrival in, what was to them a strange land, the immigration officials had come on board and, as previously arranged by the Sheik, had simply noted down carefully, the registered numbers.

Lone women, they were told, and certainly not indentured servants, were not allowed out alone in this country. So, even should they ever manage to escape from the Sheik's well protected new palace, these tattooed wrists would result in them being quickly picked up by the local Morals Police and returned to a furious Zalu for punishment.

Similarly no women were allowed to travel without the written permission of their husbands or fathers, if free women, or of their Masters if indentured servants. Thus any woman who tried to board a bus, or hail a taxi, or managed to reach the airport would also be arrested and returned to a furious Zalu. The Sheik glanced again at the monitor that showed the two beautifully curved bellies. What a delightful sight they made.

He looked at the daily written report on the state of his women that Zalu had give to him earlier on. It was two months now since they had been flown here to his new palace. Although they did not realise it, they were due to deliver their progeny any day now.

Only that morning he had visited with Zalu the new

22

concubines' foaling box as the black eunuchs cruelly called it. Here the chief black eunuch would soon be supervising a simultaneous delivery, using his cane if necessary, to bring on one or other of them. Chained together onto a twin cutaway birthing stool, the Crimson girls, now blindfolded and with their hands fastened above their heads, would finally drop their little black foals in the traditional Turkish harem way into a wicker collecting basket.

Thus, there would be no risk of either Crimson girl seeing or touching their progeny before they were taken away. There would, therefore, be no bonding and hence no rivalry to the respect and adoration both girls were expected to continue to show to their Master.

Indeed, soon there would be nothing to remind Crimson of their nine month travail, except their now heavy breasts - heavy with milk for their Master.

How amusing it would be to have a pretty young English woman similarly chained to the birthing stool! But there would be a difference. She would be dropping a pretty little girl, or even a pair of girls, to be reared as future concubines for his old age!

1 - 3 A COLLECTION OF WELL BRED YOUNG ENGLISH CONCUBINES!

The Great Idea had dawned upon Sheik Ali when he was on a semi-official visit to England.

He was the type of good looking and wealthy Arab whom many Englishwomen would dream about. He was tall, well built, with friendly smiling eyes, a short pointed beard, and slight but distinguished hook nose. He had a charming manner and was obviously highly intelligent. But he also had a ruthless manner and an air of standing no nonsense that further increased his attractiveness to women.

It was an attraction that was even further increased by his voice, for having been partly educated in England as a young boy, he spoke good English with a deep resonant voice with only a slight Arab accent.

He was a scion of a junior branch of the ruling family of Shadek, a small, remote and isolated Arab Sheikdom. The wealth of the ruling family came from the oil revenues from an island some fifty miles off the coast which the two branches owned personally.

The senior Branch of the ruling family had recognised him as a potential threat and offered him a large income for life, on condition that he left them to run their small country and, most of the time, kept out of it. Thus, with his zeal and quick brain now frustrated, he was looking for an outlet for his drive and energy.

He had toyed with the idea of taking up a new life in the West, perhaps in a position in the United Nations or in international business or finance. But, he kept telling himself, he was a very rich man. Did he really want to tie himself to an office routine, or to the Western tradition of living with only one woman at a time?

In his world it had for centuries been customary for a rich man to find his sexual partners in the slave market and to follow the precept that 'blessed are passionate women, eager to please their Master, and even more blessed is the Master who owns them and has them trained and strictly controlled.'

Knowing that Sheik Ali came from an influential family who controlled so much of the world's oil supply, the British authorities had discreetly ensured that he was invited everywhere; tennis at Wimbledon, rowing at Henley, racing at Ascot and Goodwood, polo at Windsor, opera at Glyndbourne, Royal Garden parties, numerous horse shows and even some private dances and parties.

It was the first time that he had encountered well bred young Englishwomen in large numbers. He was fascinated by the fair skinned, tall, self-assured, and intelligent young women he met: married and unmarried, divorcees and career girls.

These young women were so refreshingly different from the mainly cowed and uneducated women he kept in his harem back in Shadek - and from the semi-professional European courtesans, dancers and cabaret girls with whom he had previously dallied.

These well-off and well educated young Englishwomen treated him with flirtatious informality. They were fascinated by the aura of power and wealth that surrounded him and his entourage, and by the way that he took women for granted. Many were also, it seemed, equally fascinated by his hints of a harem of jealous but adoring young women, living a life a ease, protected from all the worldly cares of modern life, and watched over by black eunuchs.

Many seemed torn between throwing themselves at him and nervously holding back. They were clearly nervous about becoming involved with a nouveau riche, and perhaps really rather uncivilised Arab, from a backward, if immensely rich, country where women were treated as little more than chattels, to be hidden away from the sight of men. As Sheik Ali well knew, some discerning multi-millionaires in the West might devote their wealth and energies to racing yachts or breeding successful race-horses.

Others, however, enjoyed more private pleasures, such as secretly collecting valuable paintings, antique furniture, or porcelain of a certain type. These beautiful and fine 'objets d'art', acquired by fair means or foul, had disappeared from the outside world - to be enjoyed in the privacy of their owner's home.

Thus came the Great Idea - he would similarly use his wealth and energy to collect and enjoy some of these fascinating creatures in the privacy of his harem. A harem consisting largely of well bred Englishwomen might indeed sound far fetched in this day and age. But many of Sheik Ali's wealthy Arab friends secretly boasted of having the occasional European woman in their harems, and perhaps, indeed, the odd Englishwoman. He himself already had a couple of half English Lebanese girls. So why not go the whole hog?

Indeed why not? And if the truth was ever rumoured in the bazaars of the Arab world, then it would certainly make him all the more popular with the xenophobic fundamentalists. They were becoming such a powerful force throughout the Moslem world, especially here in his new home in North Africa, that he certainly could not afford to offend them.

For them, the freedom that women enjoyed increasingly in the West, and in particular in the English speaking world, was anathema. So, they were unlikely to object if it were known that he kept Western women discreetly in his harem, controlled and disciplined, in the traditional way, by black eunuchs. Indeed, this would be entirely in accordance with the fundamentalists tenants of women being kept shut up in the home! There was, however, a slight complication.

Whereas in Arabia it was quite normal for a concubine to be left uncut, here in North Africa, 'Salat', or the imposition of purity on women, was more traditional, and the fundamentalists were constantly calling for it. 'Salat' requires as a minimum the removal of the sensitive tip of a woman's beauty bud to be snipped off, to reduce what was considered to be a woman's natural licentiousness.

It did not reduce the ability of the girl to give her Master pleasure, but it did mean that she herself could now only receive it when she was actually penetrated by her Master - something for which she now became more desperate than ever and thus more submissive and pliant.

Thus, locally, it was considered that this 'partial doctoring', as it was euphemistically termed, played an import role in keeping women subservient. For this reason, although traditionally a girl was doctored when small, these days, to meet a growing demand, local surgeons had specialised in carrying it out on grown women as well.

In particular, they had perfected the ancient technique of 'full doctoring': removing not only the beauty bud, but also the inner and outer beauty lips and then letting them heal together, leaving just a little orifice, at the bottom for the passing of liquids, and for penetration by the Master. A girl who had been so treated would have just a little long scar where before had been her beauty lips. If she became expectant, then the scar could readily be cut open for the actual delivery and then sewn up again.

Sheik Ali did not have strong views on the matter. On the one hand, he enjoyed the increased physical pleasure that came from taking a responsive young woman, and, on the other, he also much enjoyed the mental pleasure of taking a girl who had been doctored by his order.

The fundamentalists Mullahs, however, would be bound to ask whether he was obeying their guidance and having his Western concubines doctored, either partially or, preferably, fully. Moreover, they would probably want to inspect one of his concubines to satisfy themselves as to his piety.

Furthermore, of all the European countries, it was England, the fundamentalists declaimed, who had caused the Arabs the most humiliation. So, seeking revenge, the Mullahs would be particularly insistent that he, as both a loyal Arab and a pious treated his English concubines in this way.

Clearly, he realised, it would be politic to have one or two of the Englishwomen doctored so that they could be shown off to any enquiring Mullahs. How many Englishwomen should he acquire? Well, he remembered his grandfather saying that a man could jog along with a dozen beautiful and well trained concubines - provided they were under the supervision of effective black eunuchs.

Of course, it would cost a lot of time and energy, and money, to acquire these well bred Englishwomen. But, then, so much the better! He enjoyed travelling. Keeping an eye out for potential concubines, and then arranging their acquisition, would give a little spice and zest to his life! And what better way to spend his money?

Yes, the pleasure, both of the chase and of later enjoying the ensnared young Englishwoman, back in his harem, would make it all well worthwhile!

1 - 4 ZALU, THE CHIEF BLACK EUNUCH

The Sheik was well aware that much of the success of his plan would depend on having an effective and ruthless chief black eunuch, utterly loyal to his Master, used to enforcing discipline in a harem, immune to the wiles of the women in his charge, and used to shielding his Master from having to bother himself with his women's tantrums and importuning ways.

By keeping the women frustrated, a good chief black eunuch ensured that they all jealously tried their utmost to out-do the other women by first catching their Master's eye and then giving him exquisite pleasure.

A good chief black eunuch was his Master's confidant, someone to whom he could confide his desires and with whom he could discuss his women frankly and openly.

Traditionally, a good chief black eunuch, as well as running his Master's harem, also kept in contact with dealers and other shadowy purveyors of women.

Fortunately, his own chief black eunuch back in Shadek, Zalu, had all the necessary attributes!

Zalu could also be relied on to ensure that the women all had the full but firm breasts and prominent nipples that he found so erotically arousing. Indeed, this part of North Africa was well known for doctors specialising in such cosmetic surgery.

The handsome young Sheik's adoring white women would, of course, hate Zalu. Like his present concubines, they would be soon be whispering to each other: 'If only our hand-some and charming young Master knew just how cruelly and humiliatingly Zalu treats us!'

But, of course, the stricter Zalu treated them, the more they would find themselves in love with their apparently easy-going, laughing, Master. Little would they realise that Zalu would be discussing the behaviour of each of them daily with their Master and taking his instructions from him. There would also be another important side to Zalu's duties: the provision of milk-maids. In his present harem the Sheik had been an enthusiastic follower of his grandfather's oft repeated dictum: "Always remember, my son, what the blessed Prophet said; 'Blessed is the woman with sweet flowing milk.'"

Zalu had therefore been instructed always to keep at least two pretty milkmaids, as he called them, in full flow, ready and eager to offer their well filled breasts to their Master. Not surprisingly, therefore, the young Sheik also practised another of his grandfather's sayings: 'A harem is not a harem without a few little swollen bellies.'

In England, a mother-to-be might be shunned sensually, but the young Sheik knew better - and so had his grandfather! Like a flower coming into bloom, he felt, a girl only achieved her full natural beauty when she was becoming a little mother.

Sheik Ali was, therefore, now determined to try out another of his revered forebear's sayings: 'The whiter the skin, the sweeter the milk.'

His grandfather, the Sheik told Zalu, had not, of course, been referring to a motherhood induced by himself. On the contrary, like all members of the Ruling Family, he was careful not to risk causing dynastic problems by having a son, except by one of his wives.

No, some of his concubines knew that their only hope of satisfying their natural maternal instincts, made even stronger by the artificial atmosphere of the harem, was to beg to be mated with another slave, white or black. Others were terrified of being forced into a motherhood they would abhor.

But it was not only satisfying their natural maternal instincts that had made some of his grandfather's women so keen to be covered.

Indeed, when training his grandfather's concubines, the black eunuchs had always taught them to kneel over their Master and to offer their hanging breasts to him to suck, even if they were still dry. This would not only excite the Master, but also thrill and arouse the girl, too.

Indeed a slave girl soon learnt that having her nipples sucked by her aged Master, was something that she adored and longed for. How even more exciting, she would tell herself, it would be if they were actually flowing with milk - and how much more likely she would be to catch her Master's eye! Indeed her Master was likely to refresh himself from his milkmaids several times a day. Oh how thrilling that would be!

So, it used to amuse his grandfather greatly when one of his exceptionally pretty white slave girls, desperate to achieve a motherhood that was otherwise denied to her, would crave on her bended knees to be covered. He would then enjoy breeding from her, just as he did from his prize brood mares or racing camels.

"But," he used to tell his grandson, "never forget the enjoyment that also comes from making a reluctant, or recalcitrant, young mother-to-be suffer the pangs of an enforced maternity. A forced pregnancy is also something that keeps the black eunuchs on their toes!"

So it was that he would cross some white slave girls with a captured white slave, so as to have future slave girls, as pretty as their mothers, for his old age. Others, with good child bearing hips, he would put to a pygmy with a record of throwing twins or triplets, or to a giant black Dinka guard.

Nature, concerned with the girl's apparent forthcoming need to feed a particularly numerous or large progeny, would then automatically ensure that her breasts grew to provide the necessary nourishment - a nourishment that would, of course, be kept for the Master.

Either way, to ensure that a girl's sole emotional attachment remained her Master, the black eunuchs always had her hooded and her mate always muzzled, when they were coupled, so that she never saw or heard her mate. Similarly they always hooded and chained a girl's hands above her head, when she produced her progeny, so that she never saw, or touched them before they were taken away to be reared as slaves.

"But," the young Sheik had said to Zalu when making his plans, "not even my grandfather had had a choice of delightful young English women to consider when making his breeding plans. It will be your task to ensure that we always have one or two white mothers-to-be either proudly parading their swelling bellies before to me, or horrified at what has been done to them." Zalu had smiled grimly as he listened to his young Master's orders. Like many black eunuchs he took a particular pleasure in supervising breeding from the women in his charge - and if it was a forced breeding, then all the more challenging, especially if the woman was a white one.

There had been, however, a new development.

Thanks to the miracles of modern medicine, Zalu could now bring on a girl's milk at any time, even without her knowledge, by putting her on a course of special pills. But he preferred the more traditional method, even though it took nine months, since it gave a better flow.

However, Zalu was horrified by the idea of one his precious charges even seeing a man other than their Master, never mind being penetrated by one. Even if they were prevented from seeing the man or his manhood, they would still feel it - and that, for Zalu, was an anathema.

Fortunately, though, another miracle of modern medicine allowed him now to dispense with one of his future young mothers-to-be having to have any physical contact with the chosen sire - or even to be aware of what had been done to her.

Furthermore, the harem was equipped with a modern ultra-sound scan, making it easy for Zalu to check, early on, that the resulting offspring was indeed female if white, or male if black - and if necessary start again.

Indeed, spurred on by Zalu, Sheik Ali had arranged to send a succession of carefully bred, pretty little girls, away to Europe to be specially brought up by nuns or foster parents, whilst the mother remained in his harem, initially, of course, in the ranks of his milkmaids.

Ample funds would ensure that the little girls were kept unaware of the identity of her real mother, or of her indentured status - a status that, as in the days of slavery, could readily be made to apply in North Africa to them too, as the registered offspring of a registered indentured mother.

Then if she grew up to be beautiful, she could be brought unsuspectingly back to join her real mother in the harem. These arrangements, he considered, would give a whole new sense of purpose to the idea of a harem of Englishwomen. Of course, Zalu would need assistance in maintaining constant supervision of these highly intelligent, and probably wilful white women. However, in these days of effective chastity or purity belt and high quality, continuous surveillance television cameras, with long playing recording tapes, there was not now the need for so many black eunuchs in a harem.

Indeed, just as technology had made it easier to prevent escape from a harem, so it had also made it easier to detect and prevent any solitary or mutual sexual misconduct by the frustrated women.

This was something about which the young Sheik Ali, like Zalu, had very old fashioned ideas. Lesbianism might seem a natural outlet for women incarcerated in a harem, but for him any hint of it, or of self abuse by a woman, was a form of unfaithfulness to their Master, scarcely less serious than adultery by a woman.

They were an affront to his manhood, and something he would not tolerate.

He was determined that fear of a thrashing from Zalu and a mixture of hidden covert television cameras and microphones, as well as prominently placed ones, would soon put the fear of God into his new English concubines and keep them as pure as driven snow!

Nevertheless his chief black eunuch would still need a few assistants. Fortunately, even in this day and age, thanks to the chaos, and frequent civil wars, in black Africa, there was still a good supply of eunuchs.

Their remorse at losing their manhood was counterbalanced by their delight at getting away from the grinding poverty of their native villages, and at starting a new life in luxurious surroundings, and in a position of power - over women, and white ones at that.

Zalu already had several keen black assistant eunuchs of differing ages who, whilst having no love for the English, did speak a little of their language.

In particular, it would be especially amusing to use his two intelligent, but uneducated, little pigmy boy eunuchs, Baza and Naka, to control his tall and sophisticated English concu-

32

bines - and to supervise them during their most intimate moments.

The sight of tall cool Englishwomen being intimately controlled and supervised by little pygmy boys would, Zalu told himself, be one that the Sheik would find irresistible. Certainly, Zalu and his team awaited the arrival of the first Englishwomen with eager anticipation!

To ensure the submission, however, of these formerly free and arrogant white women, Zalu had discussed with the young Sheik the desirability of keeping them manacled, anyway initially. 1 - 5 ACTION! SHEIK ALI IMPLEMENTS HIS PLAN Sheik Ali had brooded over the Great Plan, incubated it in his mind, dreamed about it. He would have to move out of Shadek...

He had built a new luxurious palace, with a high security harem wing. It was in North Africa, well away from all the intractable problems and internecine fighting of the Middle East itself.

It was in an ideal site: an isolated private estate, in delightful surroundings, near the sea with a discreet private jetty for his luxury yacht. It was also only a short distance from the capital of the country, which prided itself on offering wealthy Arab expatriates just the security and privacy that they needed.

The palace had previously belonged to a rich Caid. The existing building had to be modernised and extended by Sheik Ali. However, its high walls, surrounding both the harem garden and the pretty outlying park, were just what he wanted to ensure privacy and prevent escape.

There he would entertain other wealthy Arabs and diplomats and take an active part in the male dominated social life of the capital. But always he would be gloating over his secret harem of beautiful Englishwomen locked up back in his palace and waiting for his return.

His black eunuchs and the high walls, coupled with modern technology, could also ensure that a woman, once inside his harem, would never see or speak to another man - except his eunuchs, of course. Thus no matter how much they might initially resent being incarcerated in his harem, they would soon come to realise that he, now their Master, was to be their only source of sexual pleasure, or even of male companionship.

He would, of course, have to protect himself from a disenchanted young woman escaping and causing a scandal, but a reliable chief black eunuch backed up by the same high walls and modern technology, would make this most unlikely - and ensure that the women were kept out of sight from any prying eyes.

However, perhaps just in case, it would be best if each woman was kept ignorant of not only who her handsome Master really was, as were his present concubines, but even of just where the harem was! It would be enough for them to know that they were somewhere in Africa and in the power of a rich and influential man.

Fortunately, a great advantage of this part of North Africa was that although slavery as such no longer existed, indentured service was recognised and enforced by law. Originally designed to prevent black labourers on private estates, or the inmates of brothels, from running away from their Masters, it also worked well in controlling the concubines of a rich man's harem.

Not only did the Morals Police insist that women, who were indentured servants, must be registered, under whatever Harem Name their Master chose to give them, but they also insisted that, to assist instant recognition, their registered number must be tattooed on the inside of the woman's right wrist.

Under the strict rules of the fundamentalist regime, now in power in this country, any woman found outside her house, without the written permission of her husband or Master, would be quickly arrested by the Morals Police. The same applied to women trying to board a bus or taxi, or, even worse, trying to leave the country, even if they had a passport. If the woman was then shown by the tattooed number to be an indentured servant, then the woman would be quickly identified and returned to her Master for punishment.

The very existence of such a system would make his English concubines realise the hopelessness of even trying to escape, and thus make them more willing to accept their fate.

"Yes," the Sheik told Zalu, "everything's now ready for the entrapment and arrival of the first of my future collection of well educated English concubines. Oh I'm going to so enjoy having them locked up here under your control."

"Indeed, Your Highness," came Zalu's smooth reply, "and I think I have heard about some interesting possible recruits."

Zalu handed the Sheik a folder. It referred to a beautiful Englishwoman, a young, happily married, upper class Englishwoman whom Zalu had seen in Cyprus the day before.

"She would seem to be," Zalu murmured ingratiatingly, "just the type of Englishwoman that Your Highness is seeking. And, things can be arranged so that she would be very grateful indeed to Your Highness for apparently rescuing her from a terrible situation."

The Sheik read the folder. Zalu had worked it all out very cleverly. Yes, it all certainly sounded interesting: safe and not too expensive.

He would, he decided, take his private jet and fly to Cyprus to-morrow to see the girl for himself. Then, if he liked her, he would tell Zalu to put the scheme into operation.

His Great Plan was about to commence!

PART II   THE ACQUISITION OF THE HON. MRS JEREMY
RIDDLE (LOUISE), AND OF MISS SAMANTHA SMYTHE
("Mauve and Magenta")

2-1 CERTAIN PLANS ARE MADE - AND CARRIED OUT.

"Goodbye, darling!" murmured Louise Riddle as she kissed her
husband, Jeremy, at the airport in Cyprus. "See you in London in
two week's time."

They had only been married a year and Jeremy, a clever
young man making his way in the City, was still very much in
love with his wife. He turned and waved, admiring her tall slim
beauty, her calm cool presence, her high cheek bones, her long
honey coloured hair, her green eyes and above all her happy bub-
bly personality. God, he was lucky to have such a wife! And she
was a lady to boot, the daughter of a peer - even if her nearest
relations were now all dead.

Louise waved as he disappeared past the immigration
desk. She loved her husband, but there was something missing
from her marriage. He was just too nice, deferring to her every
wish. She sometimes longed for him to take charge of her - to tie
her up, perhaps even to beat her!

They had gone off to Cyprus on holiday and after a
week of bliss together, he was going onto the Far East for an
extensive business trip, leaving her to stay on in Cyprus for a
couple of weeks to enjoy the sun before returning to London.

That evening Louise felt very alone and rather sad. She
was normally such a happy carefree girl. Perhaps staying on by
herself wasn't such a good idea after all. She confided her thoughts
to the hotel manager - who next day suddenly introduced her to a
young Frenchman, Pierre!

He was attentive and attractive and took her off to see
the sights. He treated her like a princess, and did not press his
attentions on her. A pity, she thought, aren't there any real men
left? Strong and determined men who would sweep a woman off
to ... what?

Outwardly, she was a cool liberated woman of her time. So, although she loved her husband, she also enjoyed flirting with Pierre. She was drifting into an affair, but she was not all that shocked. Indeed she was disappointed and surprised at the way he had avoided any intimate scenes. It would, after all, only be a short-lived holiday romance. In a little over a week she would be flying back to England to await her husband's return and would soon forget all about Pierre.

Pierre had asked her, a few days after they had met, to meet him at the hotel pool, 'wearing your prettiest bikini'. Was it a sign, she wondered as she got ready, that he was at last showing signs of interest in her as a woman? She made herself look dazzling for him.

She was therefore rather surprised when she saw that he was sitting with a large very black looking man who eyed her up and down as if she was an animal on sale at a market. His cheeks were disfigured by tribal scars. These and his bloodshot eyes gave him a harsh and rather frightening look.

Well, if the bastard wanted to have a good look at her, then he could damn well have one! She sauntered past them, one hand on her hips, and tossed her hair disdainfully before diving gracefully into the pool. She swam a couple of lengths and then climbed out - only to see that the strange black man had gone, leaving a smugly smiling Pierre. It was a couple of days later that Pierre said that he was going to take her to a small discreet hotel to meet a rich businessman with whom he was hoping to do an important deal. Pierre said that briefly introducing Louise to him would help him to clinch it.

Intrigued, she dressed up to the nines, and was rewarded by being introduced by Pierre to one of the most charming and handsome young men she had even met. He had a short goatee beard and the slightly sallow skin of a Levantine. With his slightly hooked nose he might have been an Arab, but he was dressed in a well cut safari suit with a red cravat. He seemed unusually tall and his eyes - ah, his eyes! They were like pools of dark liquid fire - restless and ruthless!

There was an air of savagery under his charm that im-

37

mediately attracted her. This was a man who would not stand any nonsense! She wondered if he beat his women, and decided he probably did - or, had it done for him, whilst he watched. The brute! How exciting!

She was fascinated to find he knew some of her smarter friends back in London. She couldn't wait to ask them about this very attractive man. He must be very rich to move in their circles. She liked rich men and the feeling of power that surrounded them.

He asked about her husband, and looked pleased when she said they loved each other. He also seemed genuinely interested in her background, her schooling and her family, murmuring comforting words of sympathy as she described how she was an only child, left penniless when her parents were killed in a car crash. What a charming and interesting man he was.

She was very disappointed to learn that he had to leave Cyprus on business the following day. Suddenly he rose and, bowing, kissed her hand. "I hope we shall meet again soon," he said.

"I should like that very much," she heard herself saying in a fervent tone of voice, and quickly lowered her eyes, embarrassed at her forwardness.

He laughed pleasantly, and again bowed and kissed her hand.

Then he shook hands with the obviously delighted Pierre and handed him a large envelope. "You have a deal," he said formally as he left. "The materials are suitable. Final payment will be on collection after more detailed inspection."

Louise wondered what this deal all about, but Pierre was non-committal, though obviously delighted. She realised that although this mysterious man had learnt a lot about her, she really knew nothing about him. She did not even know his name or nationality. Nor was Pierre very communicative about him.

"Oh don't worry about him," he said, "he's just a rich Arab, my partner in a rather special deal I've pulled off. Now let's go out an celebrate!" Two days later, an excited Pierre suggested that they should spend a long weekend end together in a secret place in Arabia.

"A secret place in Arabia!" exclaimed Louise, inwardly rather excited at the prospect. "But where?"

"Ah, that'll be a secret until we arrive at the airport," laughed Pierre mysteriously. "It's only a few hours flight away, but it's the real Arabia. I promise you it's an exciting and interesting place - and we can be alone at last!"

"Ah, that does sound fun," agreed Louise with a smile. Then a thought struck her. "But the hotel here ... they will guess I've gone off with you ... my husband might learn the truth ... and anyway, my flight back to London is booked ... I know I can't change my ticket now."

"Don't worry! You simply tell the hotel that you have had to return unexpectedly to London. The hotel," he explained, squeezing her hand reassuringly, and excitingly, "'will simply think you have left for England. But really you'll meet me at the airport, and we'll fly off together in a private plane lent to me by a rich friend. Then after a few wonderful days together there, I'll fly you back to Cyprus in time to catch your plane. So you'll return to England as planned and no one, but no one, will ever know that you secretly spent a few days seeing the real Arabia!"

With that he took her into his arms and kissed her, passionately. "Oh, darling," he whispered, "I just can't wait to be alone with you. It'll be such fun, together!"

Louise felt all her doubts evaporating fast, as Pierre redoubled his kisses. It all sounded very neat and simple. And Pierre was so attractive - almost as attractive as that devastating friend of his! And the idea of flying off with him in a a private plane to an unknown Arab country sounded so exciting! It all went very well. They met at the airport early in the morning. Pierre had been more charming and attentive than ever, feeling her thighs through her dress and winking. Mifsud, as she now gathered was the name of place, was indeed a primitive and fascinating place, almost like something out of the Middle Ages, or the times of the Crusaders. There wasn't even a British Embassy or Consulate.

Arriving at a comfortable hotel, Louise was surprised, and slightly relieved, to hear Pierre saying that he had reserved two rooms - and under under false names. The clerk smiled knowingly as Pierre handed him a large tip.

"Officially, they're very strict here," Pierre explained as they both handed over their passports.

After a relaxing light lunch, Louise agreed to join Pierre in his room 'for a little siesta'. Alone at last, they fell into each other's arms. Pierre kissed her passionately, slowly undressed her, carried her to the bed, and began to stroke her breasts.

Suddenly, as if in response to some signal, the door of the bedroom burst open. Louise tried to pull the bedclothes up over her naked body. But the party of grim faced Morals Police, for such they were, quickly pulled back the bedclothes and photographed them in bed together.

They then arrested her, naked as she was, saying in broken English that her passport, deposited with hotel reception, showed that she was a married woman and not married to Pierre. She had therefore been committing Adultery, a very serious offence under the Islamic Law of Mifsud. The penalty was being stoned to death.

Then as she shrank back in the corner of the room, desperately trying to hide her nakedness with her hands, they sent for her luggage and 'found' drugs in it. So she was also charged with drug smuggling - an offence, they told her, that also carried the death penalty.

To her amazement, however, instead of also arresting Pierre, they congratulated him, slapping him on the back and laughing. Pierre left the room a free man without even a backward glance at Louise. She was all alone in her dreadful predicament.

Her first thoughts had been to save her marriage and avoid a scandal. Jeremy must never know about this trip, about her infidelity - or rather her near infidelity. At all costs, therefore, she must not involve the nearest British consul. Surely it could all be explained away? What did they want, anyway, with a young Englishwoman? A little judicious bribery, she felt, and she would soon free to return to Cyprus and to denounce the odious Pierre.

But her bribes were ignored.

Things moved very quickly. It was as if it had all been planned beforehand. She was allowed to dress in her smart travelling skirt and blouse. Then her hands were handcuffed behind her back and round brass rings were locked over her ankles. They were joined by a length of chain. Her ankles had been manacled! She saw that the rings fitted tight so that they would not rub.

A leather gag was then fastened over her mouth and tied behind her neck. She was now effectively muzzled.

Then, covered in a black shroud so that no one could see who she was, she was taken out of the hotel, and thrust into the back of a car, sitting between two of the silent Morals Police.

Taken to a police station, her mind was a whirl. Understanding no Arabic and still muzzled and chained, she scarcely realised what was happening as, in a matter of minutes she was formally charged in a secret court with adultery and drug smuggling, and sentenced to death.

Then she was told that her sentence had been commuted to five hundred lashes to be spread over two years, and imprisonment for life with hard labour. Five hundred strokes! Her passport was torn up and she was told that her name was now that of an Indian servant girl. There would be no official record, in the remote Arab state, that a Mrs Louise Riddle had ever been arrested, never mind sentenced to be flogged and to imprisonment.

2 - 2 LOUISE'S INDUCTION INTO PRISON

Although it was a woman's prison, there did not seem to be any wardresses. Women, Louise was told angrily, did not hold any positions of authority in this part of the world. Their duty was to stay at home and serve men.

Instead she was handed over to several Negro guards, speaking only broken English. They were smoking and carrying long whippy canes - evidently the emblems of their authority. Nervously she remembered the five hundred strokes of her sentence.

41

Still gagged and wearing her travelling clothes, she was carefully photographed, with a Polaroid camera, 'For prison records'. Then, waving their canes menacingly, the African guards had unlocked her handcuffs and made her strip naked. Her feelings of embarrassment and shame were heightened by the contrast between her own nakedness and the smart uniforms of these black guards: white breeches, peaked caps, highly polished boots and equally highly polished Sam Browne belts with a strap over the right shoulder to support a holster carrying a revolver and a short whip.

They now, mysteriously, put her into an embroidered caftan - again to be repeatedly photographed.

Then once again naked, round brass manacle rings were riveted round her wrists and ankles. Wrists and ankles were now joined by a length of chain. She saw that the manacles fitted tightly and were lined so that they would not rub. Did this mean that they would left on her permanently? My God!

"You no escape from here!" laughed one of the guards cruelly.

She was now made to stand up on a bench with her manacled ankles fastened wide apart and her manacled hands strapped above her head to chains hanging down from the ceiling. Blushing with shame, she had had to bend her knees to help the grinning black guards shave off her body hair - 'To prevent lice'.

To her horror, she realised that they were also going to shave her head. Then suddenly, a Mullah entered the room. He was a cruel looking Arab with the eyes of a fanatic. He was dressed in the distinctive black robes and turban of a Moslem cleric.

"Governor!" said the guard warningly.

The guards stood back respectfully, as the Mullah walked slowly round Louise's naked and now shrinking body with evident approval. She felt so ashamed. She felt even more ashamed when he gave instructions in Arabic for her to use what she recognised as a pregnancy testing kit. She saw him rub his hands with delight when after a few minutes, a young Negro guard had returned shaking his head. The Mullah then made an entry in a strange little red book with some Arabic numerals on the outside.

Then he apparently ordered her hair to be spared.

Her manacled hands were now temporarily released from above her head and her prison number,9-743, was neatly tattooed in Arabic numerals on the inside of her left forearm. She saw that the numerals seemed the same as those on the front of the little red book. Then her hands were re-fastened above her head and, whilst she stood helpless on the bench, the same Arabic numerals were humiliatingly, but this time prominently, painted in indelible ink on her belly.

The Mullah now produced a set of ten little silver rings.

"Keep still. Head up! Look straight ahead!" came the warning order. Louise saw, out of the corner of her eye, one of the guards coming up to her with a raised hypodermic syringe. She was horrified as she felt a little prick into her beauty lips on one side, and then another on the other side. The black guards laughingly waited for the anaesthetic to take effect, pinching her beauty lips periodically as a test.

Then, as Louise continued to strain to keep her eyes fixed ahead, ten tiny holes were punched through her beauty lips, five on each side. A silver ring was threaded through each one.

A leather cord was threaded the rings, as on a lace-up shoe. The laces were pulled tight, closing the beauty lips tightly together - and making it impossible for her to give herself any pleasure. Then, instead of the laces being tied in a bow, as on a shoe, they were held fastened together by a tiny padlock that hung down between her legs. Oh the shame!

Still stark naked and with the Mullah watching, she was again repeatedly and humiliatingly photographed with the Polaroid camera, 'for prison records'. At first she was photographed with her hands still fastened above her head. She blushed with shame as they made her thrust her belly forward to show off the numbers. But worse was to follow! Close-ups were taken of her breasts and of her now shaven and laced up intimacies.

Then her hands were released and she was photographed coyly trying to hide her breasts and beauty lips with her manacled

43

hands. It would, she realised make an erotic picture of chained and muzzled English womanhood. But to whom might they be shown and why?

The Mullah looked at the photographs and smiled approvingly. "Red cage!" he grunted.

A young and virile looking black guard stepped up. He saluted the Mullah smartly and was handed Amanda's red book. She discovered later that he was Achmet, the overseer in charge of the women in the Red Cage.

He slipped an ugly black cotton chador over Louise's head. Under it she was still muzzled. The chador completely covered her head, neck and face. Two little oblong cutouts over her eyes enabled to see out - with difficulty. There was also a small hole in the chador over her mouth. Leather straps on the side of the chador were strapped round her neck and fastened with a padlock. She would not now be able to remove the chador.

"Shameful for women to show faces," said Achmet in broken English.

Glancing in a mirror she saw that she indeed now looked like just another anonymous veiled Arab woman. But emblazoned across the front of her chador, above her eyes, was stencilled her prison number: 9-743.

"Your name now Prisoner Seven Four Three," he said harshly. "What your name, girl?" He temporarily eased the leather gag over her mouth. "Well? Say it!"

"Prisoner ... Seven Four Three," stammered Louise, feeling utterly humiliated.

He re-fastened her gag, leaving her still muzzled under her chador, round which he now painted a red band.

"This show you belong to my cage," he said in his broken English. "Any guard see you not working hard or misbehaving, you reported to me and I punish you with this." He held up his long whippy cane.

Louise shivered with fright.

"You soon desperate for Red cage to get prize for hardest work. Then I get ten per cent bonus. If not, then all my women get cane. Understand?"

Horrified, Louise nodded.

Then he handed her a long red striped prison tunic. It had slits up the side to her waist and her prison number was also prominently stencilled across the back of it.

"Put on!" he ordered. She saw that the shoulder straps of the tunic had a velcro fastening so that she could put it on despite her chained wrists. "Hurry!"

Nervously she secured the velcro fastenings. At least she was no longer naked.

"Head up! Hands on top of head!" He gave her a sharp tap with his cane across her bottom - naked under her thin tunic. Feeling rather foolish Louise hastened to obey. "Prisoners always keep hands on head outside cage or when overseer talk to them," he added. "Sign of proper respect!"

Then, gripping her by the arm and tapping her bottom through her thin tunic with his whippy cane, he led her out of the room. Louise found herself in what seemed to be a seemed to be a large, and empty, sand covered prison yard. It was now getting dark, but the yard was lit up by bright lights fixed onto high poles. Surrounding the yard were high walls with what looked like electrified barbed wire running along the top.

In the yard were several beautifully laid circular roads made of small square paving stones each placed in the sand in well laid out half moon shapes. It reminded her of the 'pavee', she had seen in the squares of many Continental towns. The roads were obviously not complete.

Then Louis noticed that, at the other end of each road, the carefully laid paving stones looked as though they were being pulled up. What, she wondered, was the point of laying the paving stones and then pulling them again? Was this what the judge had meant when he had commuted her sentence to hard labour for life?

"Prisoners not allowed walk in yard. Double march! Raise knees! And keep hands on head."

Again he emphasised his order with a sharp tap across her buttocks. Terrified, Louise pranced along behind her young black overseer, her ankle chains clinking.

Then she gave a gasp of disbelief, for there, facing her along one side of the prison yard, was a line of straw lined low iron cages, open to the sky - and crawling in each cage, or gripping the bars as they knelt on all fours, were numerous women, naked except for the chadors hiding their features. Some of the naked bodies were black, some different hues of brown, some white.

My God, she thought, my God!

2 - 3 A TASTE OF HELL

Louise looked at the cages with mounting despair. She saw, through the straw strewn on the floor of the cages, more iron bars - evidently to prevent escape.

Each cage was painted a different colour. The cages were too low for the crawling women, naked except for the chadors that hid their heads and faces, to stand up.

Hanging on a rail outside each cage was row of tunics, each with stripes matching the colour of the cage.

Only the eyes and mouths of the women were visible behind their chadors. Like her, their wrists and ankles were manacled. Some were gripping the bars of their cages with their chained hands and looking at her.

Horrified, she saw that the shaven sex lips of these women were also, just like hers, held closed by polished leather laces threaded up through two lines of little rings and pulled taut, like the laces of a shoe, and like hers, held together by little padlocks.

Just as the padlocks at the back of their necks prevented them from taking off their chadors, so, Louise realised, these ones would prevent them from getting at themselves.

She gave a start as she saw that some of the tummies, particularly the white or near white ones, were swollen - and on each of these, written in indelible ink, was a large Christian crucifix and below it, again in indelible ink, an Arabic date. On some, she saw, there was a Moslem crescent instead of the Cross.

In these cases the beauty lips had been completed covered by a chain mail pouch that was tightly held in place by little chains going round the waist and up between the buttocks, with a small padlock keeping them fastened together in the small of the back. In the centre of the chain mail links was a little grille - evidently for passing wastes.

A shiny metal trough ran the length of each cage, outside the bars. By it lay a hose.

The cages offered no privacy, even at night, for each was lit up by a bare electric light bulb to allow another black guard, patrolling up and down outside the line of cages, and each cage's own Head Girl, to check that the caged women were all behaving properly - for an essential part of the regime in this prison was the denial of any sexual relief. Sexual enjoyment, the Mullah maintained, was something women offered men - and certainly did not dare to give to themselves or to other women. "This your new one, then?" the patrolling guard said to Achmet, speaking in their common African dialect. "You're lucky, she's a white one! What's she done?"

"Oh, just the usual, Mafu, caught in bed with a man," replied Achmet with a grin.

"They never learn!" laughed Mafu. "But she'll be nice for you when she's OK to Grip the Bars. I bet you can't wait for her to have a green ribbon tied round her neck and then to proffer herself to you. It's extraordinary what they'll put up with just to be rewarded with a day off work and left resting in their cage!"

"So much the better for us!" said Achmet grinning, "but I'll have to be careful with this one - the Mullah wants her specially handled. She's very pretty and I think he may already have a buyer for her indentures."

"All the more money for us in our bonuses! She'll soon sign up for indentured service. They sign anything after a few weeks of hard work, of Gripping the Bar for their overseer, and above all a good public performance. They always do!"

He looked the trembling Louise up and down. "Yeah, the Mullah should have no problem in finding a buyer for her - unless he's going to offer her the alternative of the new Special

47

Treatment."

"I don't think he'll being doing that," said Achmet. "He thinks she's too valuable - and I don't expect he'll want to wait nine months for his money!"

"I can well understand that," laughed Mafu. He put his hand down onto her hips. "But as a fall back, with a figure like this, she'd make a good little regular earner for the Special Treatment. It's certainly earning us all a lot of money and those new pills seem to make it all the more effective. The women seem to take every time now. And the demand is as high as ever - and they say we're their most reliable source of supply. Did you know they're paying three times as much for progeny with blond hair and blue eyes - so we need some blond European women to be kept back for the Special Treatment!"

"Well, either way," said Achmet with a shrug, "this one's a valuable bit of merchandise. But the Mullah wants her subjected to the full prison regime so that, especially after the shock of a public performance, she'll soon be desperate to sign up - either for indentured service or Special Treatment ... But what about that one of yours who signed up for the Special Treatment? She realise yet what's happening?"

"No, not yet. But she's coming along nicely. And she's still performing nicely when I choose her to Grip the Bars - but up her backside now of course! It's still nice and tight!"

"Well, anyway I like that too,!" laughed Achmet, eying Louise's soft little bottom that was quivering under her thin prison tunic.

"Oh," cried Mafu, "I nearly forgot. The Mullah wants mine tied down, for the night, next to this one of yours. I've already put her in your cage. They're both English. Perhaps he wants my one to teach your one the ropes."

"Or put the wind up her!" Achmet slapped his friend on the back, and led Louise on down the line of cages. Achmet stopped in front of the cage at the end of the line. It was painted a bright red that matched the red stripe round her chador. He unzipped the velcro fastenings on her shoulder and her tunic fell to the ground leaving her now shaven body stark naked.

48

"Hang it up," he ordered tersely. "You no wear tunic in cage. Make dirty."

Louise picked up her tunic and hung it on the rail outside the cage. Achmet unlocked a small barred gate in the front of the cage and thrust Louise into it.

"Muzzle stay on until tomorrow," he said. "Help you learn no talking allowed in cages - or in prison yard."

Then he locked it again, turned on his heel and whistling a little tune sauntered off to the comfortable quarters of the black guards.

Twenty crawling women silently surrounded Louise. All she could see of them were their eyes and their mouths. Suddenly they all started gabbling at her in a mixture of Swahili, Hindi, Arabic and broken English. Muzzled as she was she could only grunt in reply.

The patrolling guard came rushing back to the Red cage. "Silence!" he shrieked, rattling his cane along the bars of the cage, "or you all get cane! Get back!

Cowed, the women fell silent and quickly crawled back out of reach of his cane.

Just then there was a rattling noise. Peering through the bars of the cage Louise saw that a large tub was being wheeled along the line of the cages by a guard. As he passed each one he would put several dollops of what looked like watery porridge into the long trough.

Louise shrank back in horror as he reached the Red Cage, but the other women all eagerly lined up on their knees in front of the bars. The guard jerked down a lever and a long barred slit opened upwards immediately above the trough. Eagerly the hungry women, gripping the bars of the cage with their manacled hands, thrust their heads hands through it.

"Hey you! Prisoner 743! Get into line!" It was Achmet. He had come back to make sure his women would all eat up properly. Nervously Louise crawled forward, gripped the bars and thrust her head and hands through the narrow gap like the others. The trough was immediately below her head. She could smell the food. She saw that none of the women had started to

49

eat.

Suddenly Achmet pulled another lever and a bar was lowered above the women's outstretched necks, holding them in place.

"Tongues!" Achmet ordered and Louise saw the tips of little pink tongues being thrust out through the little slit in the chadors. Achmet came down the line of women, looking at the numbers painted on each chador and checking them against a list in his hand. Then he thrust a pill into the back of some of the women's throats, forcing her to swallow it.

He now stepped back, looked approvingly up and down the line, and blew a whistle. Immediately the women lowered their heads and started to eat the porridge through the small slit in their chadors.

Louise had not eaten anything since her light lunch but the porridge hardly tempted her - anyway how could she eat if she was muzzled. Suddenly she saw that Achmet was standing over her. He thrust his cane through the bars and brought it down hard across her buttocks.

"Head into trough!" he shouted angrily, giving her another stroke across the backside. "Suck up through muzzle!"

To emphasise his point, Achmet pushed poor Louise's chador covered face down into the mess of porridge. "Suck it up!" he cried.

Spluttering, Louise tried to do as she was told.

Suddenly Achmet's whistle sounded again - this time two blasts. It was the signal to stop eating. The women raised their heads, but they were still prevented from withdrawing them into the cage by the bar behind their necks as Achmet picked up the hose and went down the line washing the remains of the porridge off each woman's chador. He was a fastidious young man and liked his women to be kept clean. Louise scarcely knew which was worse, spluttering from having her face immersed in the trough, or spluttering from the force of the hose played around the small hole in the chador over her mouth.

Satisfied at last, Achmet pushed the lever to raise the bar from behind the women's necks. Gratefully Louise withdrew her head into the cage.

Then came an Arabic order, that was repeated in English: "Buttocks!" The women, still lined up at the front of the cage, turned round, parted their knees, lowered their heads to the floor of the cage and pressed their naked buttocks against the bars.

"And you 763!" Achmet called out. "Move! Hurry or you get cane!"

Scared, Louise hastily scuttled round on her knees. She was now kneeling on all fours alongside a woman with a body as white as her own, presenting her bottom to Achmet in shame.

Suddenly she jumped as Achmet thrust his cane between the bars and brought it down across her back. "Press buttocks against bars!" he screamed. "Head down!"

Blushing with even greater shame, Louise copied the other woman's position. But worse was to come

"Part Buttocks!" Achmet ordered.

Horrified, Louise saw the other woman reach back with her manacled hands...

"And you!" came the angry order. It was an order which she hastened to obey.

Achmet picked up the hose and cleaned the other women and then Louise. Oh how dreadful! But that was only the beginning. Louise gave a little start as she felt him putting grease on her rear orifice, and then she tried to scream a protest from behind her muzzle as she felt something being inserted.

Her temperature was being taken! Her temperature and that of the other women. Achmet noted them down carefully in each woman's red book. He was monitoring their monthly cycles! Then he closed the books with a snap and strode off, whistling, to have his supper. A bell rang out across the large prison yard. It was the signal for the women to be put to bed.

Louse saw the other women lie down on their backs alongside each other with their hands holding the bars behind their heads. Hesitantly she followed suit. Moments later she felt a light chain being passed through the loop in her wrist chain. She, too, was now held, helpless, lying on her back, with her hands fastened to the bars behind her head.

It was indeed a very simple way of ensuring that the naked women in each cage did not, despite the laces, try to touch themselves, or each other, during the night. It also kept the expectant women lying helplessly on their backs, feeling something strange moving in their bellies, and peering down at their mysteriously swelling tummies.

Parting their outstretched legs as far as their ankle manacles permitted, the women could still, of course, spend a penny through the laces, or through the grill of the chain mail pouch, onto the straw beneath their buttocks, with the liquid running away through the bars to the sand below.

The cage was now silent except for the occasional clinking of a woman's ankle chains as she vainly tried to lie on her side.

My God, Louise was thinking, am I going to spend the rest of my life here? No one, she realised, except for the odious Pierre, knew she had gone to Mifsud. Even the hotel register did not show her real name - nor did the records of the Court or the Prison.

But at least Jeremy would not know. And he must never find out. How terrible it would be for him if he ever learnt that his precious wife was being kept caged like an animal, in a remote Middle Eastern prison, supervised by a young Negro overseer with a cane. She blushed in horror at the thought.

But Jeremy would have no idea what had happened to her - or even that she was in an Arab country. For him, his lively, amusing and easy-going young wife would have just mysteriously disappeared.   2 - 4 THE MULLAH Back in the air-conditioned office, the strict fundamentalist Mullah was smiling as he looked out on the illuminated prison yard. He nodded with approval as he saw the new prisoner, Number 9 -743, looking in horror at the line of cages and saw Achmet putting her into his Red cage. The girl could earn him a lot of money and Achmet was one his best overseers.

He unlocked a safe, took out a file, and glanced through it. Everything was going to plan - and a financially very rewarding plan at that! He locked the file away again. Louise would have been astonished had she seen that it was marked 'The Hon. Mrs Louise Riddle' - and that it contained a good deal more information on her than merely the sentence of the court, including certain payments made to a certain Pierre, discussions with a certain black eunuch named Zalu, and indeed a substantial payment in advance from a certain Very Important Person.

He looked at the Polaroid photographs and nodded approvingly. He would send them to Zalu to show to his anonymous, but clearly very wealthy, Master. Their very eroticism should make him keener than ever to own the girl, or rather her articles of indenture.

But the Mullah did not feel entirely committed to Zalu. Pierre had previously arranged for other women to be sent, very profitably, to his prison and, if Zalu and his, at present, unknown Master reneged on their financial commitments, then he would discreetly circulate these photos amongst certain other wealthy Arab gentlemen! Alternatively, of course, she might prove to be a very profitable candidate to 'volunteer', like another Englishwoman had already done, for his new Special Treatment. The Mullah smiled to himself as he remembered how the prison had been established at the insistence of the fundamentalists to serve several small neighbouring Arab states. It was originally intended to be a centre for disciplining recalcitrant women - particularly foreign servants used to greater freedom, or local feminists influenced by their Western sisters.

Such ideas were, of course, complete anathema to the fundamentalists, who were determined to stamp out the Western concept of sexual freedom for women. 'God has made men to excel over women. Go ye therefore and enjoy them and if they rebel, scourge them.'

Women's role in life, the Mullah and his colleagues held, was, therefore, merely to give pleasure to men, and to produce and rear his children. Women were a source of evil and temptation and must be confined, under the threat of the lash, to their homes.

The key feature of the prison was therefore its harsh

regime: intended both to act as a punishment for any woman not complying with the subservient and humble role envisaged for women by the fundamentalists, and to act as a terrible deterrent to any dissidents.

Women found guilty of not being fully veiled in the presence of strange men or in public, or their hands hidden in thick gloves and their ankles in ugly boots, or of being out of their houses without the written authorisation of their fathers or husbands, could be sent here by the religious courts. So, too, could errant wives, accused of adultery, or unmarried women, accused of fornication.

The very existence of the prison, whispered between even educated women in frightened tones, served as a terrible warning to all women to remain in the humble and subservient role that the fundamentalists prescribed.

It also served as a prison for women, usually foreign servants from India, Sri Lanka or the Philippines, who were genuinely or falsely accused of theft, laziness or disobedience.

Furthermore, the Mullah believed that he was particularly following the tenets of the True Faith, when the women concerned were the hated Western women, caught in a sexual misdemeanour. Moreover, like many of the other lighter skinned women, these white women could often be disposed of at considerable profit - especially if no one knew they were there!

He provided, he felt, a service to good Moslems with a certain wealth - a service that had died out with the closing of the slave markets. The Mullah had also developed another highly profitable little sideline for the women in his charge, in conjunction with a particular Adoption Agency based in Cyprus. They had clients from all over the world and needed to be able to supply merchandise of all colours - including the most highly prized ones of all: little blond boys and girls with blue eyes.

They also needed, however, a regular source of supply and didn't worry too much about how they got it. This suited the Mullah very well. He was able to take advantage of the isolated women's natural maternal instincts - and their fear of the constant threat of public flogging and of the prison regime.

In general the whiter the merchandise, the more the Adoption Society could charge their clients, and the more they paid the Mullah.

Ironically, it was the miracles of modern medicine, developed in the West, that enabled the Mullah to arrange these financially very rewarding matters so neatly with so little fuss, or emotional involvement. Not only did the women have no contact with the sires but, being strapped down blindfolded, with their hands chained above their heads on the day of deliverance, they never saw or held their progeny. Once again it was all done very neatly, and tidily, with no emotional involvement.

And the women concerned, especially the white ones? Their maternal instincts seemed as developed as those of their less well educated sisters. Encouraged by the cultural shock of this prison, and then the experience of their first public flogging, the first of the many such floggings to which they had been sentenced, they soon enthusiastically volunteered for their new role, as a spoilt little mother-to-be. Indeed the Mullah would boast that after only a short spell in the prison, they would do anything, sign anything, in exchange for an easier life.

And now Mrs Louise Riddle was to brought into a state where she too would sign anything. He did not think it would take very long! The Mullah was well aware that the virile young black guards had needs that must be satisfied in a controlled fashion, or else they would take the law into their hands with results that could upset the carefully laid plans being made for some of the women.

Accordingly each guard was allowed to take one of his women each evening before they were fed. There were, however, four strict rules.

The first was that, so as not to offend against the fundamentalists own rules against rape, the girl must offer herself to her overseer. To get her to do that, the overseer may, of course, have offered the girl a day or two of rest in her cage, away from her back-breaking work in the prison yard. But just why the girl offered herself to her overseer did not concern him.

The second rule was that it must only be a woman on

the list kept by the Mullah of those who had recently come into season, and so was wearing a green ribbon round her neck signifying that it was now safe to use her. The Mullah certainly did not want any unplanned half black progenies!

The third rule was that women who were being got ready for Special Treatment and being given Fertility Pills were strictly off-limits; they were being prepared for a quite different type of conception! A coupling with their black overseers might ruin everything.

The Mullah laughed out loud at the thought of how he had introduced the international No Entry sign to denote the bodies of such women.

Once she had been given the Special Treatment, however, there was no objection to her being used, since the chain mail pouch would ensure that only her rear orifice would be available to her overseer's manhood.

The final rule was that just to make sure, all couplings had to be carried out simultaneously, in front of the Mullah so that he could check that no unauthorised women, or those bearing No Entry signs, were being mounted.

Moreover, the sight of a line of half a dozen young black buttocks thrusting in and out of their chosen women provided an amusing spectacle for his guests.

2 - 5 ANOTHER ENGLISHWOMAN!

Louise longed to be able to speak to the white woman lying chained on her back next to her - the same woman who had knelt alongside her to have her temperature taken. But, of course, her gag kept her muzzled.

But later that night when the other women were sleeping and the patrolling guard had gone off to make a cup of coffee, she heard a little whisper: "Are you awake. Can you hear me? I know you're muzzled. I was, too, for my first night. But we're both English! So just give a grunt if you can understand me."

The other white woman was an Englishwoman - and speaking in an educated voice! Eagerly Louise grunted.

"This may be my last chance to talk to you. Normally I'm kept in the next door cage, but tonight I've been put into yours. None of the women in my cage understand English properly and I'm so longing to confide in someone, even if they can't reply. Can you understand me?"

Again Louise grunted eagerly.

Just then they heard the footsteps of the patrolling guard and the woman fell silent. But over the next hour she was able to whisper briefly an extraordinary story to Louise. She was, she said, a Miss Samantha Smythe, an attractive 35 year old career girl, earning a good salary. Suddenly finding herself being made redundant by her struggling firm of stockbrokers, she had gone to Cyprus alone for a holiday to meet new friends and get over it all. Then, she had met Pierre with the same result as Louise, except that there had, evidently, been no mysterious prior meetings with a hideous black man with tribal markings, nor with the handsome young bearded Arab gentleman.

Her wrists and ankles had been manacled. Then, apparently delighted by her slim beauty, the Mullah had also ordered her hair on her head to be spared, but not that over her beauty lips.

She had been horrified at being in the charge of a young male Negro overseer, Mafu. She had been even more horrified when he started taking a keen interest in her womanly cycle, recording her temperature daily in her little red book and checking each month her now hairless beauty lips for any signs of coming into season. Then, a little later, a green ribbon was tied round her neck as a sign that intercourse with her was now 'safe ', and she could be listed as available for her overseer's lust.

She had indeed been appalled at the casual way he would daily use one of the women in his charge, provided she was wearing a green ribbon. He would tell the poor girl that if she gave herself to him willingly and eagerly, then she could enjoy a couple of days of rest in the cage - whilst her companions sweated under the hot sun. It was rare indeed that a girl refused his offer.

He would beckon the nervously trembling girl to crawl out of the cage, and then, with his cane point to her to bend over, still naked, facing the other horrified women, still in the cage, and to grip the bars.

Indeed Gripping the Bars, as it was apparently called, and offering their bodies to satisfy their overseers, was a service that all the women were invited to carry out, in turn.

Never would she forget the first time she herself came into season, as the guards callously called it, and then had the green ribbon tied round her neck. For several days a grinning Mafu offered to let her spend two and then three days resting in the cage - if she would let him have his way with her. Meanwhile she seemed to be being treated more harshly than ever during the work in the prison yard.

Exhausted and with her back almost breaking, she finally agreed to proffer herself to her black overseer. But he insisted she offered herself willingly and keenly, something that made it all the more difficult to bring herself to do it. But finally she did!

A few days later, it was her turn to be beckoned out by a cruelly grinning Mafu, to Grip the Bars. Terrified of his cane, she too had bent over, facing her companions and gripping the bars in front of her, as he forced his large manhood up her.

But at least it had been at a time when she was quite safe - thank God!

Then had come the day of her first public flogging. It had been terrible, the most terrible thing in her life. She, a woman, to be flogged with a rhinoceros hide whip in front of a jeering crowd. The pain and humiliation had been quite awful. And yet, it had only been twenty strokes.

The thought of another four hundred and eighty strokes to be applied over the next few years had driven her almost mad - especially since she never knew, as each Friday came round, whether or not she was going to be sent off for the next batch of strokes. It was, she said, a terrifying sword of Damocles hanging over her head the whole time.

Then, one day she had been marched in to see the

Mullah. She had been scared lest she had not been meeting her daily quota of work, picking and laying those awful paving stones, and that she was going to be thrashed. But the Mullah had been all charm, saying that he was sorry she was going to be flogged in public again and again, until her sentence of five hundred lashes had been applied in full.

However, there was one way of deferring this terrible punishment - perhaps for ever. "Tell me! Tell me!" she had begged him.

He told her that, by law, expectant mothers could not be made to work, nor flogged. He had then paused whilst she took in the implication of what he had said. It was true she knew, that she had always longed for motherhood - her maternal instincts were so very strong. Might she now satisfy these instincts and at the same time make life in this prison bearable?

"Naturally," the Mullah had said as if in answer to her unspoken question, "no one would ever know, but your life here would be transformed: no road building and no public floggings. All you have to do is to sign a contract to be a surrogate mother."

"A surrogate mother!"

"Yes, your child would be brought up in the lap of luxury - and, although you would remained chained, even during your moment of delivery, your life here would be one of ease. It really is an offer you simply cannot refuse."

Samantha had gasped. Indeed could she possibly refuse such an offer. Did she even want to refuse it? She had always longed for the excitement of carrying a child. How jealous she had been of her married girl friends when they had proudly announced they were pregnant.

"And," went on the Mullah, "I can authorise the ultimate threat of public floggings, hanging over your head, to be reduced by two hundred strokes for each live white child you successfully deliver in the prison. Think of that!"

Again he had paused.

"Of course the choice is yours: regular public floggings and the full harshness of the prison regime, or a motherhood, that you, in any case, have probably been secretly longing for: to

59

fulfil your destiny as a woman."

She must, he added, have noticed that there were several other white women in the prison who were in an expectant state: they, too, had opted for motherhood.

"You don't have to make up your mind now," he said smiling. "Why not wait until after your next flogging?"

"No! No!" she had cried. "Give me the contract to sign now."

The Mullah had then handed a contract saying that of her own free will she was willing to be a surrogate mother. She had been taken back to her cage, but not before a bright red circle had been painted on her chador and again on her belly. It looked, she thought, like the international road sign for No Entry. But no entry to what, she had wondered, puzzled.

At first life had gone on much as before and she continued to have to work on the road making. However, she noticed that Mafu no longer chose her, to her great relief, for Gripping the Bars and she was not selected for another public flogging. At times she began to wonder if she had simply dreamed about signing the contract.

But now Mafu was making her take some strange pills every morning and evening. They were obviously important, for Mafu made sure she swallowed them, holding her head back and thrusting them down her throat, like a dog being wormed.

She wondered what they were for and why only certain other women were also given them. Greatly daring she had asked Mafu what they were for, but he had just angrily brought his cane down across her buttocks and told her it was none of her business.

Then, a couple of weeks later, she had been taken by Mafu to the prison sick quarters for what Mafu had said was called Special Treatment. She was going to be given a little reward, he told her, for all her hard work. She had been thrilled. A little reward! Oh, how exciting!

The Mullah had been there, smiling and rubbing his hands. She had seen a carefully locked refrigerator. She wondered if she was going to be allowed a glass of iced champagne and a sumptuous meal - her first since since she arrived at the prison.

Then Mafu had invited her to lie down on a special couch. She was still rather excited at the thought of being rewarded. Then to heighten the surprise, they told her, she was going to be blindfolded. Lying on the couch, unable to see and eagerly awaiting being given her reward, her head had been lifted and a fizzy drink had been put to her lips. Thrilled, thinking it was champagne, she drank it eagerly. But it did have a funny taste for champagne.

She began to feel drowsy. The drink must have been rather strong! Vaguely she was aware of another man's voice talking to Mafu and the Mullah. She heard laughter and the noise of the refrigerator being opened and then shut again. Another bottle of champagne? How exciting!

Instead of the popping of a cork, however, there was a noise as if something was being prepared in a metal dish. She had felt her prison tunic being lifted up and her knees being raised and held wide apart. But then she could no longer keep awake and had dozed off.

When she awoke she was back in her cage and could remember nothing more. But the strange thing was that, just as she had noticed on some of the other women, she was now wearing a silver filigree pouch over her beauty lips. It was held tightly in place by little chains that went round her waist and up between her legs. They, too, were held padlocked by a little padlock in the small of her back, like the one on the back of her neck that kept her chador locked in place.

She felt something slippery and oily inside her. She wanted to wash whatever it was out of her body. But with her beauty lips hidden under the chain mail, she was quite unable to do so, or even to feel and explore inside herself and see what this mysterious substance was.

Moreover. she saw, Mafu had inscribed a Christian cross on her belly, in indelible ink, together with some strange Arabic figures which she could not understand.

She had been astonished when Mafu had called her out

to Grip the Bars. How could he use her, when her beauty lips were covered by the chain mail pouch? But he had, pulling aside the chain that ran up between her buttocks and thrusting his huge black manhood up her backside, using her rear orifice. Oh the shame! A few weeks later she had started to feel strange and had sometimes been sick in the morning. She had been frightened that Mafu would punish her, but he had simply smiled and seemed unconcerned. However, after a weeks or two, he had taken her back to the Sick Quarters for examination.

There, Mafu had made her take off her prison tunic. Then, naked and blushing with shame, she had to stand up on a stool in the usual position for Inspection, her manacled hands clasped behind her neck, her head up, and looking straight ahead.

"Part legs and bend knees!" he had then ordered, raising his cane menacingly. Her tummy was now level with his face. "Thrust out more," he had shouted, reaching round to tap her sharply on the buttocks. Then he had come behind her and unlocked the padlock holding the grille in place over her beauty lips. Oh the feeling of relief as she felt her released beauty lips open up like the petals of a flower.

Then she heard a door open behind her and a strange male voice, speaking to Mafu in Arabic and laughing. She did not dare to turn round. Suddenly she felt a man's hands clasping her waist from behind. Out of the corner of her eye she saw that the hands were brown. They reached round and began to feel her tummy, knowingly.

He came round to her front. He seemed to be dressed in white, but she did not dare to look down.

"Belly out!" Mafu now ordered. "More!" Blushing she had thrust her tummy out, but then had not dared to move a muscle, as she felt his hands parting her now exposed beauty lips. He held them open for the man in white to start expertly feeling up inside her.

Then, laughing mysteriously, the man in white had run a strange object over her bare tummy. Suddenly he had pointed excitedly to something showing on a monitoring screen. Triumphantly he held up two fingers. Grinning enthusiastically, Mafu patted him wildly on the back, like a footballer congratulating a fellow member who had just scored a goal.

She waited, standing there ignored and not daring to move or say a word, as the Mullah was sent for, to see for himself. She herself tried to look down to see what they were so excited about, but a stroke from Mafu's cane had made her quickly raise her head again and go on looking straight ahead.

When the Mullah arrived, and looked at the screen, he grunted in approval and turned to pat her tummy approvingly. Then, still pointing at the screen, he began to question the man in white in Arabic. Then, smiling, and with a final pat on her naked tummy, he had left the room.

An obviously delighted Mafu had replaced the chain mail grille, and led her back to her cage, telling her in his broken English that the doctor said her sickness was just indigestion and reaction to the unusual prison food. He had told her not to worry, even if she felt strange things going on in her tummy, and not to be surprised if it started to swell and if she started to miss. It would all eventually settle down.

She was now excused her daily quota of work and was left in the cage all day - fastened down on her back, just as she was at night, with her hands chained above her head, unable to explore the strange goings on in her tummy.

She had remembered that strange contract of motherhood, and she had excitedly wondered vaguely wondered if she was pregnant. But she knew that she could not be. She had, she said to Louise, been arrested before she could make love to Pierre, and although here the awful Mafu had taken her repeatedly it had only been either when the green ribbon signalled that she was safe or up her bottom.

Sometimes she felt frightened and had vainly tried to get a finger under the tight chain mail pouch. At other times she felt a pride in whatever was going on inside her. It made her feel wonderful and strangely fulfilled. In any case the little chains that held the chain mail pouch in place, seemed to be getting tighter, keeping her more mystified than ever.

She had longed to talk to another European woman

about it all, but had no chance to do so until now - and then the other woman was muzzled. It was all so frustrating! Behind her chador, Louise's eyes had been out on stalks as she had listened to Samantha's story. Poor girl! Was this what she herself was in for? If only a handsome white knight could come and rescue her! Rescue them both!

But it was a conversation that had also been listened to, with approval, by the Mullah up in the Governor's office - thanks to a discreetly placed microphone.

He was delighted to hear that Samantha was still uncertain about her state. In his experience it was always better if white women were kept uncertain about what was going on for as long as possible. Then they did not fret so much - not that they could do anything about it, even if they wanted to, thanks to the chain mail grille.

The Mullah was also delighted that Samantha had told her story so graphically to her fellow Englishwomen. Anticipating it, he had given instructions that they were to be secured for the night next to each other.

Doubtless Louise's heart had gone out to her fellow Englishwoman. All the better, for a new plan was going through his mind as a way of disposing of Samantha even more profitably than using her as surrogate mother.

Moreover her state would be used to make her all the more valuable - for Samantha was carrying twins, girl twins, white girl twins!

2 - 6 HARD LABOUR

It was now dawn, a few days after Louise's incarceration in the prison, and the Mullah and her overseer were both pleased at the way she was settling down to the degrading regime.

The women had already had their morning feed. Achmet now unlocked the entrance to the Red Cage and gave three sharp blasts on his whistle. The women crawled out, Prisoner 9-743 amongst them. By now she knew what she was expected to do.

They all silently lined up on a trestle bench in front of their cage, naked below the neck, manacled hands on their heads, manacled ankles well apart, knees bent and tongues thrust out through the little hole in their chadors. It was the humiliating position prescribed for inspection, enabling Achmet to examine the women in his charge without having to stoop.

It might be humiliating, Louise thought, but she could not help also feeling that it was rather exciting having to present herself like this to a virile young man.

Achmet came slowly down the line. Clearly Louise was not the only woman to find it secretly rather exciting, for there was a scent of female arousal in the air. Indeed, Achmet enjoyed playing with his women.

Louise did not dare look down as she felt him part her shaven beauty lips and, as usual, start to play with her beauty bud. It was something that the virile young overseer was very good at. To her shame, like that of the other young women in her cage, she found herself looking forward to it each morning.

A moistening of his fingers and a glistening of her beauty lips told Achmet that he had indeed aroused her. He took his had away - it would never do to allow this white slut to climax. Louise found herself giving a little sob of frustration. How this young black man knew how to play on a woman's feelings!

Then he drew a white silken handkerchief through her now well moistened lips. He shook his head, disappointed. He could hardly wait to have this girl wearing the green ribbon and for the Mullah to then allow him to have her Grip the Bars. Perhaps an early public flogging would bring her on. He would suggest this to the Mullah.

He again blew his whistle and the women all jumped down and ran, still naked except for their chadors, to a long low trough full of water. They all squatted over it, their knees bent. Crimson with shame behind her chador, Louise prepared herself.

As Achmet tapped each woman with his cane, they one by one released their wastes for his inspection. He was responsible for their health and this provided a simple daily check. He put a series of ticks or crosses against each number on his clipboard. Later he would transfer them to each woman's little red book.

Only when each had performed to his satisfaction were they allowed to run over and join the women from the other cages, to be put through a simple form of dip. It was long, narrow and eight feet deep.

Quickly, one behind the other, and driven on by the guards' canes, the naked women had to jump into the end of the dip. Each woman would completely disappear under the soapy water that was well laced with chemicals to kill any fleas, ticks or other parasites that they might have picked up.

Slobbering and spitting out the foul tasting liquid, Louise struggled down to the far end of the dip, where it shallowed sufficiently to enable her to step out. Then, her chador clean but dripping wet, she had to run back to the Red Cage, put on her prison tunic, and then run off, raising her knees high in the air, to pick up her first load of stones of the day.

As she did so, she was thinking, yet again, how awful it would be if her husband ever had any idea of what she was going through here. Supposing he had seen her arousal as that brute Achmet inspected her intimately? Or had seen her squat over the trough, waiting shamefacedly for the tap of Achmet's cane? Or had seen her being put through the animal dip? It was all too awful to think about. Her black overseer made her do things that she felt so ashamed about that she wondered if she could ever look a white man in the face again.

Her thoughts we interrupted by a shout from Achmet. "Number 743! Get those knees up properly - or you'll get the cane!" Louise stood rigidly at attention in front of the black chief prison warder. She was breathing heavily after having had to run, raising her knees even higher than ever, after being reprimanded by her overseer. She was also breathing with relief that he had not called her over to be caned on the spot.

Still holding out her manacled left forearm to the black man for his inspection, she was balancing a heavy basket of stones on her head with her right hand.

"Number 9-743, Sir," she repeated. The fat warder looked at her arm and made a note in his ledger. Then he pointed his finger.

With a little sob of despair, Louise lifted up the front of her tunic with her right hand to display her now bare beauty lips. All the surrounding hair had been removed. Shamefacedly, she parted her legs and bent her knees in the required sign of respect to this fat Negro, whom she feared as much as she did her own cruel overseer. But, she wondered, as she felt her beauty lips suddenly moisten, was the shame partly because of the animal arousal, that being treated like this seemed to induce?

She was longing to brush away the sweat that was running down her forehead and into her eyes, but she did not dare to do so. How lucky for Samantha that she was left behind in her cage, even if she was strapped down on her back with her hands fastened to the bars so that she couldn't interfere with what was going on in her belly.

The chief warder was in no hurry as he sat relaxed under the shade of a large sun umbrella. He took a sip of his iced drink. It amused him to keep a European woman waiting in this humiliating position. It was revenge for all the humiliations that his race had suffered from the European colonisers.

It would also make her have to work all the harder to catch up and meet her quota of loads.

He grinned to himself as he saw the telltale way in which her shorn beauty lips were glistening. It was extraordinary how the stricter you treated these women, the more they secretly seemed to enjoy it.

He took another sip of his iced drink.

Louise jealously licked her lips, wondering how long it was since she had enjoyed even a sip of anything iced. Certainly not since she had so mysteriously been sent to this terrible prison. Like all the guards in this woman's prison, the chief warder was black and male. Most of the guards were young Negroes, chosen for their splendid physique. No true Arab would demean himself by acting as a guard in a woman's prison, and the idea of giving women power to supervise other women, even in a prison, was of course anathema in this part of the world.

The position of warder was a well paid job that required little exertion and which offered certain perks. For behind the high walls that surrounded the large prison yard, this prison was different from Western ideas of what a prison should be like in this enlightened age - though not all that different, perhaps, from a concentration camp.

Instead of spending most of the time locked up in cells, here the prisoners were forced to work in the yard from dawn to dusk. Indeed there were no cells - just the row of straw covered cages open to the elements.

Up to twenty women slept in each cage, and each cage had its own black overseer responsible for the discipline, health, feeding, cleanliness, intimate hygiene and punishment of its occupants. He was also responsible for recording her monthly cycle, something that that the clever system of green ribbons encouraged him to do with meticulous care! Behind the seated black chief warder stood one of the prisoners. She was a pretty young Filipino woman who had come to Arabia to earn her dowry.

She had, however, had the temerity to resist her Arab Master's sexual demands. To bring the girl to heel, her Master had had accused her of stealing a brooch. A few months, he had reckoned, in this terrible prison would make the girl far more amenable, especially since, under the terms of the parole on which she would be released, was the constant threat of being sent back there if her behaviour was not completely acceptable to her Master.

Indeed many of the foreign women in the prison, often from the Philippines or the Indian sub-continent, had been sent there by their Masters or Mistresses on trumped charges for a short sharp shock - and to ensure that from then on they were virtually slaves, forbidden to leave the country and terrified of being sent back to the prison at the whim of their Master or Mistress to complete their sentences.

There was fear in the Filipino girl's eyes. Anxiously she was fanning the gross figure of the chief warden as he sat, naked to the waist, watching with his cunning eyes all that was going on in the prison yard. She knew that the slightest sign of sweat running down his forehead, or between his plump shoulder blades, would result in several angry strokes of the cane and, if it was repeated, would result in her replacement. Her's was a much sought-after job. Anything was better than the awful back-breaking road making.

The chief warder looked down at his watch. It was a gold one that he had removed from one of the white prisoners, a young French woman who had been a governess in the household of a leading local Arab family. Like the Filipino girl, she had refused the advances - this time of her Mistress. She would not now do so again, when she was sent back to her!

Prisoners, especially white ones, were not allowed watches or calendars - nor, indeed anything that they might associate with their true former identity. There were two sharp blasts of a whistle.

Immediately all the women prancing across the prison yard stopped, grateful for the hourly break. Those with baskets loaded with heavy paving stones balanced on their heads put them down. It was a chance to get their breath back and to go quickly over to the big water trough to quench their thirst.

Louise knew she had a just five minutes before that cruel swine of a chief warden blew his whistle again. By then she must have left the trough with its crowd of scrambling women, have run back to her basket, and have lifted it back on top of her head again. Then the moment the whistle went, she would have to resume her high prancing action and run across to where another Negro guard, also sitting in the shade of a large umbrella, was responsible for weighing the loads.

Louise could scarcely hold the heavy basket as she lowered it to the ground. She did so very carefully, scared lest the small square shaped paving stones might spill out and make her waste precious time loading them again.

She ran over to the trough, still raising her knees as high in the air as her manacled ankles and the slits in the side of her tunic, permitted. Even during the short rest periods the women all had to move at the regulation pace. The slightest slackness in raising her knees up high could result in a guard calling out her number, printed in large Arabic numbers across the back of her tunic, and across the front of her chador. Then he might order her to double on the spot for five or ten minutes, whilst he periodically urged her, with painful strokes of his cane, to raise her knees yet higher.

Quite apart from this being exhausting, and preventing her getting at water trough until the next rest period, it could also prevent her from reaching the standard quota of fifty full loads of paving stones.

Several times in the past few days she had suffered the degradation of having to perform in this way before a simple black man as he screamed at her: "Up! Up! Higher!", punctuating each command with a slash of his cane across her back or buttocks.

She was certainly not going to risk that happening again, she resolved, as she pranced across the yard to the water trough.

But the trough as surrounded by desperate women, each silently trying to get at the water. At last she managed to push her way through the milling crowd and lowered her head into the trough. I'm acting just like an animal, she thought, but this was no time for manners. It was every woman for herself.

Hastily she ran back to her basket, taking care yet again to keep her knees raised high. With a struggle, she lifted the basket up onto her head and balanced it carefully with both hands. She was just in time. A few seconds later came the chief warden's whistle.

Fighting hard to retain her balance, for to fall now would be a disaster, she ran across the yard at the regulation pace to the weighing machine. Sweat was pouring down her back again under her thin prison tunic as she lifted the heavy basket onto the scales.

The Negro nodded contemptuously, enjoying his moment of power over a white woman. He kicked a large plastic ring across the sand towards her. She went down on her hands and knees and picked it up with her teeth. She gripped it tightly, like a retriever bitch bringing a slipper to her master. She knew

70

she would have to earn fifty such rings buy nightfall, if she were to avoid a beating. She ran to where the circular road was now being laid. It was a road that was never finished, for as fast as some prisoners carefully laid the small paving stones in a pretty pattern at one end, others were lifting them up at the other.

It all seemed so pointless.

However, there was nothing pointless about the punishment that awaited any woman who had not laid fifty loads of paving stones before dark.

Several other women were laying their stones as she started carefully placing hers. Idly she wondered wheat nationality she were. With only their eyes and mouth showing from under their chador it was impossible to tell. She often longed to talk to them and ask them why they had been sent to this terrible prison. But she never dared to do so. The young guards were too alert and any talking was strictly forbidden.

One of the guards was standing on the section of newly laid paving stones. Louise knelt down and with her manacled hands carefully began to lay hers in the semi-circular pattern required. Each stone had to be fitted tightly into the stones next to it, with just the regulation amount of sand between each one. The top of each stone also had to be exactly level with its neighbours.

Suddenly she saw the Negro's high polished boots moving. She could not help trembling with fear. Please let him be pleased with my efforts, she prayed fervently. She saw him run his boot over the top of the stones just laid by another white skinned woman, testing that they were level. She saw the woman put her head down and kiss one of the Negro's boots, humbly licking the dirt off the soles. She saw the gleam in the Negro's eyes as the woman debased herself in this way to gain his approval for her work.

Then his boot caught in the raised edge of a stone. With an angry curse, he brought his cane down across the kneeling woman's back. He kicked several of her stones across the sand. Humbly she scuttled back after them, her ankle manacles clinking, and began to relay them, taking even more care than before.

As Louise worked on, keeping her head down, she no-

71

ticed that the shiny boots were now coming directly towards her. She saw them testing the levelness of the stones that she, too, had just laid. Her heart was in her mouth. She did not dare to stop working. Controlling her natural repulsion she reached forward, thrusting her tongue out through the little hole in her chador, to lick the sole of the boot that the other white woman had not touched. It was important to placate this guard's quick temper.

It tasted horrible. The guard must have deliberately walked in filth. She pulled her head away nauseated. But the grinning young guard raised his foot as if to kick her stones away. He also raised his cane high in the air. Desperately she forced herself to put her head downs again and lick his revolting boots. To her horror, as she did so, she felt a sudden arousal between her legs at being made to perform so submissively. Being utterly dominated by a man seemed to satisfy some primeval need - something which had been so lacking in her marriage.

The guard looked down and smiled. It made him feel a real man to make a white woman do that. Then, after a pause, he walked away, satisfied, grinning up at the window behind which the Mullah had been watching the scene he had carefully arranged.

Louise was indeed being rapidly broken in!

Shaken, she finished laying her stones. With her teeth she then picked up the precious ring, which she had dropped onto the sand in order to lick the Negro's boots, and ran back across the yard to where the women were picking up the previously carefully laid stones.

She knelt down in front of yet another Negro guard and, like a well trained dog, dropped the ring into a bowl at his feet. It was proof that she had picked up and laid correctly, a full load of stones.

She held out her left forearm, lifted up the front of her tunic with her right hand, parted her legs respectfully, and called out her prison number. Slowly the Negro turned the pages of his ledger. It amused him to keep a white woman waiting. Then he put a tick in the ledger and kicked her away.

Quickly Louise crawled to the end of the road. She tried to remember how many loads she had now completed. Was it 26 or 27? Or only 25?

The guards never told a woman how she was doing. This kept them working hard all day, just in case they had miscounted, for no woman would risking not completing her quota.

2 - 7 A PUBLIC FLOGGING

It was Friday, the Moslem holy day, the day of rest. It was Louise's first Friday in the prison.

After the usual early morning session of road building in the prison yard, the bell had rung - the signal, on a Friday, for the women to run back to their cages.

After hanging up their tunics, Louise and her companions. like the occupants of the other cages, were made to stand in a line up on the long bench facing their cage. Achmet harshly them ordered them to assume the humiliating position of Inspection.

But, Louise was alarmed to see out of the corner of her eye, it was not his white silk handkerchief that he was holding as he slowly came down the line of women, feeling each one between her parted legs, but a pot of green paste.

As she stood with her head up, her hands clasped behind her neck and her eyes looking straight ahead, she heard little groans from the women he had passed, and sharp intakes of breath. They seemed, she thought, to be writhing in pain, straining to hold position and not squeeze their thighs together, or to rub their intimacies with their hands.

She was trembling all over by the time Achmet stopped in front of her. "Number 743!" he warned her, checking with the number across the front of her chador, "you keep head up! You not look down ... and bend knees more! Wider apart!"

Terrified and feeling utterly degraded, she obeyed.

Suddenly she felt him rubbing the paste down along her body lips and over her now hairless mound. Desperately she tried not to look down. She felt him part her beauty lips. Oh the shame! However, she could also feel a rising excitement at the

73

thought of this being done to her by her virile young overseer. Was she, she wondered, beginning to fall in love in with the cruel brute?

The she felt him part the now moist lips and rub a little paste inside them.

He stood back and smiled. Suddenly she felt a burning sensation. Like the other women, she caught her breath as she strained not to break position.

"You keep quite still - or you get cane! Keep hands behind neck and legs wide apart."

She gave a little groan and started to writhe in pain. Oh, how she hated him.

"Keep still," he warned. "You not look down. You let paste burn off all new hairs. Paste keep nice and smooth. Every Friday women get paste."

After a time the burning sensation began to ease slightly.

"Good," grunted Achmet. "But you keep legs wide apart and let paste work."

He moved on down the line, leaving Louise still writhing in pain and humiliation as the little hairs that had been beginning to sprout again were burnt off.

Then, after a pause, Achmet unlocked the straps at the backs of the chadors of all the women, except Louise and Samantha, and ordered them take them off. Astonished, Louise saw that most of the women were completely bald, giving them a strange, almost inhuman look. She remembered how her own her head had nearly been shaved. She had never understood why it had not. She also remembered Samantha saying the same.

The Negro overseer ordered the women to kneel down on all fours on the bench, facing him, but with their eyes down, proffering their bald heads. He went down the line again, this time rubbing the green paste into their craniums. They had to keep quite still for several minutes whilst the paste did its work.

Then they were ordered to replace their chadors and he locked the retaining straps into place behind their necks. The chadors would not be removed again until the following Friday.

Achmet hosed down each woman as she crawled, naked except for her chador, back into the cage. Then he and the other overseers left, leaving one guard to patrol up and down the line of cages to make sure there was no talking or misbehaviour.

As it was Friday, the women would be allowed to rest for the remainder of the day. But instead of looking pleased and lying down, Louise was mystified to see, the women were restlessly crawling round the cage. The eyes peeping through the small eye holes of the chadors were all looking nervous, if not distraught.

Louise heard the midday call to prayer from the minaret of a nearby mosque. The women seemed even more restless. Shortly afterwards, peering through the bars of the cage, she saw the young smartly dressed overseers come out of their comfortable air conditioned living quarters, sauntering and laughing. Each made his way to the cage for which he was responsible, a sheet of paper in his hand.

Louise saw the other guards call out the numbers of a small number of women. They crawled out of their cages, put on the tunics and formed up into a line. Louise saw that their eyes had a terrified look, and that, under the hole over their mouths, they were biting their lips to keep back the tears.

Achmet also looked at his list and called out a number, but in Arabic which she did not recognise. Suddenly he pointed at her.

"You! Number 743!"

Scared, Louise crawled to the front of the cage and was taken out. She, too, was made to put on her tunic and then to stand with the others. She seemed the only white woman. She saw Samantha eying her, full of pity, from behind the bars.

The fat chief warder barked a word of command and the women all turned smartly to their right. The were now in line, one behind the other. Louise followed suit. What else could she do? Half a dozen young Negro guard overseers were watching them, each carrying a cane, ready to punish the slightest sign of ill-discipline.

The chief guard again barked an order. The women held their arms out in front of their bodies as far apart as their wrist manacles allowed. Again Louise followed suit.

Two young guards came down the line, one on each side, fastening the women's wrists to two long chains. They were now fastened in a coffle with one chain linking all their left wrists and another all their right ones. Each woman's wrist manacles now lay taut across her belly.

Another word of command was shouted. Stepping off smartly with the right foot, the coffle broke into a brisk trot, their ankle manacles swishing in the sand. They ran past the line of cages and then across the yard to where a large open truck, with high sides, was waiting.

Bemused, Louise ran in step with the other women. They were loaded up into the truck like cattle. Two guards, armed with sub-machine guns, climbed onto a little platform, looking down onto them, their guns at the ready. The fat chief warder climbed into the cab beside the driver.

The truck started off across the yard with a jerk that flung Louise to the floor. Then, peering through a slit low down in the wooden sides, she saw the prison double gates being opened by armed guards: one was opened first, the other only after the first had closed.

Suddenly they were out in what seemed desert. Then streets began to appear. Louise saw trees, houses, people, cars and even the occasional European man or woman - they were free, she thought ruefully, whilst she was a prisoner, and in her black chador and striped prison tunic, she did even look European.

The truck turned into the native quarter, the old part of the town. It went down narrow streets and suddenly came out into a large square. Louise saw that it was filled with a huge crowd of Arabs, all looking up at a raised platform. She saw a powerful looking Negro, standing on the platform, naked to he waist, his muscular torso gleaming.

At his feet was what appeared to be a crouching man.

Horn blaring, the truck forced its way through the crowd. It came to a stop alongside the platform. Many of the crowd turned to look at it, laughing and pointing.

Louise heard shouts, and then the rattle of a drum. The crowd all eagerly turned back to the platform. Louise saw another Mullah, dressed in black, like their own dreaded prison governor, climb up onto the platform.

He turned to the crowd which fell silent. He read something from a paper. There was a roar of approval from the crowd. Then he turned and nodded to the half naked Negro. He looked, a terrified Louise thought, like an old fashioned executioner standing up on a scaffold, as he raised a large glittering scimitar high above his head.

There was a sudden silence from the crowd. Louise held her breath. Suddenly he brought the scimitar down. There was a thud and a terrible scream. Again the crowd roared.

Then Louise saw the Negro bend down and pick something up. He held it aloft. The crowd roared their approval. It was a severed hand, the blood still dripping from it. She almost fainted in horror and fright.

There was a pause. Something else was going on. Then she saw the huge Negro pull the victim up onto his feet. He was a small dark skinned man in a simple prison robe. The Negro raised the stump of the man's arm. It was now covered in black tar. Again the crowd roared their approval. The wretched thief was hustled away.

Now the crowd turned towards the truck carrying the women. They shouted and jeered. The Mullah raised his hand for silence and began to read from a sheaf of documents. Horrified Louise recognised her own number amongst the rest of the unintelligible Arabic.

The back of the truck was let down. The chief warder came up into the truck and unfastened Louise from the coffle of women. Again trembling with fear, she let herself be led down from the truck and up the steps to the scaffold, her ankle manacles clanking. Dear God, was her hand going to be struck off, too, in this mad, remote, place?

"What have I done?" she cried out through the little hole in her chador. But no one heard, nor understood.

The crowd surged forward. The Mullah proudly read

out something that sounded like Inglezi and Roumi, which she now knew meant English and Christian. The crowd picked up the words and started to chant them, overwhelmed with excitement and anticipation.

The chain linking Louise's manacled wrists was seized by the huge Negro. He fastened it to another chain that hung down from a beam high above her head. Then he turned a handle and Louise found herself being raised up by her wrists until she was standing on her toes.

The big Negro picked up a long black, stiff, whip like those which Louise had seen on television being used by the police in South African countries. It was indeed a sjambok, some six feet long, and made of rhinoceros hide. It was a whip that could kill in inexperienced hands, or inflict exquisite pain in experienced ones.

The Negro came to the front of the scaffold and faced the crowd. He held the sjambok in both hands and, his bulging muscles rippling, slowly bent it in a tight curve. The crowd roared and laughed.

Then he gestured to a boy in the crowd. The boy threw a packet of cigarettes into the air. With a flick of his wrist he struck it with the tip of the whip. and split it open, the cigarettes cascading down in all directions. The crowd roared their appreciation of his skill.

Then he made several exploratory strokes with the sjambok, swishing it through the air in an alarming fashion.

Louise was petrified. She had not understood the proceedings of the Islamic Court, but she knew that she had been sentenced to five hundred lashes as well as to hard labour. But she certainly had not understood that she was going to be publicly flogged. She remembered what Samantha had said of her own experience - and what it had made to agree to.

Desperately she looked around for a friendly European face in the crowd. There were none. She tried to cry out in protest but this was greeted with a new roar of delight from the increasingly excited crowd. It was not every day that a white woman was publicly flogged for committing adultery.

Louise could not take her eyes off the heavy, long, stiff whip. It seemed so terrifying, much more so than the, relatively harmless, thin whippy canes used in the prison, and they were bad enough.

The Negro now came behind her. She tried to look round to see what he was doing. But he tapped her with the sjambok and made her look at the crowd. She dropped her head, ashamed to look at the sea of eager faces. But again, pushing her chin up with the end of the sjambok, he made her raise her head.

But the crowd were shouting for more. They wanted to see her every grimace and hear her screams of pain.

The Negro smiled and with a sudden jerk, ripped her cotton chador apart. Her blond hair cascaded down. Her pretty features were displayed. The crowd gave a roar of approval. Now they could see that she really was an Inglezi, a Roumi.

Suddenly she was aware of the whip running down her back, across her buttocks and down her thighs, as the big Negro examined just where her body was under the loose thin prison tunic. Then he raised the thick black whip high in the air. There was a sudden hush.

"In the name of Allah, the Compassionate, the Merciful," intoned the Mullah, his eyes gleaming. Louise heard a swishing noise and then her buttocks seem to have been hit by a line of liquid fire.

She gasped with the pain, tottering on her toes - much to the amusement of the crowd.

There was a long pause. Louise wondered what was happening.

"In the name of Allah, the Compassionate, the Merciful." intoned the Mullah.

The whip again struck her across the buttocks with a crack. This time she screamed and screamed. The crowd enjoyed that. Then after another long pause came the third stroke, and then the fourth and finally the fifth. Louise was screaming and sobbing, and dancing on her toes with the pain.

Suddenly her wrists were released. Instinctively she rubbed her buttocks with her hands to soothe the terrible pain.

The crowd was enjoying itself as they watched the pretty young woman rubbing her bottom as she still danced up and down with the pain.

She turned to leave the platform, glad that it was all over.

But the burly Negro blocked her way. As the crowd laughed, he sternly pointed back at the beam and at the chain hanging from it. He tapped her with the terrible rhinoceros hide whip and made her go back. Again he fastened her wrists to the manacles, and again he raised her up on her toes. Again he raised the whip. Again the crowd fell silent. Again the Mullah intoned his incantation.

There as another long pause, Poor Louise was almost out of her mind with fear. She moved her buttocks awkwardly under her thin tunic as she awaited the next stroke. Horrified, she felt herself becoming aroused just as she had when Achmet had caned her. There were knowing laughs from the crowd. Oh the shame!

Then suddenly the whip came down hard - not across her buttocks but right across her shoulders.

She was completely taken by surprise and her scream of pain was heard right across the large square. Four more strokes followed, also across her back, protected only by the thin tunic. Then her arms were again released.

Again she assumed that it was all over. Again she was driven back by the grinning Negro. But this time her manacled wrists were not left drawn taut above her head. Instead the Negro made her bend over, tightly, and face the crowd.

With her buttocks now pressed against the thin material, the Negro was able to get at the tender back of her thighs. Slowly and methodically, encouraged by the incantations of the Mullah, and the cries of the crowd, he brought the whip down five times. The pain was appalling. Louise screamed and yelled. After each stroke she jumped about the scaffold like a demented woman.

The Negro waited for her to become quite still again, before applying the next stroke, positioning her carefully with the end of his whip. As before, however, he was careful not to draw blood, or to injure the girl permanently. He knew that Louise was far too valuable a commodity to risk that. But he was an expert with the whip, and when, once again her manacled wrists were released, Louise just collapsed onto the scaffold - unable, it seemed, to stand.

The Negro gave her a few moments to recover. Then, again much to the delight of the crowd, he made her crawl right round the edge of the scaffold, for all the crowd to see, and then back to where the hanging chain awaited her again.

This time, the five strokes were more lightly applied, but on the front of her body - her breasts, belly and the front of her thighs all received attention - just as they had from Achmet's cane. But this was in public!

At last it really was all over. A sobbing Louise was carried back through the crowd to the truck, slung over the shoulder of the Negro who had just flogged her. The crowd were cheering and patting him on the back.

The chief warder seized her hands and quickly recovered her head and face with a fresh chador that also had just two little eyeholes and a small hole over the mouth. Then he refastened her to the coffle of women as two women, with coffee coloured bodies, were unfastened and led up together to the scaffold. To provide a little variation for the crowed, they were to be thrashed together, facing each, and flogged simultaneously, with the big Negro and one of his assistants beating each of the them with a sjambok.

As the square rang to the cries of the two women, the chief warder spoke in broken English to the still sobbing Louise.

"Court ordered you have five hundred lashes. You now had twenty. Four hundred and eighty left." Louise gasped, Four hundred and eighty more stokes! She could not possibly stand it. Not another stroke!

The chief warder paused to let his words sink in. Then he went on: "Sometimes you flogged twice a month, sometimes once. Sometimes not once in one month and twice in next one. Sometimes on first Friday of each month, sometimes on last.

You ever know and you never how many strokes. Sometimes just ten, sometimes many more. So you thinking all time if your number going to be called next Friday. Soon you think of nothing else - and of whether kind Governor, the Mullah, will offer you special deal."

Special deal! My God, Louise was thinking, like Samantha?

"Alternatively -" Louise's heart was in her mouth. Yes, yes, she wanted to scream. "Alternatively, of course, we put you on list for next Friday!"

"No! No!" she cried. "Please not next Friday ... Please not ever. I'll do anything ... Anything! I'll sign anything ..."

The chief warder smiled. The Mullah would be glad to hear what the girl had said. But perhaps another little game of cat and mouse might make her even more amenable.

2 - 8 THE EVENING INSPECTION

It was several days after Louise's public flogging.

Just as Achmet had forecast, the shock of Louise's flogging quickly brought her into season, as Achmet described it. He reported this development to the Mullah who carefully added her to his list and gave Achmet a green ribbon to tie round her neck - a ribbon that was to be returned to him after ten days.

At last he could now take her - provided, of course, she first agreed to offer herself to him! At first she haughtily refused his offer to let her rest in the cage provided she offered herself to him. The very idea! She a sophisticated Englishwoman proffering herself to an uneducated black guard!

But then, she thought, why not if it would ease her terrible life in the prison? Who would ever know? Anyway, she had been intrigued by the sight of Achmet's large manhood when other women from her cage had willingly Gripped the Bars for their virile overseer's pleasure.

Yes, she told him, he could have her!

He watched her gloatingly as she ran off to the dip.

82

Every evening the women were put through it again, to wash off the sweat and, this time, also to wash their tunics.

Then she had to hang up her tunic to dry overnight, and crawl back naked into the cage. There she lined up with her companions, on all fours, gripping the bars, as she anxiously awaited the evening feed. But first there would come the terrifying formalities of Evening Inspection.

Achmet left the small barred gate open and stood outside the cage, flexing his cane in a terrifying manner. Louise and the other women's eyes were all fixed on it. For, they all knew, the moment of truth was at hand. Evening Inspection was now about to start.

The Mullah came across the prison yard to the line of cages. He was accompanied by the Negro guard who kept the ledger that showed how many loads each woman had picked up and satisfactorily laid.

He was also accompanied by several other Arab men, dressed in spotless white robes, or, like him, in the black robes of a Mullah. Both contrasted starkly with the nakedness of the caged women. The strangers had been invited by the Mullah to the Evening Inspection to see for themselves just how strict a regime he maintained. Invitations to the Evening Inspection were much sought after.

As the party passed each cage, its overseer ordered the women to lower their heads to the floor in silent respect. Louise was trembling with fear, like the other women, as the party reached the Red Cage at the end of the line.

The Negro with the ledger said something to Achmet, showing it to him.

"Prisoner 743! Short of three loads," shouted Achmet. "Six strokes. Out!"

Oh my God, Louise was thinking as she crawled out and then stood up naked on the trestle bench in front of the black robed Mullah, in the degrading position of Inspection. Keeping her head up, she saw out of the corner of her eye, that the Mullah's guests seemed very interested in her.

The Mullah ran his hand down her belly and then stood

back and nodded to Achmet.

"Down!" ordered Achmet.

Terrified, Louise stepped down from the bench. She knew what she had to do. She had watched in dread as other women had been punished each evening. Somehow she had avoided it so far. But now it was her turn.

Already sobbing with fright under her chador, she went to where a small leather padded wooden horse stood in front of the cage. She looked at Achmet in hesitation. Was she to present her front or back? Which would be worse?

"Front," ordered Achmet.

Keeping her knees bent, Louise lowered her back onto the wooden horse, gripping the tops of the legs behind her head with her manacles hands. Her body was now arched back - nicely presented for the application of Achmet's cane.

She gave a gasp as she felt his hands between her beauty lips. Immediately she felt them moisten. Oh the shame. Then Achmet stepped back. Grinning he pointed to the girl's now glistening beauty lips. Several of the guests laughed appreciatively.

Six times there came a whistling noise. But she realised, she was only being quite lightly caned. A strong muscular brute like Achmet could half kill a woman. It was obviously more for effect than to inflict serious pain. What was she being spared for, she wondered.

Nevertheless, it hurt enough to make Louise scream six times through the little hole in her chador, whilst the men watching all laughed. But she did not let go the bars as the thin whippy cane descended, twice across her belly, twice across the front of her thighs, and, finally, twice across her breasts. And between each pair of strokes, Achmet again stroked her beauty bud, bringing the wriggling young woman, blushing under her chador, almost to a climax.

Finally he put his cane down and with both hands parted her beauty lips, displaying to the Mullah's guests her now increased arousal. Louise felt overwhelmed with shame.

"It's a strange fact of life," explained the Mullah, "that a good caning will often arouse a woman even against her will, particularly if she's white and the man beating her is black. It makes these Christian sluts feel so excitingly helpless."

Then he and his guests moved on to see the same scene being repeated outside other cages.

Meanwhile, discreetly watching the scene through binoculars, from the window in the Governor's office, was a large black man. His distinctive tribal scars on his cheeks and his bloodshot eyes gave him a particularly frightening look.

He was comparing the white body he was looking at through his binoculars, the one that being caned, with photos that he was holding in his hand. These were the photos that had been taken of Louise on arrival at the prison - the ones that showed her both dressed and naked. They had been sent to him with a request for a further payment in advance, for services rendered so far. It had been a request, which his Master, seeing the photos, had willingly paid.

With expert eyes, he compared the hang of the breasts, the swell of the hips, the flatness of the belly, the length of the legs, the turn of the ankles. Yes, it was the same body - even if the face was hidden by the chador. She was being given the agreed harsh treatment.

He watched as Louise crawled back into the cage, desperately trying to ease the pain, and feeling utterly humiliated at being aroused by Achmet and the caning.

My God, she was thinking, I'll make sure I complete my quota tomorrow, even if it kills me. But the Evening Inspection was still not over. The ceremony of Gripping the Bars had yet to take place.

So it was, that after the Mullah and his party had gone done the line of cages, watching the caning of any other women who had failed to meet her quota, they came back to the Red Cage.

The fat chief warden blew his whistle.

The black guards in front of each cage pulled off their well polished boots, slipped off their breeches, and put their boots on again. Still wearing their military style caps, tunics and Sam Browne belts, they were now incongruously naked below the waist

- except for their boots.

Behind her chador, Louise's eyes, like those of the other women, were peering, fascinated and yet horrified, at Achmet's long black hanging manhood, surmounting the big manly testicles.

Up in the Mullah's office, the watching Negro smiled. Let the girl look at the overseer's manhood! Soon, where she was going, she would never see another one again, except for that of her Master, of course!

Zalu turned to leave. He had seen enough. He could report back to his Master that plans were developing very satisfactorily. The strict life in the Sheik's harem would be nothing compared to this! Every evening, a horror-struck Louise had watched as one of the naked women, wearing a green ribbon, had been silently beckoned by Achmet to crawl out of the cage. Blushing under her chador, she was then made to bend over the leather padded wooden horse in front of the cage, the tiny padlock holding the laces closed over her beauty lips was unlocked and the laces eased.

Then her ankles would be fastened wide apart to the feet of the wooden horse and a strap passed round her waist, holding her down onto the horse, and making her bend her knees. She was now held wide open, ready for the eager attentions of Achmet. Finally the chosen woman had to grip the bars of the cage - from which action this little daily ceremony got its name.

Now, in obedience to his shouted order, all the women knelt on all fours in front of the bars of the cage, their heads up and their bare breasts hanging down invitingly beneath them, as Achmet walked down in front of them, deciding which of the women wearing green ribbons, and not marked with a No Entry sign, he would choose. As he did so, Louse noticed with mounting horror, his manhood was rapidly showing signs of arousal.

How long would it be, Louise kept asking herself with a shudder, before she was beckoned out of the cage by a gloating Achmet? She was horrified when this thought, coupled with the sight of Achmet's now erect manhood, made her feel aroused. What a helpless animal she was!

Suddenly out of the corner of her eye she saw that a naked white woman was crawling out of the next door cage in answer to the beckoning of its overseer, Achmet's friend, Mafu. On her black chador was the ridiculous and degrading No Entry sign. It must be Samantha! Oh no!

Although Louise was, of course, no longer muzzled, she still had had only the most fleeting opportunities to speak to Samantha, since she had poured her heart out to the gagged Louise on that first dreadful night in the cage.

Indeed, just as the Mullah had given Mafu instructions to fasten the two Englishwomen side by side on that occasion, he had since told him and Achmet to keep them well apart. Nevertheless, Louise's heart went out to her. In particular she had noticed that, although Samantha could not believe that she might be expectant, her tummy did seem to be slightly swollen above her shame-making laced up beauty lips.

"But you can't, she's -" Louise rashly began to cry out as Samantha crawled out through the little gate of the next door cage.

As if expecting such an outburst, Achmet thrust his cane through the bars and brought it down hard across Louise's back.

"Silence in cage!" he shouted, his manhood now becoming erect.

The Mullah smiled. His plan was indeed beginning to work. The relatively simple deal that Zalu had initially proposed on behalf of his wealthy, anonymous, Master, might well become rather more complicated and wider in scope - and much more financially rewarding for himself!

One the watching guests pointed to the Christian cross emblazoned on Samantha's belly.

"That," explained the Mullah in Arabic, with a smile, "signifies that she is a Christian bitch, a little mother-to-be who, although she may not yet realise it, has been well and truly inseminated with the seed of a blond Scandinavian boy, whom she's never even seen."

"But how did you manage to get hold of his seed?" asked the guest.

"Well," replied the Mullah with a laugh, "you see he was a cabin boy who rather rashly strayed into a rather dubious part of a nearby port - and then got lost."

"And?" persisted the guest.

"Being a rather pretty boy, he was taken to the establishment of a certain ...dealer ... who specialises in providing certain rich men in these parts with such white youths - once they have been castrated, of course."

"But in that case, surely -?" the guest began to object.

"Ah," said the Mullah, tapping his nose with his finger, "but before being castrated, the boy was kept caged with his hands chained behind his back so that he could not get at himself. Once a day a pretty girl was put into his cage with orders to 'milk' him. So a good supply of the boy's seed was obtained - which I was able to acquire, and put to good use!"

The guests glanced admiring at the Mullah. He certainly knew how to keep these arrogant Western woman in their place.

Then he pointed to the tightly laced up beauty lips.

"All our little mothers-to-be are volunteers - keen volunteers, who have begged to be allowed to conceive. But even so, I like to have them them laced up whilst the seed is doing its work, and kept like that afterwards - just in case they are tempted to change their minds! The first time they feel the kicks is often a traumatic moment, as they realise just what they have signed up to do. You sometimes see them trying to tear at the laces. But then they soon settle down again as nature takes over."

The was ripple of cruel laughter from the guests.

"Yes," went on the Mullah, "I like to give my prisoners the opportunity to earn their keep, especially the white ones. I allow them certain privileges but, as you will see, they still have to perform certain duties."

"Bars!" ordered Mafu.

With a sob of despair, Samantha bent over the horse and bent her knees. She knew she must appear eager to please her overseer if she were to be allowed to continue her present easy life.

Her feet were fastened as wide apart as her ankle

manacles permitted. The chain mail pouch was now nicely displayed to the Mullah's watching guests. Immediately above it was her enticing rear orifice.

"Now you can see how these pouches are a very effective way of preventing these sluts from getting at their little progeny," explained the Mullah in Arabic, to his cruelly smiling guests, "whilst still enabling our virile overseers to take a well earned reward from further behind."

Suddenly Louise saw that a grinning half naked Achmet, his own large manhood now half erect, beckoning to her. Oh no! She had known that he would take her one day. But today! Not whilst her friend Samantha was also being taken by her overseer only a few feet away.

"Out!" ordered Achmet, and, half hypnotised by the sight of his huge manhood, Louise obeyed. She too bent over the horse in front of her cage. Her manacled ankles were soon similarly fastened wide apart. She realised that her hairless beauty lips, neatly held together with the zig-zag lacing, were now on display to the Mullah's guests.

Straps were put over both women's waists and pulled down tight. They were held quite helpless. Both women reached forward to grip the bars of their cages. They turned their heads and looked at each other's eyes, peering through the little eyeholes in their chadors. They had still never seen each other's faces.

The head guard now blew his whistle again. Louise looked on open mouthed as the big Negro, Mafu, began to push against Samantha's buttocks. A cry of protest and pain from Samantha, coupled with a roar of triumph from Mafu, and a sudden tightening of Samantha's grip on the bars announced a successful penetration - of her rear orifice.

Seconds later Louise herself gave sharp cry as she felt her own rear orifice being greased and then penetrated, and unbelievably stretched by Achmet's large manhood.

Further down the line of cages, other pitiful female cries and male roars announced that other cage overseers had also achieved penetration - though not usually in the same way as Mafu and Achmet. No attempt had been made to warm the women up or to prepare them for their ordeal. The Mullah liked his young guards to take their women cold.

It was therefore a fascinating scene that the Mullah and his guests enjoyed as they looked down the line of cages, with in front of each a pair of taut black buttocks thrusting rhythmically in and out of the, usually lighter coloured, body of a naked but veiled, and tied down, young woman.

Both Samantha and Louise were screaming in a mixture of pleasure and pain as the strong young Negroes thrust deeper and deeper into them. Then as each woman's overseer began his own rhythmic movement, the grip of both their hands on the bars of their cages, began to tighten and then momentarily relax. Louise saw that Samantha's bottom was beginning to thrust back to meet the thrusting belly of Mafu, and then found that her own bottom was doing the same.

Oh, once more, the shame! Just as Samantha's body was betraying her, so her own one was betraying herself, aroused by Achmet's sheer masculine virility.

"It is interesting," commented the Mullah to his guests, "how these sluts, no matter their colour, nearly always find themselves, in the end, responding to what is being done to them."

"Yes, indeed," pompously said one of his guests, another stern faced, black robed, Mullah. "Women cannot control their lust. It is for that reason that it is right that women should not be allowed out of the home."

Suddenly Samantha screamed again as she felt the overseer's seed drenching her and seconds later her screams were joined by those of Louise. But were their screams ones of utter outrage, or partly of sheer excitement and disappointment at not being allowed to reach their own climaxes?

My God, vowed Louise, if I ever get a chance of getting out of this awful place I shall certainly try to take poor Samantha with me, despite her present state.

The green ribbon was now in place round Louise's neck. All day, as she sweated in the prison yard, she had worried whether or not she was going to called out again that evening to Grip the Bars - and this time have her laces unlocked and eased, so that Achmet could thrust up her normal channel of intercourse.

Achmet seemed to enjoy playing a cruel game of cat and mouse with her, choosing another woman for his pleasure, whilst telling her that it would be her turn next. Then, just as Louise would be breathing with relief at not being chosen, he would change his mind and, with a stroke of his cane, send the woman scurrying back into the cage, and slowly beckon out the cringing Louise.

Oh, the uncertainty and fear! And this coupled with the even greater uncertainty and fear that her name was going to be on the list for the following Friday. It was all driving her mad!

Friday came. The young Negro came to his cage and read out the names of the women to be flogged. Hers was not included. The relief was almost overwhelming, as she watched the line of women running off to the truck.

Then Achmet came back to the Red Cage. He called out Louise's number as if he had missed it earlier by mistake. He beckoned her forward.

"No! No! Not me! Please!" she screamed. "I said I'd do anything, sign anything."

But Achmet grimly continued to beckon her forward. "Good," he said, "then you'll be able to tell the Mullah just that."

The Mullah! Was she going to be made the same offer that he had made to Samantha? An astonished Louise was taken out of the cage and hustled, not to the waiting truck, but along a corridor to what seemed to be a beauty parlour, manned by two pretty black youths with strangely high pitched voices.

Instead of being cuffed and thrown into the truck, her chador was unlocked and removed, and she was pushed into a luxurious foam bath. Then, stark naked, she was strapped down onto an inclined couch.

Her hair was washed and dried, and then combed and brushed. Her eyes were beautifully made up. Her finger nails and toe nails were carefully painted, her cheeks rouged, her breasts powdered and any remaining hairs on her beauty lips removed. Then, a final humiliation, the zig-zag laces over her beauty lips were carefully polished.

Then, leaving her wrist and ankles manacles still on her, the two black youths draped over her shoulders a beautiful and half transparent long negligee with a wide satin sash.

Nothing was said to her to in English by the two black boys as they prepared her and laughingly chattered to each other. Greatly daring, she tried to ask them what was happening. Was she going to be released? But if so, why had she been dressed in such a revealing and provocative manner?

But they ignored her questions.

Then Achmet came back into the room. In one hand he was carrying his cane and a leather dog collar and lead. In the other a pen and a legal looking document, written in Arabic with an English translation.

He looked approvingly at Louise. "Crowd in square enjoy watching you flogged dressed like that," he laughed.

"No!" gasped Louise. "I said I'd do anything ..."

"Then you'd better hurry up and sign this," he said, pointing to the document. "Another truck waiting for you and this time you get thirty strokes. And because you make people wait, this thirty not count against your two hundred - just an extra thirty strokes."

"My God! No! Please, no! I'll sign it. I'll be a good little mother. I promise."

"Well, you lucky girl, instead of becoming a little mother, a rich Arab Sheik has come to rescue you."

"Rescue me!" cried Louise astonished. She couldn't believe it. "You mean take me away from this awful prison?"

"Yes, and no more public floggings - provided you agree to become his indentured servant for rest of prison sentence. You enter his service and he responsible to Court for you."

"Enter his service? As a servant? An indentured servant?" queried Louise, her voice trembling.

"Yes," laughed Achmet, "but only if he find you sufficiently attractive to be put into harem."

"What! His harem!" gasped Louise.

"Yes, lovely life of ease and luxury with not a care in world. Of course, if you prefer stay here, then next truck waiting take you for next public flogging. You get thirty strokes this time."

"Oh, my God!" cried Louise. "Thirty strokes! And what's this Sheik like?"

"He rich and powerful. He like English ladies. He want rescue them from this prison."

Greatly relieved, a sudden thought crossed Louise's mind. "But, if he's rich and powerful, likes Englishwomen and wants to rescue them, then could he also rescue Samantha, my English friend in your friend Mafu's cage? We'd keep each company in his service ... Oh, but I forgot. Would he still be interested in her in view of her ... state?"

Achmet laughed again. In this part of the world, her state would make her all the more interesting - and valuable! The Mullah's plan looked like working out rather well - which would mean an extra big bonuses for him and Mafu. And, although Mafu was due, in any case, to get a bonus when Samantha safely delivered her progeny, that would not be for months, whereas this bonus would be paid here and now.

"You make Sheik want you first," he replied cunningly, "and then if he likes you, you tell him about Samantha. Maybe he willing be responsible to Court for you both - willing to buy both your indentures. Have you both in harem."

He did not tell her that in anticipation of the Sheik asking about her, Mafu was already beautifying Samantha in a next door room and putting her into a similar negligee which could be pulled back to show off her prettily swollen little belly.

"Oh, I wouldn't mind it so much if there was another Englishwoman with me!" Louise felt almost happy for the first time since she entered the terrible prison. Obviously no Arab could really keep Englishwomen in his harem and anyway they could always escape!

"But first you sign agreement - if not, you go back into truck for flogging."

Eagerly Louise seized the pen and signed. She would have signed anything to avoid another flogging. In her relief she did not noticed that the English version was headed "Indentures for Life Service".

Achmet fastened the collar round her neck. A white woman treated like a dog! That should excite the Sheik. He gave a sharp tap with his cane and told her to get down on all fours. Then he led her crawling along a corridor with her silken negligee hanging down around her. Stopping at a door, he told her to wait outside, still kneeling on all fours.

Louise was so thrilled at the thought of being taken away from the prison that she hardly noticed the humiliating way she was being treated. Instead, she was thinking more of how she could impress this Sheik, so that he really did take her away - and Samantha. He was probably some awful old man, but at least she would have an educated Englishwoman as her companion.

"When door opens, you crawl in, crawling to show submission - like indentured servant. You keep eyes down. You see shoes of important Sheik sitting on sofa. You crawl up to him and lick his shoes. You humbly beg him to rescue you, to take you away. You call him Your Highness and Sir. You promise be obedient servant girl. You say you want to please him, to give him much pleasure."

Give him pleasure, thought Louise with a sudden feeling of repulsion. But he was her only chance of getting away from here. Much better be an old man's slave than a prisoner here!

"You beg nice and humbly, then may be, only may be, he sufficiently pleased to buy your indentures. If not, you sent back to waiting truck to have next public flogging. Remember thirty strokes this time."

"That'll kill me!" cried Louise.

But Achmet had not finished brainwashing her to show herself off properly. "He already interested instead in another girl," he lied, "a younger girl. So you must try all the harder to

94

catch his eye."

"Another girl instead! A younger girl! No! No, it's me he must rescue. Me! He must choose me! I'll do anything to make him choose me!"

"Then you tell him how grateful you will be!"

"Oh I will, I'll worship him as my God, my saviour!" Louise cried, thinking all the time of those thirty strokes - an extra thirty. "I'll beg him humbly to take me into his service."

"Alright, but you just remember, I standing right behind you holding you by lead, with my cane raised."

As she knelt humbly outside the door, she could hear the voice of the Mullah and of another man. It sounded somehow familiar. But they were talking in Arabic.

Suddenly the door was opened by the Mullah. Achmet gave her a sharp tap on her now bare bottom with his cane. Desperately anxious to please, she crawled in, her wrist and ankle manacles clanking, pulling against her lead, her eyes down, but seeking the sofa and the shoes of the man who might save her.

Right ahead of her she saw the sofa. She saw the spotless white robes of this strange Sheik, the man who liked English ladies. She saw his highly polished Italian shoes, expensive looking, made of crocodile skin.

She must, she realised, make a highly provocative sight as, her lead held by Achmet, she crawled servilely towards her rescuer, her saviour. Her head was lowered humbly. Her hand and ankle manacles were clinking. Her hanging breasts were only half concealed by her nightdress. Her hips were swinging entrancingly and her bottom was pressed against the silk of the negligee. Her slim waist was set off by the tight sash. Her long hair blond hair hung down over her face. Her beauty lips were kept tightly by the well polished laces.

She blushed at the thought of it all, but if this was what it took to get away from this terrible place, then who cared? But, she realised, the thought of pleasing this man was starting to arouse her. She could feel herself becoming moist. Oh why did her body always let her down!

In complete silence, she continued to crawl towards the

expensive looking shoes. Then as she had been told to do, she put out her tongue and licked. She could feel herself becoming more aroused as she did so. Oh what a slut she was: a slut who was always longing to be forced into submission.

The Mullah closed the door, smiling. This little scene alone, he thought, would enable him to almost double the price that that the young Sheik would be willing to pay to get the girl.

Still nothing was said. Then a hand came down and gripped Louise's hair. Her head was pulled up sharply. Her head swam. She was about to see the man who was going to buy her indentures, the man whose service and harem she would be entering - if she pleased him! 2 - 10 ACQUIRED! Louise gasped in astonishment. There, looking down at her as she knelt at his feet, was not some repulsive old Arab Sheik, but the handsome and charming young man she had met with Pierre in Cyprus. The man she had longed to see more of.

He was a Sheik and he was he was her rescuer! Her handsome saviour! Oh how wonderful! Somehow he had heard of her plight and had come to get her out!

Eagerly she put her head down and again started to lick his shoes, just as Achmet had told her to do. He raised one shoe offering the dirty sole to her tongue. It was a test! It tasted foul, but she eagerly licked that too. Anything to be taken away from here!

She raised her head, and holding the hem of his spotless white robe with her manacled hands, kissed it reverently. She remembered what Achmet had said about another younger girl, and of begging him to take her into his service and of impressing him with her gratitude. Yet again she remembered the truck waiting outside, waiting to take her to be flogged. Thirty strokes! She redoubled her humble kisses.

She raised her head and looked up at him piteously.

"Oh, please, Your Highness, do save me, I beg you. Please take me into your service! Please!" she begged in her prettiest girlish voice. As the words tumbled out, she now alternatively held his hand, covering it with fervent kisses, and raised her eyes to look up at him submissively and humbly, as she pleaded.

"I'll do anything you want! Anything! I'll give you such pleasure! But please, Sir, please save me. Please take me away from this awful place. I shall be so grateful, Sir. Grateful for the rest of my life. Please! I beg you, I will thank you for ever. I will for ever be in your debt. I will ..."

"And what would you say," came the smooth attractive voice of the young Sheik, speaking in fluent English, "if I required you, as my indentured servant, to enter my harem so that I can keep you locked up? In that way I could account for you properly to the Court that sentenced you?"

Louise hesitated, but only for a moment. It was now or never. This was the moment of truth. She must not throw away her chance of getting away. She looked up into his fierce and dominating eyes. She felt another surge of arousal and moisture in her loins.

"Then I would say, Sir," she said now speaking slowly and deliberately, but with genuine fervour, as a cultured young Englishwoman, "Yes, take me and put me into your harem. Make me your humble servant. Make me your submissive slave. I long to please you, and ... to love you, and to adore you."

There was silence for the moment, as the Sheik revelled in what he had so carefully planned to bring about: a beautiful and well educated Englishwoman, a married woman, a sophisticated woman of the world, begging him to take her into his harem - to make her his slave! She really must have gone through hell to have brought herself to beg so prettily to enter his service. And who was he to refuse the pleadings of such a pretty woman!

Then the Mullah nodded to Achmet who, giving a jerk on Louise's lead, made her stand up in front of the sofa, her negligee hiding her body. He gave her another tap with his cane and quietly murmured an order. Hastily she stood up straight, raised her head, looking now at the wall above the sofa, and put her manacled hands behind her neck.

There was a long pause as Sheik Ali looked at this clearly well disciplined and lovely creature who had just begged to be his adoring slave.

Again the Mullah nodded to Achmet who, still holding her lead taut, came round and untied her sash. Slowly he drew back the negligee, disclosing, as in a slave market of old, the young woman's firm full breasts and her slim waist, her beautifully smooth and hairless mound, the line of her equally hairless beauty lips held pressed together by the neat lacing.

The Mullah smiled to himself as he saw the way the young Sheik's eyes increasingly lit up as Louise's body was slowly and erotically displayed to him. So much depended on how the merchandise was displayed! How right he was to have had Louise brought in half naked on a lead, crawling on all fours, her manacles clanking. He would now bargain with the Sheik over the price, just as in former days a slave dealer would bargain over the price with a rich buyer, attracted by a particular young woman who had been erotically displayed to him.

"I must warn you, Your Highness," smoothly lied the Mullah in Arabic, "that in view of this young married woman's very serious offence, the Islamic Court require a much larger price for her articles of indenture than I had expected. But I'm sure we can reach an agreement that will satisfy them."

Sheik Ali nodded. He had been expecting this - but this girl, Louise, would be worth every penny he had to pay for her. She was just the sort of aristocratic Englishwoman he wanted for his harem - and, thanks to the arrangements that Pierre had made, no one would ever know where she was.

Indeed, like an eager buyer at an old fashioned slave market, he could hardly wait to get the girl home - even if meant paying a little more than he had originally arranged with Pierre.

"Show respect to Master!" ordered Achmet.

Blushing, and keeping her eyes fixed on the wall behind the Sheik, Louise parted her manacled ankles, bent her knees and thrust her belly towards the handsome young seated Sheik. Her beauty lips were now on display, glistening with arousal.

"As you can see, Your Highness, she is a natural slave," said the Mullah, pointing to her evident signs of arousal. He nodded to Achmet who deftly unlocked the little padlock hanging between her parted legs, then undid the laces from the little rings.

Louise blushed as, her head still raised, she felt her released beauty lips open like the petals of a flower. She blushed even more, but still did dare to look down, as she felt Achmet part her aroused beauty lips for the young Sheik's inspection.

There was another long silence, as Sheik Ali put his hand down and felt up inside her. Louise held her breath. Was he going to save her?

The handsome young Sheik pointed down to his feet. Louise sank down, back onto her knees. Again she licked his shoes. Again she looked up imploringly. A few weeks of prison life had made her delightfully submissive, he thought. She had the makings of a willing and pleasing concubine.

"Save me, You Highness, please," she begged.

"Very well," came the reply, "but do you realise that I shall be responsible for your future conduct?"

"Do with me what you like, Sir," begged Louise. "But please, please, take me away from here. Let me be your slave."

"Very well, then"

Louise burst into tears, tears of relief. She felt the handsome Sheik's hand reach down and stroke her head. Eagerly she seized it and smothered it with passionate and humble kisses.

"Oh, thank you, Sir. Thank you. I promise I'll be your humble slave for as long as you like."

Suddenly she remembered Samantha.

"Oh, Sir," she said, greatly daring, "if you are keen to rescue English ladies, do you know there's another one here, my friend, Samantha Smythe? We would be friends in your service."

The Mullah smiled. He had, of course, planned to mention her to the Sheik at the appropriate moment, but much better that it came from Louise.

"Oh?"

"Oh, do save her. I think she may be expecting, but she's an English lady just like me."

"A little mother-to-be! Well, very interesting," murmured the Sheik, remembering his plan to follow his grandfather's maxims with his Englishwomen. He would now be able to make a start right from the very beginning. Splendid! Moreover now that the Crimson twins had both delivered their mulatto progeny there were no prettily swelling bellies in the harem. This possible new acquisition would instantly rectify that.

Better and better, thought the Mullah, rubbing his hands.

"Can I see her?" the Sheik asked him in Arabic.

"Of course!" replied the Mullah Ten minutes later, Louise was again kneeling on all fours outside the door. Her lead had been fastened to a ring on the wall. A few moments earlier she had seen Samantha being led in, just as she had been, crawling on all fours, through the door, bathed, beautified, made up and dressed in a similar negligee to her own.

Louise was panting with excitement. Soon she and Samantha could be on their way - taken away from this terrible prison. Suddenly she realised that she still did not know the name of the Sheik, the handsome young man who was going to be her Master, and perhaps Samantha's, too. Nor did she know where he was going to take them. But no matter - provided he took them away!

It had been the first time that she had seen Samantha not hidden in her chador, the first time she had seen her face and her hair. What an attractive woman she had turned out to be, with gentle soft eyes, over honey coloured hair. With her peaches and cream complexion, she seemed the very epitome of English womanhood.

This, too, had been Sheik Ali's first impression, as she, too, had been brought in crawling on a lead, her manacle chains clanking. And how delightfully, and in an educated English voice, she, too, had begged him to take her away! Eagerly he had read the notes on her background, supplied to the Mullah by Pierre. She, too, was just what he was looking for. And she, too, could disappear into his harem without a trace.

Moreover, when Mafu had untied her sash and pulled back her negligee, just as he had earlier with Louise, he had been fascinated to see the signs of a little swollen belly, on which were neatly inscribed a Christian cross and her expected date of deliverance. He was even more fascinated to learn that she still did not fully realise that she had been successfully impregnated, and apparently still thought it was all just indigestion!

Then when she too had been made to Show Respect, he had been fascinated to see the little chain mail pouch, similar to that used by Zalu to ensure that a girl did not harm her progeny when the truth finally dawned on her.

"Your Highness is pleased?" asked the Mullah in Arabic ingratiatingly, as he mentally calculated the extra price he could ask for her - and for her progeny.

"Perhaps," replied Sheik Ali nonchalantly, trying not to show his excitement, "though it's a pity she's not younger."

"A more mature career woman will feel her new servitude all the more," smiled the Mullah. "And in the West, a woman is in her prime in her thirties - and indeed into her forties."

He gave another order to Mafu. Still holding the woman still with one hand, with the other Mafu lifted up one of her firm large breasts, holding it up for inspection.

"See how it's getting larger as nature prepares it for its proper, predestined, new role," the Mullah laughed. "See the prominent blue veins. See how the nipple is looking a darker red, ready to be enlarged for your delight. Oh, yes, this one will make a splendid milk slave."

Again the young Sheik's eyes lit up, as he remembered his grandfather's maxim. Yes it would be delightful to tell Zalu to keep her in milk and to have this beautiful woman brought to him to offer him her refreshing milk.

"And," asked the Sheik, "tell me more about the child."

"Twins!" interrupted the Mullah with a smile. "Twins - so the milk will be even more plentiful! And both little girls are probably beautiful little blue eyed blond ones, that before too long will, in turn, be ready for your harem. See for yourself!"

He switched on the scanner.

"Position for Inspection!" ordered Mafu, giving Samantha a tap on the buttocks with his cane.

Hastily, biting her tongue to overcome her embarrassment, Samantha straightened up, her ankles together, her head raised, her eyes on the wall, and her manacled hands clasped behind her neck.

She blushed prettily as she stood, her body half naked and exposed, in front of the sofa on which this good-looking and immaculately dressed young Sheik was seated. How wonderful that he was mysteriously interested in rescuing her - and, apparently the other new English prisoner as well.

"Belly out!"

Blushing yet more, she thrust out her swollen tummy, towards the seated Sheik. Oh how shame-making! But what a charming looking young man. And why all this interest in her tummy?

She felt the Mullah moving something slowly over her tummy, but, with Mafu's cane still tapping her bottom, she did dare to look down to see what it was - nor down at the monitoring screen.

The Mullah pointed to the screen and broke into voluble Arabic.

Samantha had no idea that the Mullah was proudly pointing to two strange tiny objects, now clearly showing on the screen. Not did she know that the Mullah was equally proudly enlarging on the role of the silver filigree chain mail strapped over her beauty lips with the pretty little square grille in the centre.

"I suppose they were sired by her black overseer?" said the Sheik disparagingly.

"Oh no, Your Highness!" protested the Mullah. "She was fertilised, unknown to her, with the precious seed of a beautiful blond Scandinavian boy, taken before he was castrated. But we have used his seed on other white women prisoners and the results have always been beautiful blond little girls."

The Mullah again pointed to the little creatures on the screen. "These might well grow up into very suitable entrants for our harem," he said in a persuasive tone.

"Indeed," murmured the Sheik his eyes glistening.

He was thinking of the arrangements that Zalu had persuaded him to make for any little white girl progeny of his English concubines to be sent to Europe to be reared in a convent that he had endowed particularly well. Then when they reached maturity, they would be sent back to their guardian - ignorant of the fact that, by an old North African Law, the daughter of a Registered Indentured Servant can herself automatically be registered an Indentured Servant.

Well! He could make a start with this woman's twin girls.

"Imagine," said the Mullah in Arabic, interrupting the Sheik's reverie, "just imagine, the delight of having this girl paraded before you every day, still chained, to display her prettily growing belly."

He nodded to Mafu who with his cane made Samantha come right up to the seated young Sheik.

"Belly out!" he again ordered.

"Feel it Your Highness, feel it for yourself. Admire its little curve. Imagine it when it gets really well swollen - and still with the lips tightly compressed by the silver filigree pouch or, if you prefer, still tightly laced together."

The Mullah nodded to Samantha's overseer.

"Keep still!" warned Mafu, "Eyes fixed ahead!" Then he quickly unlocked the small padlock in the small of Samantha's back. The chain mail pouch fell away, disclosing her hairless beauty lips - just as those of Louise had earlier been shown off.

The Mullah ran his hands down the lips. "No problems here," he murmured. He ran his hands over the blushing young woman's hips. "Good child-bearing hips, too."

Samantha gasped as she now felt the young man's hands running over her thrust-out tummy, cupping it.

Oh yes, the Sheik was thinking, it really would be delightful to have this creature in his harem. As Mafu parted the lips, he ran his fingertip down between her legs.

"And the Court would also allow this woman's indentures to be bought?" he enquired. "And, of course, with a special discount for taking two."

"Indeed," replied the Mullah, inwardly gloating. "I'm sure I could persuade the Court to accept a reasonable figure. But there would also, of course, be the expense of breaking her contract of motherhood. My clients in Cyprus will be very disappointed not to take delivery, especially of white twins!"

The Sheik gave a contemptuous laugh. It would be a delivery, the Sheik was telling himself, that would, instead, now be made in the secrecy of his harem - the first, perhaps, of several involving his Englishwomen. Perhaps, indeed, the other Englishwoman might also make a very suitable little mother-to-be. The Mullah now gave orders for Louise to be brought in, to join Samantha. They were both now standing in front of the Sheik, their leads held taut by Achmet and Mafu. Their negligees were slipped off.

The Mullah gave an order and, giving them both a tap with their canes, Achmet and Mafu ran their stark naked charges prancing up and down in front of the Sheik, their knees raised high in the air. Samantha's softly swollen belly contrasting with the flat tautness of Louise's.

It was, thought Louise, rather like a pair of mares being trotted up in front of a prospective buyer. How exciting! Horrified she felt herself becoming moist with arousal.

Horrified, she saw the Mullah pointing out, to the handsome Sheik, her beauty lips, now glistening with arousal through the lacing.

"A natural slave!" he said. "And with her good childbearing hips she'd make a fine little mother, too."

Despite the humiliation and embarrassment both women were anxiously smiling across at the handsome Sheik, silently pleading with him to take them away with him - no matter where.

What a magnificent pair they'd make, the Sheik was thinking, if only they were both expectant. How delightful it would be when their little progeny was delivered and, first one, and then the other would proudly come into milk. Zalu and his team would supervise it all very well. The women's natural jealousy would ensure that they would compete for being his favourite milkmaid.

And how delightful they looked in their wrist and ankle manacles. He would have them left on for the time being.

As the women continued to be pranced round the room by their proud overseers, the serious bargaining commenced ...

and was finally concluded with the Mullah handing the young Sheik the two women's little red books.

"Your chief black eunuch will find here all the information he will need about your two new acquisitions," said the Mullah with a smile. Then pointing at Louise's flat stomach, he spoke quietly in Arabic.

"Forgive me, Your Highness, but it occurred to me that as you evidently found the state of the second young woman of interest, then perhaps before this first girl is loaded onto your plane, you might like to take advantage of my facilities here, and of the fact that she happens today to be nicely ripe for conceiving, to have her ... discreetly given the same Special Treatment as her friend has had? ... Two swelling bellies in your harem! And one delivering her progeny several months after the other."

"Ah!" cried the young Sheik eagerly. Then a frown crossed his brow. "Would she," he asked anxiously, "know what had been done to her?"

"Oh no!" the Mullah assured him, rubbing his hands. "Half the amusement for you would be that, like her companion, she would not realise her state - until your black eunuchs decide to tell her. It is extraordinary how long a little mother-to-be will accept that she is just suffering from a bout of indigestion. And even when she does realise the truth, she will have no idea how it could have happened."

The Sheik laughed. "Alright," he agreed. "But can you use the same white seed as you used on the other young woman, so that they'd be carrying sisters, pretty white sisters!"

"Indeed, Your Highness, we do have enough of that left." The Mullah paused and then coughed. "There would, Your Highness, of course, be a small extra charge ... But I will throw in a silver filigree chain mail pouch for her, free of charge."

The Sheik laughed. This Mullah was incorrigible! But why not? Zalu would be delighted to have two reluctant white mothers-to-be in his power - and so quickly after Crimsons had delivered their progeny. Moreover his own grandfather would have been proud of him! "all right," he agreed. "His Highness will be taking you both away with him on his private jet," announced the smiling Mullah shortly afterwards to the two delighted, but still stark naked women. A very large cheque was sitting in his pocket. "But it must, you will understand, be done discreetly. But don't worry - a little drink, a lovely long sleep and then, when you wake up, you will be hundreds of miles away from here!"

The blushing women smiled. Anything to get away from here - and the Sheik was so charming and civilised. Obviously he wasn't really going to use them as indentured servants in his harem. He probably didn't even have one in this day and age. That was all just all talk to keep the Mullah happy.

No, soon they would be free! A few hours later, the Sheik's private jet arrived at the airport in North Africa. It taxied to a discreet part often used by Sheik Ali. He was met by a smiling Zalu.

The Sheik drove off in a large Mercers. A truck remained behind. Zalu supervised the unloading of two wooden crates from the aircraft, They were marked 'Pregnant Livestock - Handle with care'.

He noted the little air holes in the lid, through which straw could be seen, and smiled at the noise of deep breathing as from a sleeping animal.

The baggage handlers, retainers of the Sheik, made no comment as they loaded the crates into the truck which drove off to the Sheik's palace - or, rather, straight to his harem.

Zalu was smiling cruelly and rubbing his hands as his assistant black eunuchs unloaded the still sleeping women from their crates. He particularly smiled when he saw that not only was Samantha still locked into her chain mail breeding belt, the key to which he now held, but that Louise would wake up in the young Sheik's harem astonished to find that she, too, had been locked into one.

Just as Samantha had been reassured by her prison overseer that her mysterious morning sickness and increasingly swelling tummy were just indigestion, so too Louise would be similarly reassured by Zalu - much to the amusement of Sheik Ali.

Indeed both sleeping women would be blissfully unaware that, under each of their chain mail breeding belts, they

106

were now carrying little twin, white girl, embryos, progeny for their new Master, albeit with widely different dates of delivery.

Zulu smiled again, this time more cruelly, at the thought that both women were also blissfully unaware of sort of life that awaited in his harem. They may have escaped the fear of an occasional public flogging, but they would soon learn that this had been replaced by the constant fear of Zalu's cane - and of the whips of his assistant black eunuchs.

Oh yes, Zalu told himself, he would certainly enjoy taking charge of these two white women - and arrogant Englishwomen to boot! Expectant or not, it would not be long before they felt his cane on their backsides!

PART III THE ENTRAPMENT OF MRS ROBIN SEYMOUR (AMANDA - 'Royal Blue')

3 - 1 THE TRAP IS SET

Oh, what a fool I've been, Amanda kept telling herself.

But it was too late now. To have gone to the casino at all was mad. And for her, a pretty young woman with green eyes and a good figure, to have done so day after day, whilst Robin was away back in London on business, was even crazier.

But she had been bored, bored stiff with being alone in Beirut. It was a boom town again, now that the dreadful civil war was over, full of wealthy Arabs from the oil sheikdoms who had come looking for fun in a safe place with a decent climate.

Perhaps, she thought, if she went to the casino, she might meet someone amusing - amusing and rich. She was ripe for a little flirtation. Robin was all very well, but he wasn't there. She knew that she was pretty and attractive to men. Why shouldn't she have a little innocent fun... So, she had her hair done and went to the casino, dressed up to the nines. She cashed a cheque and bought a few chips, a trifling amount really.

Rather daring, she sat down at a low minimum bet roulette table. next to a rather handsome young man. He was evidently a rich Arab, tall and good-looking, with a short beard, a slightly hook nose and eyes that seemed to burn right through her.

His voice was resonant and attractive, with a slight Arab accent. He was very well dressed in a well cut yachting blazer with black buttons, that must have come from London, and white trousers. He looked, Amanda thought, like a millionaire who had just stepped off his yacht - which indeed he was. And how exciting, he seemed rather interested in her!

She wondered why he was not playing on the top table. Perhaps it amused him to play with the hoi-poloi.

Before long he introduced himself: a Sheik Ali. He asked her about herself. She told him that her husband was away and that she could not afford lose very much. He suddenly seemed very interested in her. How exciting! She wondered if perhaps he might be deciding whether to invite her out to dinner!

But then, politely excusing himself, he suddenly got up and went across to the cashier to cash in his chips.

Hiding her disappointment, she watched him speak earnestly to the cashier. He was pointing at her and seemed to be giving the cashier a very large tip! Well, what it was to be rich!

She thought she saw the cashier showing him her own cheque that she had cashed to pay for her chips. He glanced at it, as if impressed by her name and by the fact she banked at Coutts Bank in London. He seemed to be writing down her name. Well!

Indeed, Sheik Ali was thinking, this very attractive young married Englishwoman certainly seemed to come from the right background - and if she was alone in Beirut - and said that she could not afford to lose very much ...He was also thinking: well!

Well indeed! But Amanda would have been appalled had she realised how very different his thoughts were to hers.

He glanced across the room towards Amanda and smiled - and in his quiet, ruthless, way decided to put certain plans into operation ... Amanda was disappointed that the handsome Sheik did not return to the gambling table, but almost immediately put him out of her mind as suddenly her combination of numbers came up. Holding her breath, she left half her winnings on the same combination. It came up again.

Amanda was thrilled. All that money! Several hundred pounds! She bet again again on some adjoining numbers and won again ...and again. It seemed that she could do no wrong.

"Congratulations, Mrs Seymour" came a deep voice from behind her.

Startled that someone should know her name, Amanda turned round. It was the handsome young Sheik.

"But if I were you, I would call it a day now and come back tomorrow," he added in almost faultless English. "You might do even better then - and at the top table, now. That's the one I usually play on."

Then he had bowed and turned away.

Shortly afterwards Amanda took his advice and cashed in her winnings. They came to over a thousand pounds. She could hardly believe it. Hoping to see the handsome Arab again and also to win again, Amanda returned the next day, and played at a higher table. There was no sign of the handsome Arab, but her winnings continued to mount.

Excited and thrilled by what, to her, seemed huge winnings, she moved to the top table where the stakes were much higher. Again she won. It seemed as if she was on a winning streak and just could not lose.

Running out of chips, she asked her neighbour, a friendly Arab businessman, to lend her a couple of hundred chips - a relatively small sum of money. She had chatted with him the day before at the other table and had borrowed the odd small amount from him, always paying it back from her winnings.

As usual he was delighted to oblige. This time, however, he asked her to sign a rather complicated looking receipt. Without looking at it closely, she signed and gave it back to him.

Then she lost ... and lost again. Her neighbour offered her another couple hundred. Again she signed a receipt for him. This time she noticed that he had the receipts witnessed.

Suddenly she found that she lost everything. How lucky, she thought, that it was only a relatively small sum - really not much more than her winnings. What a fool she had been not have stopped when she was winning. Oh well!

She collected her coat and went out to her car. Suddenly, as she walked along to the car park, a car came up silently alongside her. A door opened and she was pulled inside. It was all over in a second.

She was pushed down onto the floor. A gag was thrust into her mouth. Her hands were handcuffed behind her. Desperately she looked around. Sitting on the back seat of the large car was the man who had advanced her the money.

On either side of him were two Arab thugs. It was they who had pulled her into the car, silenced her and immobilised her. One of them now seized her hair and jerked her head up to face the man sitting in the middle. She remembered his name: Mr Mohammed Achmud.

"So, Mrs Seymour, we meet again. You still owe me, I think, four hundred thousand dirams."

Four hundred thousand! That was getting for a quarter of a million pounds! She shook her head desperately. She had borrowed, perhaps, four hundred not four hundred thousand! Indeed, he had only given her about four hundred - and that was what she had lost. And on leaving, she had given him a cheque for the equivalent of four hundred. He had then torn up what she assumed were her receipts. Once again, she shook her head desperately; there must be some mistake.

"No, Mrs Seymour, there has been no mistake. Here are your receipts. Look! Two hundred thousand each and each witnessed independently by a different friend of mine."

Frantically she looked the receipts. Yes, each was for two hundred thousand. Had they been carefully forged? The signature was perfect. Had he copied the signature from the receipts she had signed the night before? Or had she just signed without looking, not wanting to interrupt her play?

"So, Mrs Seymour, you can see that you still owe me four hundred thousand dirams. There is no point disputing this. I have witnesses who will say that you asked me twice for two hundred thousand, that I gave you this amount, that you signed the receipts that were promptly witnessed, and that you then lost both amounts."

There was a long pause as Mr Achmud let his words sink into her distraught mind.

"Now listen carefully. I know, and you know, that neither you nor your husband can quickly lay your hands on four hundred thousand dirams. That's why we're going to a remote beach. That's why your car is being driven along behind mine. That's why your clothes are going to be found abandoned on the beach, near your car. That's why you decided that the only way out, rather than face the disgrace and ruination of both yourself and your husband, was to drown yourself. We shall be arriving at the beach in a few moments, so prepare yourself.

Frantically Amanda moaned behind her gag. Frantically she fought to free herself from the handcuffs. But all to no avail. The two thugs were still holding her down on the floor. She could not even struggle.

These mad people are going to kill me, she thought. They were going to drown me. And there was nothing she could do about it.

The car slowed and stopped. One of the thugs opened the door and pulled her out. Standing in the road, she saw her own car come up behind her. She was still gagged, still hand-cuffed, and still held by the two thugs.

"Now, Mrs Seymour, it's time to remove your clothes,"

She struggled, but the thugs held her still. Mr Achmud went behind her and started to unhook the back of her scrapes dress. In a moment it was round her ankles.

"A very pretty sight, Mrs Seymour. You're going to do very well for my purpose."

His purpose? Surely, she thought, his purpose is to drown me?

Slowly and methodically, he proceeded to strip her. Her shoes, her stockings, her slip, her bra, her panties. Held as she was, there was nothing she could do to stop him. He opened her bag. He opened her diary and tore out a page. He took out her pen.

Then, as she watched, horrified and scared out of her wits, he and one of the thugs went to the back of his car and took some things out. One was a cane, which he swished through he air.

"The bastinado!" he said, "the traditional way, in this part of the world, of disciplining young women without marking their bodies."

She noticed that one of the thugs was now carrying a sort of hinged wooden stocks with two semi-circles cut of each half. He fastened it round her ankles, and then threw her down onto the sand of the beach. He put his foot down onto her throat and lifted up the stocks holding her ankles. With her hands still handcuffed behind her back she was now held down quite help-

112

less on her back with her feet raised high in the air.

"Hold her still," she heard Mr Achmud say. Then there was a whistling noise and he brought the cane down across the soles of her feet.

The pain was terrible. She tried to scream but, of course, all that came out through her gag was a little whimper. She tried to wriggle but one thug still had his boot on the back of her neck and the other was still holding up the stocks.

Again came the whistling noise. Again the terrible pain and again the little suppressed whimper. The pain was appalling. Why was he doing this? What did he want her to do? She would, she thought, do anything to stop him giving her another stroke with that awful cane.

"I'm going to give you six strokes," came the voice of Mr Achmud.

No! No! Amanda tried to scream, desperately trying to wriggle away from the terrible cane. But there was nothing she could do and slowly and relentlessly the cane came down again and again.

At last she was released from the stocks, and pulled to her feet. She could hardly stand and the thugs had to hold her up. Mr Achmud pulled back her hair so that she had to look him in the face.

"So, Mrs Seymour, you've now felt a little pain." A little, Amanda thought! My God. "But was it enough to make you do what I want you to do? Or would you prefer to have another half dozen strokes of the bastinado?"

Terrified, Amanda shook her head. "No, no more!" she tried to scream.

"Well, will you do what I want, or... " he held up the bastinado.

Almost out of her mind with fear, Amanda desperately nodded her agreement.

"Good! Well now, Mrs Seymour, you're going to write a little message, a farewell message to your husband, on this page torn out of your diary, using your own pen. You're going to write what I dictate. And if you don't then you'll get another six of the

113

bastinado - and then another six, until you do. Well, are you ready to write?"

Again Amanda nodded desperately - and kept on nodding.

"The fact that you are trembling and that your writing will look shaky, is all to the good. You're supposed to be in shock after losing four hundred thousand dirams!"

He nodded at one of the thugs. Her hands were freed. Her pen was thrust into her right hand. One of the thugs gripped her tightly by the neck. The other twisted her left hand up behind her back. There was no chance of escaping.

"Now start writing: "'Darling Robin, I have been such a fool, We shall be ruined if I stay alive. This is the best way out. Forgive me. Amanda.'"

She scarcely understood what she was writing, for she could hardly take her eyes off the cane. How shame-making! She, a grown-up woman, being threatened with a caning!

Someone, she realised, perhaps the man who had driven her car, was holding a torch so that she could just see what see doing. He was wearing gloves, perhaps, she thought, to prevent any fingerprints, other than her own, from appearing on the wheel of the car.

Mr Ached took the piece of paper. He put it prominently on top of her pile of clothes, with a stone to prevent it from fluttering away. The two thugs then put the handcuffs back on her wrists behind her back.

"Put her back in my car," Mr Achmud ordered. The boot was opened, She was thrust in. The boot was closed. She was alone in the dark.

She felt the car start up and move off...

3 - 2 AMANDA LEARNS THE TERRIFYING "TRUTH"

It was the following evening.

Still stark naked, Amanda was standing at attention in front of a table in a cell-like room. Behind the table sat Mr

Achmud. On either side of him stood the two thugs. Across the table lay the dreaded bastinado. She could not take her eyes off it, she was so frightened.

Some time during the previous night she had been carried out of the boot of the car and put into a locked cell next to this one. She had been thrown onto a thin mattress on the floor, There was a bucket in the corner, nothing else. Later, some biscuits had been thrust into the cell under the door. Now she had been dragged out by the two thugs into this cell.

"Right, Mrs Seymour, or, as I shall prefer to call you, Amanda, may I present myself? But not in my official guise as Mr Mohammed Achmud, the well known goldsmith, but rather in my other role as a dealer in women, though the clients for both roles are often the same: wealthy distinguished Arabs who come to my humble premises both to buy and sell gold - and women. They come to see what little treasures, both golden and female, I have to offer them, especially pretty young European women like yourself. I must confess, however, that we rarely get women of your background - so all the more interesting for my clients!"

"But - but -"

"Officially you are dead. Look at the evening paper." He thrust an English language newspaper under her eyes. "Look, your clothes and abandoned car were found by the police, on the beach road early this morning, as was your suicide note. The police enquires are already closed. They've said it's a simple case of suicide following a disastrous visit to the casino. I have already shown the police your signed receipts for the four hundred thousand dirams. I told them that, clearly, I will now never be repaid. In the sad circumstances I have waived any right to proceed against your husband, your widower."

"But my parents ... they're Colonel Humphrey Newsome and the Lady Cecilia Malby, the daughter of the Earl of Hawfield," said Amanda, hoping that the mention of these rather grand names might frighten him into letting her go.

"Yes, I know that. I had you checked out when you first started to come to the casino, Then, it was not difficult to bribe the croupier to fix the table so that you won and won - before

115

losing of course."

Amanda gasped. Indeed, what a fool she had been.

"Doubtless your parents would try and ransom you. But why should I risk trying to get a ransom for you when with little effort I can sell you for a small fortune! An upper class English-woman of genuine aristocratic birth! A rare catch! And one that can be sold very well to certain discerning Arab buyers."

"Sell me!" Amanda exclaimed. "You can't be serious!"

"Oh but I am! You are going to be one of the little trea-sures whom, as I told you, I like to display to my more discern-ing clients."

"Oh my God!"

"Yes, Amanda, in a few days time, you will be sold to a wealthy Arab to be put away in his harem. You will bring me in a very large sum of money."

"But my husband, I love my husband!" Amanda cried out.

"Good, all the better! There's always been something very satisfying for a rich Arab in putting the weeping and pro-testing wife of another man into his own harem, especially if she is still in love with her husband, and especially if she is European - and a Christian!"

"Oh!" gasped Amanda.

"Yes," said Mr Achmud, "and you're going to help me get a really good price for you when I auction you in a few weeks' time." He did not bother to add that there would be high reserve on her price - to enable a certain Sheik to play the role of her rescuer.

"Auctioned! Oh no! No!" screamed Amanda.

"Oh yes! That is the traditional way we sell women in this party of the world - an auction preceded by an opportunity for the agents of the potential buyers to examine the goods. ... And you know what will happen to you at the slightest sign of reluctance," he said, picking up the cane, bending it and then swishing it menacingly through the air. "Do you not?"

Terrified, Amanda nodded.

"Yes," went on Mr Ached blandly, "I have just received

a consignment of several pretty young Eastern European dancing girls and you will be auctioned with them. They had signed contracts, as they thought, to appear in several Middle Eastern night clubs, but their first and only public appearance will in fact be at my auction - for which they, like you, are now going to be prepared."

"Prepared?" gasped Amanda

"Oh, don't you worry your little head about that," laughed Mr Achmud. He was looking at her naked breasts as he spoke. He always maintained that the value, on the block, of every women could be enhanced by a little breast enlargement or firming up. His friendly surgeon had done this to the other girls. It was a pity that there wasn't time to have this one done, too.

His eyes dropped to her beauty lips, still half hiding behind the little blond curls. He could see the flesh of the inner lips gently protruding. She would have also have looked prettier on the block after the hair had been removed, if her little womanly obtrusions had been snipped off. A snip or a tuck! Either way, rich elderly Arab gentlemen liked the resulting little girl look, even if the girls' beauty buds were not touched.

"Of course, you future Master will have this," Mr Achmud said moment added, producing a legal looking document. "These are your indentures - in this part of the world, they effectively make you as good as a slave for an indefinite period."

"Oh!" cried Amanda. "I can't believe it!"

"Oh yes! Here is your signature , carefully witnessed by people swearing that you signed the document willingly. Look!"

Amanda saw her signature. "But -" she started to protest.

"Enough of that! Now listen carefully. You're going to be put back into your cell. You're going to keep it spotlessly clean and you will eat up the food that is given to you. These two guards will supervise you. They speak no English and will be inspecting the cell twice a day, and if they are not satisfied, then they have the authority to use the bastinado. So don't antagonise them!"

He paused.

"My two guards will teach you a display routine. Make sure you learn it carefully. This is the routine you will put on at the auction. Just remember that the bastinado will be waiting for you if don't learn quickly, or if you don't make yourself look beautiful and erotic at the auction. I certainly wouldn't like to be in your skin if you don't make the reserve!

There would, of course, be little chance of that, he laughed to himself. He gestured to the guards to put the girl back in her cell. But it would still be as well to take precautions in case the Sheikh backed out of what was, for Mr Ached, a very profitable contract. It was important to make the Sheikh realise that he was acquiring a really desirable young woman -but, if he changed his mind, well there would always be the other buyers!

3 - 3 AUCTIONED!

Later that day, the two huge guards brought a girl into Amanda's cell. She spent several hours washing and brushing Amanda's, hair, painting her toe and finger nails, and waxing her arms and legs.

The two guards stood over her, making sure she did not try to speak to the girl. They made her lie back whilst the girl ran an electric razor over of her mound and down the line of her body lips. It made her fell more naked than ever.

The display routine that the guards now taught her to perform to music was unbelievably humiliating. But the threat of the cane was enough to make her learn to perform it perfectly and abjectly. It was awful but she was made to go on practising it, over and over again.

The following day, Mr Achmud came to watch her. He too had a cane in his hands and Amanda knew she had go through the routine without making a single mistake. He made her do it several times. Then, nodding with approval, he congratulated the guards and, without a word to the blushing Amanda, left the room. The next day, Mr Achmud again came to her cell. He was accompanied, as usual, by the two thugs. This time he was pointedly carrying a rather frightening looking leather switch, which he tapped impatiently against the the palms of his hands. Following along behind him was the girl who had done her hair and body.

"Auction this evening!" he announced. "You will be on display to several buyers. This girl will get you ready. I shall want to see you moving as seductively and provocatively as possible - just as you've been taught."

He pointed to the leather switch. "And don't you forget it!" he added. He was thinking of the extra fee that he would earn provided that Sheik Ali was able to make himself appear as the girl's saviour, rescuing her from a terrible fate. But as the young Sheik had made quite clear, there would be no fee and no purchase of the girl if she suspected that it was really all a put up job. The girl had to be genuinely terrified.

"But first you will be displayed and examined by their chief black eunuchs. Doubtless they will wish to see your ability to perform in a womanly way for their Masters."

Black eunuchs! Oh, my God, thought Amanda. An hour later Amanda was standing naked on a low table, with her wrists fastened above her head to either end of a bar hanging from the ceiling, so that her belly would be at eye level. In this way it would be easy to reach down to inspect her intimacies, feel her breasts, examine her teeth, or walk round behind her, to judge her back and waist, and to assess the firmness of her buttocks.

Her knees were slightly bent and her ankles fastened wide apart to provide easy access to her beauty lips.

A pot of slippery oil was placed between her outstretched legs to make it easier to feel up her from both in front and behind - something to which, Mr Achmud had told her, these experienced judges of soft female flesh attached great importance if they were to advise their Masters properly.

And she was blindfolded.

Standing helpless on the table, unable to see what was going on, she was horrified to hear heavy footsteps approaching and then to feel hands, many hands, touching and probing, probing deep inside her. Ashamed and humiliated, she heard the high pitched voices of eunuchs as they laughingly exchanged views

119

on the body they were so intimately examining on behalf of their Masters.

But then, as if that was not enough, she felt herself being deliberately aroused by experienced fingers playing with her beauty bud, rubbing her nipples and stroking her body lips. Her body began to respond. She could feel frantic twinges of fire leaping from her breasts down to her womb and back. Her breasts felt larger than ever. There were approving comments as her blushes spread from her cheeks to her neck and breasts.

Tied as she was there was nothing she could do to prevent nature from taking its course, a course that the watching black eunuchs wanted to see, so as to be sure that she could be made to be highly responsive in her Master's bed.

As she began to approach her inevitable climax she felt, to her horror, additional fingers probing to feel her wetness and so satisfy themselves about the genuineness of her arousal.

Then there was sudden silence as all the fingers except one were removed. Writhing, crying out, tugging frantically at the straps that held her, she was expertly brought to a frantic climax.

Then her blindfold was removed, and, overcome with shame, she screamed as she saw that she was surrounded by a group of black men, many of whom were busy scribbling in notebooks. One of them, a huge brute of man, was still stroking her intimately. He must be the one who had brought her so unwillingly to that devastating climax. He lifted up her chin to look in her eyes, and she gasped as she saw his cold bloodshot eyes and the distinctive tribal markings on his cheeks.

Finally, as if satisfied with their inspection, the party of black eunuchs left the room, leaving Amanda shocked and horrified. For the next hour, Amanda was treated like a dog being prepared for the show ring. She was washed, shampooed, powdered, and dried all over. Great care was taken with her make-up, her hair, her cheeks and every other feminine detail. As she looked in the mirror, she had to admit that she looked lovelier than she had ever looked - even on her wedding day.

Then she was dressed - if that is the right word. The

motif was to be gold.

She was put into gold high heel shoes. A gold chased belt of black leather was fastened round her waist to emphasis her slimness, which contrasted excitingly with her full breasts and her good child bearing hips. A shiny gold plated flexible collar was locked round her neck. It had a large ring on the front.

A half cup gold lace bra was put around her breasts. A triangle of similar gold lace, suspended by thin golden cords from her waist belt, was put over her hairless beauty lips. Over it all a beautiful long cloak of golden gauze from placed over her shoulders. It only seemed to accentuate her nakedness. Half naked, Amanda stood nervously and silently, under the eyes of the two thugs, in the examination room in which she had been so shamefully inspected. It was, she knew, next to the auction room.

She was mentally running through the routine that she had been taught.

In one hand she held a white card with an Arabic number written prominently on it. This would be used to help identification during the forthcoming parade. Mr Achmud had told her that half a dozen rich Arabs had come, or sent their black eunuchs, to bid specifically for her.

Through the open door she could hear voices coming from the big room next door. They were talking in Arabic. They must be the men to whom she was about to be displayed, questioning their black eunuchs about her suitability.

A bell tinkled. The voices died away. Amanda shivered. She knew from the rehearsals that the curtains of the little stage next door would now be drawn back and the lights in the small auditorium would be dimmed, leaving only the catwalk leading out from the stage brilliantly lit, together with a spot light trained on the entrance onto the stage from the preparation room.

The bell tinkled for a second time. One of the thugs nodded at Amanda. How she hated being ordered about by them! He raised his cane. It was enough. Amanda straightened herself. Then, as she had rehearsed so many times, she walked onto the stage and down onto the catwalk. One hand was nonchalantly placed on her hip, the other displaying the numbered card. Her

121

buttocks and and shoulders were swinging provocatively in the exaggerated walk of a top class model.

As she did so she was acutely aware of the way her breasts, only partially restrained by the little lace bra, bounced under the silken material of her gauze cloak. She slowly walked down the catwalk, pirouetting periodically. Mr Achmud, in an auctioneers rostrum on one side, started to describe her in Arabic.

Because of the way the bright lights were trained on the catwalk, Amanda could scarcely make out the faces of the watching audience. She turned and walked back up the catwalk, continuing to pirouette, smiling towards the invisible watchers, before turning back down the catwalk again.

Amanda was breathing heavily under the emotional strain of what she was going through. She shivered as she heard the crack of a whip. Her knees felt weak, but the frequent practices proved their worth as she went through her performance in a daze.

Two little black boys ran in and took off her cloak. Once again she started to strut up and down the catwalk. She heard Hassan calling for opening bids. The bids were just starting when again the two little black boys ran in again. This time they unfastened her bra. Blushing with shame, she set off down the catwalk again, her bare breasts bouncing more than ever, and her painted nipples gleaming under the spotlights.

Mr Achmud would now, she knew, put her through an erotic display intended to show how this once proud Englishwoman could be trained to perform to please her Master. As she reached the end of the catwalk, Amanda heard what she was expecting - the crack of Hassan's whip. Instantly, just as she had been taught, she froze with her head up and her hands clasped behind her neck, her firm breasts thrust out.

Again the two black boys ran in, and this time removed the tiny triangle of gold lace from over her beauty lips. The whip cracked again and a shamed Amanda thrust her bare beauty lips forward. Then again there was the crack of a whip. This time, keeping her back straight and her hands still clasped behind her

122

neck, she parted her legs and bent forward so that her breasts hung down, tipped by her painted nipples. Her beauty lips were now also well displayed from behind, between her parted legs. It was an erotic sight and having to hold this awkward posture showed off both her state of training and her fear of the whip.

At last it cracked again, flicking her buttocks. She straightened up and swung her arms high, keeping her fingers straight and raising her knees level with her hips as she marched back towards the stage. As she did so, the bidding rose to a crescendo.

Now the lights were turned up to help Hassan control the bidding, and out of the corner of her eye Amanda saw the terrifying face of the black eunuch who had so shamed her that morning. He was actively bidding for her! Dear God, she prayed fervently, don't let that swine buy me!

Then she noticed a familiar figure sitting splendidly alone on a sofa dressed in a well cut yachting blazer. He calmly raised one finger and Hassan quickly acknowledged his bid. As he did so, Amanda recognised him: the handsome and friendly young man she had seen wearing yachting clothes in the casino! Good God! Had come to rescue her from a terrible fate?

Then the whip cracked once again. Still gripping her hands behind her neck, Amanda pranced down the catwalk, raising her knees high in the air.

The bidding rose. The whip cracked and she knelt down on all fours. The young boys again ran in ran up, and snapped a lead onto her collar. Then they led her, crawling on all fours, slowly along the catwalk and back again.

Suddenly she heard the hammer fall. She had been sold, but to whom? Overcome with emotion she burst out crying. There were cruel laughs.

3 - 4 THE TRAP SNAPS SHUT

The cruise was like a honeymoon, a honeymoon that she came to pray would never end. They were always out of sight of land and she did not bother to enquire just where they were.

How she dreaded returning to her old way of life with Robin, with all the worries about money, about entertaining, about servants, about keeping up with her correspondence, and again about money. Decisions, decisions! Here with the Sheik she had no worries, no responsibilities and had to make no decisions.

All she had to do all day was to make herself look beautiful for him, her handsome, charming and virile lover. Oh how she adored him! He was so masterful! And, he was her saviour, the man who unselfishly had paid a huge sum to rescue her from the that awful white slaver, and from the threat of ending up in the harem of some equally awful rich Arab.

If only her life could go on like this!

She began to wonder if she could spin out staying in the Sheik's palace. "There'll be no hurry for you to leave, you'll soon see," he said encouragingly. "But meanwhile let's just enjoy this little cruise. Then we must see about returning you to your husband and your family."

"Oh, yes, they'll have given me up for dead."

"Indeed," laughed her lover. But like all good things, the cruise had to end. The yacht docked in a small harbour early one morning. It was only just getting light. Amanda could not make out the jetty's surroundings. The Sheik had sent her off to bed early the evening before to get a good night's rest before she saw his palace in the morning. She had no idea where they were and when she asked him, he simply shook his head and smiled.

"Ah that would be spoiling the surprise!"

Two large cars with Arab drivers had been waiting for them on the small jetty. One was for the Sheik and the other a special woman's car that, he had told her, would take her to his palace. It would never do, he laughed, for a man of his position to be seen by the fundamentalists driving in a car with a woman! Women were not supposed to leave their houses except on rare occasions, and then only if accompanied by their husbands or fathers.

The car windows were all tinted black - on both sides. No one would be able to see who was in the car, nor, she was very disappointed to find, could she see out. She couldn't even see through the window between herself and the chauffeur.

After a time, the car turned off the road and onto a rather more bumpy track and stopped. She heard voices, challenging voices, and a reply from the chauffeur. There was the noise of a gate being opened, and then closed behind them. Then another gate was opened and again the car went forward and continued now along what sounded like a private drive. There was the noise of gravel crunching under the car's tyres.

Despite herself, Amanda shivered. She was entering what seemed to be a well guarded and very private world. But she quickly dismissed her concern. She was visiting the palace as the honoured guest of her wonderful young and handsome Sheik and no harm could come to her.

He loved her! The car stopped and the door was opened. A veiled woman, evidently a servant, beckoned her through a small door. She had a glimpse of what seemed to be large building made of white marble. It looked more like the White House than an Arab palace. She saw the Sheik's car parked outside a large shaded portico held up by high marble columns. The contrast with the insignificant little entrance to which she had been taken was marked.

She had a glimpse of armed guards standing at attention and of numerous men dressed in immaculate white robes greeting the Sheik on his return. The contrast between his reception and just the beckoning woman who was greeting her, was also marked.

She had the impression of a park, surrounded by a high walls and of another even higher wall that joined the building near to where she was stand and which she seemed to shut off part of the palace. She wondered why.

Amanda followed the woman along a long marble, white painted, corridor that led to an iron studded door, in front of which armed guards kept watch. They challenged the woman, and then satisfied, unlocked the door and opened it. Amanda followed the woman through the doorway.

A few yards further down the corridor they were confronted with a beautifully worked, large, gold painted locked grille. It was decorated with a crest of crossed scimitars and stars - the same crest as she had seen on the yacht and which was even embroidered on the underwear she was wearing. It had made her feel, deliciously and reassuringly, that she somehow belonged to the Sheik, that she was under his protection, now that he had saved her from the terrible slave dealer, Mr Achmud.

Through the door came the voices, as if from a nursery, of several excited young girls. How strange, she thought, to find a nursery in this palace.

The woman pressed a bell and a large black man appeared. He was dressed in white silken baggy Turkish trousers, and a red waistcoat with a strange looking white hat on his head, like an upturned flowerpot, wider at the top than at the bottom. Round the top was a gold ring, like an insignia of rank.

He held a long, beautifully worked, leather dog whip in his hand, like a badge of office. It had a red tassle on the end. Tucked into his large cummerbund was a short handled black whip with a long coiled up lash. It reminded her of the whips used in circuses to crack and to intimidate the performing animals. Were there animals here?

His eyes were cold and bloodshot and his face was disfigured by tribal scars. With a gasp of horror, Amanda recognised the man who had so shame-makingly brought her to orgasm with his hands as she stood up on the examination bench at the establishment of the terrifying slave dealer.

What was he doing here? She remembered Mr Achmud saying that the Negroes who had so callously examined her were the chief black eunuchs who ruled the harems of his rich clients. God! Surely this could not be the chief black eunuch of the Sheik. He had never said anything about having a harem... Zalu nodded to the servant woman, who turned and left through the heavy iron studded door, which was slammed shut behind her by the armed guards on the other side.

Then he went to an electronic lock at the side of the grille and pressed a complicated sequence of numbers. The grille opened and Zalu beckoned her through it. Hesitantly she stepped

126

pass the grille which was immediately slammed shut behind her.

She saw that a strange looking copper strip ran across the floor of the corridor, several yards beyond the grille and wondered what it was.

Immediately after they had stepped over it, the frightening black man led her into a little room off the corridor. She saw a large photograph of the Sheik on the wall. His hand on his hip and holding a coiled up whip, he was proudly looking down on a line of prostrated women, their hair flung forward over their lowered heads.

Subservience and submission!

The large black man turned to Amanda and presented her with what seemed to be a very pretty wide choker collar. It was made of flexible chromium plated links, like a metal watch strap. Some Arabic writing and numbers were engraved on a small plate at the side of the choker, together with the crest of the Sheik. There was a strange little bulge at the back.

He smiled and gestured to her to put it on, pointing to a mirror in which she could admire herself wearing it. Fascinated she put it round her neck. It fastened with a click. She admired herself in the mirror. The choker was surprisingly wide and came up high under her chin, making her neck look almost ethereally long and slender.

What a lovely present! How thoughtful of the Sheik to have arranged for her to be given it on arrival. Perhaps this frightening looking black man wasn't so bad after all! Suddenly Zalu clapped his hands. Amanda gasped as two beautiful, and almost identical, young women of her own age ran into the room.

She gasped again when she saw that they were being driven along by a little black boy, running behind them and cracking a small whip like a child's hunting crop. How awful to be treated like that by a mere boy, she thought. Or was it just a joke? Some sort of a game?

The boy seemed so small that she wondered if he was a pygmy. She had never seen one before. The little boy was dressed just like a miniature version of the big black man, the eunuch. He was cracking his whip with one hand and, in the other, held a smaller version of the big black man's dog whip.

The two girls were closely chained together by the neck, almost giving the appearance of being Siamese twins, their bodies joined together at the sides. They looked almost European - except for one thing: each had a large well polished brass ring hanging down from her nose and reaching down to her chin. These big nose rings gave them a strangely erotic, and almost animal, look.

Amanda gasped again as she saw that they not only did they look alike, but they were dressed alike in cutaway crimson coloured transparent silken trousers, which left their hairless beauty lips and mounds shamelessly on display.

She gasped again as she saw that prettily tattooed on their tummies was a coloured crest. She recognised it as the same crest, of green crossed scimitars and a black star, as she had seen on all the clothes that she had worn on the yacht, on his silver-ware, on the funnel of his yacht ... on everything that he owned.

She gasped yet again as she saw that neatly tattooed below the crest were some Arabic numerals. She remembered, back in England, seeing grazing cows branded with their herd numbers. These girls had been marked like animals! Then she gasped as she saw the two lines of rings going down their beauty lips, the well polished tight laces and the little padlock hanging down between their legs. She had heard in Beirut of little Arab girls being sewn up to protect their virginity, but these girls were grown up!

She saw they also wore identical crimson embroidered boleros which did not meet in front and left their very full breasts. The scarlet painted, strangely prominent nipples, were exposed. Their dress was completed by identical little crimson caps on their auburn coloured hair and by little crimson Turkish slippers.

With a sudden burst of jealousy she saw that they, too, were wearing shiny metal chokers, just like her own one. She now noticed that the chokers all had a small ring in the ring at the front and another at the back, like the ring in dog's collar used for attaching a lead. The short chain that kept their necks close together was fastened to the rings on the fronts of the chokers.

The two girls stopped in front of Zalu, standing up at attention as if awaiting orders. He nodded to the boy who coiled up his little whip and proudly tucked it into his small cummerbund, then went and stood quietly in a corner of the room, his eyes watching the three women.

Before Amanda could say a word, Zalu silently beckoned the three girls back into the corridor. He went to the grille and pressed the buttons of the electronic lock. The grille swung open. At the same time the guards outside opened the iron studded door and stood there grinning. Both they and Zalu gestured to the girls, as if offering them their freedom, through the open grille.

But the two girls, still chained together by the neck, shrank back in horror, looking at the copper strip in the floor.

The black man shrugged his shoulders. Then, turning to Amanda, he made a gesture as if inviting her to leave via the grille. She could hardly wait! Eagerly she ran towards the grille. Then, as she approached the copper strip across the corridor, she felt a series of little shocks in her neck, apparently coming from the beautiful choker collar. They got worse as she she approached the strip. With a cry, she tried to pull it off, but it seemed locked round her neck. She ran back away from the grille. The shocks ceased.

The fat black man waved an admonishing finger and pointed at the copper strip on the floor. She remembered seeing advertisements for a similar system for stopping dogs from straying from their owners' houses or gardens. My God! That was just how she was being treated. No wonder the other two girls had shrunk back when invited to approach the grille. Did that mean she was now a prisoner? Not a prisoner of the handsome young Sheik, her passionate lover, surely?

"No," she screamed, "there must be some mistake. I'm here at the invitation of the Sheik - as his guest. Take off this awful collar! At once! Do you hear? At once!"

But the big black man merely smiled and let her go on ranting and tearing at the collar. A sudden burst of girlish laughter came from further down the corridor. Zalu frowned and drew his long whip out from his cummerbund and uncoiled it. Calling out something to the watching young black boy, he strode off down to where the noise was coming from.

Moments later Amanda heard his high pitched voice shouting something, accompanied by several loud cracks of a whip. The noise stopped immediately.

The two chained girls stepped forward. One of them put a consoling hand on Amanda's shoulder. "You must learn to accept your fate, just as we all have had to do," she said in almost perfect English.

3 - 5 AMANDA LEARNS HER TRUE FATE

"What fate?" demanded Amanda angrily. "I'm here because I was invited by my lover - we'll be spending the siesta together."

"I doubt it," murmured the girl sympathetically. "Not unless the Master chooses you at the parade. We have been told to get you ready. We should have started already."

"What do you mean? What parade? What Master? And who are you? And who's the other girl? And why are you both dressed identically and chained together?"

"That's an awful lot of questions!" The other girl also spoke good English. "But we must start getting you ready, or there will be trouble... You see, the Master is your so called lover."

"What!"

"Yes, and this is my twin sister. To amuse the Master, Zalu likes to keep us chained together as if we really only one person but with two bodies. That's why we both have to answer to one name, Crimson, and have to wear the same coloured clothes."

"How dreadful!" gasped Amanda. Surely her handsome Sheik, her wonderful lover, would not do anything so cruel. "But who's this Zalu? He sounds terrible."

"He's the Master's chief black eunuch," replied one of the girls called Crimson.

"The man who put you into your slave collar," added the other one.

"Slave collar!" cried Amanda. Suddenly she remembered the indentures she had signed and how the awful Achmud had said they virtually made her into the slave of the person who bought them - the Sheik!

"And whatever Zalu says here is law and you want to be careful not to upset him. He's a cruel swine and treats us like animals - and that damn dog whip of his can hurt like hell. He's in complete charge of all the girls here in the harem."

"Harem! But the Sheik never said anything about a harem. You mean I'm now in his harem?"

"Of course! That's the fate that you've got to accept, just like all his other women."

"Other women," cried Amanda incredulously. "But he told me he was married."

"That's right. He hasn't yet chosen any wives. But that doesn't stop him from having a harem of concubines, like you - and us."

"What! I'm certainly not going to be one of his concubines. There must be some mistake!"

"Oh, no!" laughed the other of the girls. "There's no mistake. You're just one of us now - under the control of Zalu and the other black eunuchs."

"Other black eunuchs?"

"Yes, Zalu's got several assistant eunuchs." She nodded towards the small pigmy boy watching them from the corner of the room. "You'll never be out of sight of one them, or," she added, pointing up to a little moving lens in the corner of the room, "one of the watching internal television cameras."

"But why? What's ..."

"Don't be silly - it's to make sure we never ease our frustration trying to play with ourselves - or each other." She pointed down at the polished laces between her legs. "Not that, with these damn laces there's much we can do!"

"Oh! You mean that ... that little boy is going to watch me to make sure that ..."

131

"...you're kept pure? Yes! Even at night there's always one black eunuch patrolling up and down in the dormitory making sure that none of us have our hands under the bedclothes. And don't ever get caught alone or alone with another girl - or you'll get twelve strokes for Attempted Adultery... come on, we really must get you ready..."

"But I'm not going to take part in this disgusting parade!" cried Amanda angrily.

"You must," answered one of the girls in an anxious voice. "Don't you see? It's to make the Master feel you're now in his power! Oh please, do hurry. We might even get twelve strokes for Disobedience."

Amanda looked at the clothes they were offering her with dismay. They were so scanty! And her smart suit made her feel different from these other girls.

"Oh do hurry! Zalu will be back in a moment!" cried the twins in genuine fear. "He'll be furious if he finds you still in your European clothes. You're going get us both thrashed. Do hurry."

"But ..." cried Amanda still loathe to give up the freedom that her European clothes represent. "But ..."

"No buts, here you just do as you're told," came the furious high pitched voice of Zalu, speaking in a mixture of English and Arabic, as he re-entered the room, his face a blaze of anger.

He turned to two girls called Crimson, his dog whip raised. "You idle, chattering, disobedient pair of useless girls. I told you to get this new girl properly dressed for the harem, and you haven't done so. So bend over, both of you. And take your trousers down. Go on. Now, Baza, go on and give them a proper hiding!"

Scarcely believing what she was seeing, Amanda watched horrified as, struck dumb by Zalu's outburst, and biting their lips, the two beautiful Chained girls slipped their silken harem trousers down to their knees and presented their now bare bottoms to young Baza. These two poor girls, half European, were going to be beaten by a little black pygmy boy, punished

132

like naughty children - and it was all her fault!

My God, was this how discipline was maintained in the handsome young Sheik's harem?

"Four!" Baza announced proudly, his eyes flashing with anticipation as he played with his little whippy dog whip, bending it with both hands. There was a sharp intake of breath from the two girls. Four strokes!

"And then," said Zalu, "if you don't then get the new girl stripped and dressed ready for the harem, whilst I count ten, then you'll both get another four - from me! And this time," he added, turning to Amanda, "you'll get four too! So you'd better start taking off your clothes now."

"Bend over!" Baza ordered the twins.

My God, thought Amanda, how awful to have to submit to being beaten by a little boy. Terrified, she found herself struggling with the buttons of her coat, as, watched approvingly by Zalu, Baza slowly and ponderously raised his dog whip high in the air and then brought it down hard, first across one soft little bottom and then the other, leaving a bright line across each.

Two little cries rent the air, making Amanda shake with fear as she now almost ripped off her blouse, disclosing a pretty lace bra with the crest of the Sheik, embroidered just below each nipple. Blushing, she hastily pulled this off too, disclosing her small pert little breasts.

Zalu was pointing to a spot on one the bottoms just below the new red line. "Let's see you put the next stroke, exactly half an inch below the first one," he said to Baza.

Zalu liked to see a good ladder effect when a girl was thrashed. Any fool could just leave a crisscross mesh of stripes. He liked to have each stroke neatly placed below its predecessor, no matter how many strokes she was to receive. It had a most salutary effect on the other girls as they later saw the tidy and methodical effect through the girl's transparent harem trousers.

Zalu also liked to have a long pause between each stroke when a girl was beaten. It made the punishment so much more effective. It made the girl look back on the waiting with as much fear as the actual pain itself.

So, whilst the two terrified girls called Crimson waited, trembling with sheer fright, he turned and looked at Amanda. He took in the small size of her firm little breasts. He had first noticed this when inspecting her at Mahmud's establishment in Beirut.

Clearly they would have to be enlarged. But perhaps the master would agree to using the traditional harem way of calling in nature to give a helping hand. If she were to carry a couple of large black creatures sired by, say, a Dinka giant, then nature would soon respond accordingly, to meet what it expected would soon be their extra large nutritional needs.

He turned back to the now quivering bare bottoms, and nodded. Twice, young Baza again brought his dog whip down again, expertly leaving another red line just below the first.

Two more little cries echoed round the room. Zalu did not mind girls crying when being beaten. It increased the deterrent value for the watching girls - this time the terrified Amanda, shortly to assume her new harem name of Royal Blue.

He saw that she had now slipped off her skirt and was already lowering her silken panties. He glanced at her hips. The bone structure seemed alright. The girl had good child bearing hips. There should be no trouble delivering even a half Dinka progeny. It was time she had he first child. He would have to speak to the Master about it.

He glanced at Amanda's beauty lips. They would look better, he decided, nicely ringed.

He turned to the twins, and put his hand to feel between both girls' legs. Yes, despite the pain and fear, their laces were both wet with arousal. Beating a girl, he knew, rarely failed to have this effect.

It was time for the third pair of strokes.

Amanda was desperately pulling off her stockings, her last garment, as the final strokes fell. Zalu now began to count slowly; "One ... two ..."

Scared stiff of the prospect of a further four strokes, the two girls literally fell upon the now naked Amanda, pushing her legs into the dark blue silken trousers and her arms through

134

the holes of the matching bolero. They encountered no resistance, for Amanda, too, was scared out of her wits at the prospect of also having to proffer her bare bottom to Zalu's dog whip.

Zalu was slowly intoning: "Eight ... Nine ..." as one girl jammed the pretty little dark blue embroidered harem cap on Amanda's head whilst her sister put the remaining matching Turkish slipper onto her feet.

Panting all three girls straightened out. Their task was accomplished. Amanda no longer looked like a sophisticated European woman. She looked like what she was: the pretty new concubine of a vigorous young Sheik.

"...Ten."

Zalu lowered his dog whip. "All right," he said. "Pull up your trousers!"

Greatly relieved the two girls did so.

Then he produced a short length of chain. "Come here, Royal Blue!" It was the first time that she had been addressed by her new harem name. At first she didn't realise that he was talking to her.

His whip caught her across her bottom, making her cry out with the unexpected pain. "Move when I call you," he shouted. "You always run when a black eunuch gives you an order. Do you understand?"

Trembling with fear lest he gave her another stroke with his terrifying dog whip, she nodded.

"And don't just nod when I speak to you. You say 'Yes Sir' - or you'll get six for Dumb Insolence. You understand? Well, do you?" He raised his whip again.

"Yes, Sir," shouted Amanda, scared out of her wits. "Yes, Sir! Yes, Sir!"

"Good," said Zalu. "But don't you forget! Any more insolence to me or the other black eunuchs and you'll get six on the spot. And don't think you can go crying and complaining to the Master. Here in the harem what we eunuchs say is law - and that's what he wants."

"Yes, Sir. Of course, Sir," cried Amanda, remembering the girls' warning not to upset him.

Zalu produced a short length of chain. "Go and stand behind the other girls," he ordered.

Amanda ran across the room, and silently stood behind the other two girls, feeling like a beaten puppy dog. Grim faced, Zalu fastened one end of the little chain to the ring at the front of Amanda's collar. The other end, he fastened to the middle of the chain already linking the collars of the two girls, Crimson. He liked to couple a new girl to a more experienced girl when she was first introduced into the harem. He also liked to take the precaution of rendering her helpless. Seizing Amanda's wrists, he bound them behind her back.

Amanda was indeed now helpless, coupled to the two girls, Crimson. She looked at herself in the mirror. A half naked Eastern houri, dressed in a wildly erotic way, stared back at her. The shameful cutaway in the front of the silken harem trousers framed her smooth mound and beauty lips, shamefully. They had, of course, been depilated before the awful auction.

She looked up at her breasts. Having her hands fastened behind her back, made her small naked breasts stand out.

Zulu looked her and down and then nodded with approval. He turned to Baa.

"Take them down to the pool, to see her little companions and let Crimson introduce her to her two countrywomen, Mauve and Magenta. Then put her into play with the ball - I want to see her breasts tautened up."

Little Baza pulled his miniature riding whip out of his cummerbund and gave it a crack. "Run!" he ordered.

3 - 6 THE GOLDEN CAGE

Amanda gasped with astonishment as they ran into a beautiful large room surrounded with pillars and colonnades. The floor was of smooth pink marble and in the centre of the room was a large circular swimming pool with a pretty fountain playing in it.

Half a dozen naked, olivia skinned, dark eyed, girls were playing in the shallow end of the pool, throwing a large and apparently heavy rubber ball to each other. Their long hair hung down their backs like that of young girls. Several were wearing big brass nose rings, like those of the twins.

They were being watched from the side of the pool by a hugely fat black eunuch, dressed just like Zalu but without the gold ring round his strange shaped cap. Amanda was horrified to see that he carried a long carriage whip with which he was reaching out to the playing girls. He was making sure that each, in turn, lifted the heavy ball high above her head, tautening her breasts as she did so, before throwing it to another girl. But, she realised, he could also use his long whip to stop any illicit fun and games in the pool.

One girl's nipples seemed to be bound with silken threads so that they were exceptionally long, more like teats. Was that how the twin's nipples had been elongated. Indeed several of the girls seemed to have unnaturally large breasts and elongated nipples. Were they in milk? Would that be done to her, too? Oh, my God!

At the other end of the pool, several girls were swimming naked, using the breast stroke, under the eye of another hugely fat black eunuch, this time holding a large net, strong enough to catch and land any one of the swimming girls. My God, Amanda thought, we really are treated like animals.

Several girls, each wearing a different coloured harem cut-away trousers and bolero like her own, were playing with a skipping rope - laughing and crying like young children. How, she wondered, could grown up girls play like little girls?

Then something else caught her eye: the sight of two young women, with strangely white skins, and strikingly blond hair, like her own. They were practising belly dancing in an alcove off the pool. Horrified, she saw that their wrists and ankles were manacled and linked by a length of shiny chain. They also wore the same terrifying collars, so the manacles couldn't be to prevent them from escaping. It really must be just for the greater amusement and arousal of the Master. How could such an apparently charming man be so cruel?

The backs of the two women's chained hands were

touching above their heads and their bellies were thrust out provocatively as they gyrated erotically to the sensual Arab music. They were following the movements of an olivia skinned instructress who was facing them, also dressed in transparent trousers and a matching bolero, perhaps another of the harem girls.

Like herself and the two girls Crimson, the two white skinned young women were dressed in slightly different dark reddish coloured trousers and bolero. They must be Mauve and Magenta, her fellow Englishwomen!

Through the cut-away in the front of their transparent trousers gleamed something silver. She saw that each of their beauty lips were hidden beneath a silver filigree chain mail pouch held firmly in place by little chains locked round their waists. One of women looked definitely pregnant and the tummy of the other one was also beginning to show a pretty curve.

How cruel, Amanda thought, to make girls belly dance in their state. But then she looked again. Magenta's greatly swollen tummy made her belly dancing look quite natural, more so really than Mauve's. Well!

Would she, too, have to learn to belly dance in order to catch again her lover's eye? Oh no! Would she, too have her wrists and ankles manacled? Goodness! Perhaps catching the Sheik's eye was the reason why the harem seemed so preoccupied with swollen bellies - and breasts in milk.

How dreadful! Overcome with the isolated and artificial atmosphere of this harem were some of the women driven to begging Zalu to be mated? But with whom? How awful! Might she herself, desperate to catch the Master's eye, reluctantly submit to motherhood, just to be in her lover's arms again?

But then, she thought looking around at the beautiful women in the harem, and not least at the two Crimson girls, might she find herself jealously competing against them to be selected for it? Oh, what a dreadful idea! She felt a sudden pang of jealousy. What did all these women know about pleasing her handsome young lover? She had just done so for three consecutive nights! What even did Mauve and Magenta know about pleasing their Master compared with her? Then, she remembered that they were being trained by Zalu to perform in his bed as a team. Again she felt madly jealous.

One of the Crimson girls had whispered to her the significance of the big nose rings. She had, she told herself proudly, already received the Master's seed up all three orifices on the yacht, at least once. Two more times to go! Oh, how embarrassing and painful it had been, when the Sheik had gently insisted on taking her from behind. But would those times count towards earning her a nose ring that seemed to be so prized? What a shameful thought! Was she already being brain-washed by the sensual and all female atmosphere of the harem?

As she watched spellbound, looking over the shoulders of the two Crimson girls to whom she was still chained, she saw that the English women were desperately thrusting their tummies forwards and backwards in time to the music. What an erotic sight! She remembered what she had been told about belly dancing being a mime of making love. Well, their dancing was certainly explicit alright, even it was still a little amateurish.

Kneeling in front of the girls was another little black pigmy eunuch boy, wearing, like Baza, a miniaturised version of Zalu's dress. He was holding a long feather up to where the two young women's beauty lips were thrust out by their dancing, past the cutaway front of their transparent harem trousers!

The two women were trying to rub their beauty lips against the feather! And the boy was teasing them in turn, first tickling each girl and then taking the feather away. Oh how frustrating it must be for them! And how shame-making for their arousal to be controlled in this way by a young boy who hardly came up to their waists. But, what a clever way of making the women exercise their tummy muscles, thrusting forward and backwards in their efforts to catch the feather with their beauty lips.

She looked at the two women's right wrists as they held them, their backs touching, above their heads. Yes, there on the inside of each of their right wrists some Arabic numerals had been tattooed, just like the girls Crimson. So they were registered indentured servants, too!

Looking around the room, Amanda saw through a line

of large windows covered in iron bars, a pretty garden and beyond that a very high wall, with an electrified fence at the top. Running across the garden, near the bottom of the wall, she saw a long brass strip, just like the one at the entrance to the harem, that had so painfully triggered off her collar.

My God, there really was no escape from this harem!

In despair she turned away and saw that many of the girls were wantonly glancing up at a balcony high up on the inside wall of the harem. As they did so, they were flirtatiously tossing their long hair, fluttering their eyelashes and shaking their half naked breasts.

The lattice work on the balcony would hide anyone in the balcony from the women down in the harem, but she thought she saw a shadow behind the wooden grille.

Moments late Amanda fund herself smiling up at the balcony, tossing her hair, fluttering her eyelashes and shaking her half naked breasts, too.

3 - 7 INSPECTION BY THE MASTER

Suddenly a bell rang. Pandemonium! The girls in the pool all ran out. Mauve and Magenta stopped dancing. The Crimson girls ran towards an alcove, dragging Royal Blue behind them, and crying out to her: "That's the signal for the parade. We've got fifteen minutes to get ready. Hurry!"

Amanda found herself in a long room. Along one side was a line of tables and mirrors, like a chorus girls' dressing room in a big theatre. Along the other side was a row of narrow lockers with names in Arabic letters and in English: the concubines' slender wardrobes!

Standing in the middle of the dressing room, a brush and comb in his hand, was a young black eunuch hairdresser. Meanwhile the girls, nearly twenty of them, were pouring into the room, excited and whispering, laughing and chattering jealously. They stood in front of the line of dressing tables and mirrors, brushing their hair or rouging their cheeks, or rushed to the lockers to dress in their different coloured, but identical harem dress.

Meanwhile the young hairdresser was going down the line of chattering girls, adjusting one girl's curls, and painting the lips, nipples or beauty lips of others.

When he came to Amanda, he deftly outlined her eyes and mouth heavily in kohl, giving her a typical Middle Eastern look. With her hands still tied behind her back, she was helpless to prevent him also outlining her nipples in the same black kohl - and then he did the same to her beauty lips, giving them a strangely erotic look. No two girls were made up in the same way. Was this to be the way she was to make up in future, she wondered as she picked up hair brush and began to brush her long honey coloured hair.

A quarter of an hour later, there was a sudden respectful silence as Zalu entered the dressing room, his beady bloodshot eyes darting here and there, as the girls nervously eyed his long dog whip dog. Amanda, too, found she could not take her eyes off it.

He barked an order, and the women all ran out and lined up in two rows on a thickly carpeted platform, raised some three feet above the tiled floor, in front of a small balcony. Amanda found herself in the second row, immediately behind the two girls Crimson to whom she was still chained, coupled like a foxhound puppy to two older hounds.

Alongside her was Mauve. There seemed something familiar about her. Magenta was in the place of honour in the centre of the front row. The cutaway part in the front of her harem trousers had been pulled back to emphasise her curved belly - clearly considered here a matter of beauty and pride.

The hugely fat black eunuchs were patrolling up and down in front of the platform on which the girls were paraded. The eunuchs' whips were uncoiled as they enforced strict silence.

Behind Amanda, and behind Magenta and Mauve, were the two young black eunuch boys - using their little whips to tap the bottoms of their half naked charges warningly.

There was a long wait. None of the girls dared to speak

141

or move. Amanda glanced at Mauve. What a pretty woman she was, she thought jealously. How many times, she wondered, had the Master taken her - and how? But she'd never had him all to herself for days on the yacht! Mauve smiled back at her, a friendly conspiratorial smile. Perhaps they could be friends! Suddenly a bell rung. The black eunuchs all cracked their whips and the women dropped to all fours in a clearly well rehearsed movement, their breasts hanging down prettily beneath them.

"Get down! The Master's coming," whispered Mauve, out of the corner of her mouth, her wrist manacles clanking. Then she added: "Welcome to the harem!"

It was the first time she had heard Mauve's voice and she was astonished to hear her talk in the distinctive tones of a Sloane Ranger. Goodness, she thought, how on earth could a girl like that end up here? But then the same question could just as well have been asked about her!

As she dropped to her knees, Amanda saw that the horrible little Baza had moved away.

"Who are you?" she whispered to Mauve, as she knelt there, her forehead to the floor. "I'm Amanda Seymour."

"Any relation of Robin Seymour?"

"Yes, I'm his wife!"

"He's a cousin by marriage! I'm Louise Riddle and the girl ahead of us, dressed in magenta, is Samantha Smythe. But shush! Don't let them catch you talking during a parade!"

But the warning came too late. "Silence during parades!" came Baza's boyish voice, back behind them again. Amanda flinched as he reached up and brought his whip down across her back - but not hard enough to mark.

Suddenly there was the noise of a door opening and Sheik Ali stepped out onto the front of the balcony from behind the wooden grille.

Again the bell rang, again there was a cracking of whips, and this time the women all humbly prostrated themselves, on their knees, lowering their foreheads to the carpeted floor of the platform. Their hands and hair were flung forward, with just their buttocks raised and gleaming through their silken trousers.

"Part your legs!" whispered Mauve. "It's a sign of respect to the Master."

Blushing, Amanda hastily did so. She could feel the cutaway in her trousers neatly framing her bare beauty lips, now on display between her buttocks.

She heard footsteps on the balcony and the strong voice of the Sheik, speaking in Arabic. She heard Zalu replying in his strangely high pitched voice. Were they discussing the women? Was the Sheik enquiring how they had behaved in his absence? Was Zulu pointing out one or two to the Master?

Amanda longed to raise her head and look, but did not dare to do so. She was aware of a strong scent of female arousal all around her. At the same time she was aware of her own suddenly growing moistness. How shame-making!

Was it just nature taking over, the natural reaction of a group of helpless women being displayed to a man of power and wealth for him to choose from? Or was the strange effect of the harem, of the exciting feeling of being kept helpless for the pleasure of one man? Or was it the women's naturally excited jealousy as they found themselves competing against the other equally frustrated women, for the Master's attention?

What ever it was, Amanda found her former anger and shock leaving her. Now she, too, was just a slave: an excited, aroused and submissive one, and one who was desperately longing to attract the Master's eye.

There was just nothing she could do about it as she knelt in front of the wonderful man who was now her Master and who had, until that very morning, been her passionate lover. Sheik Ali, with Zalu standing obsequiously behind him, stood proudly gripping the rails of the balcony, looking down on his well disciplined harem. A satisfying feeling of power swept through him. It was nice to be back again!

He was dressed in an immaculate long white robe and white Arab headdress with golden ropes, that contrasted vividly with the half naked women with their skimpy but brightly coloured harem dress.

He smiled, with a proprietary air, as he looked down on

the two lines of humbly prostrated women: his women, his concubines, his registered indentured servants, effectively his slaves,
his property.

He smiled again as he saw three sets of blond hair flung
forward, from one pale still slim body and from two rather more
interesting ones.

The first of his collection of Englishwomen! It was
slowly building up and already he had three, with several more
in the pipeline. And two already with a little swelling bellies!
Moreover, they all seemed to have fitted into the harem with the
minimum of fuss. Well done Zalu! Amanda now caught her
breath, as keeping her head down, she peered up, and saw, out of
the corner of her eye, that the Sheik, her Master, her erstwhile
lover, was stepping down from the balcony. Followed by Zalu,
his whip at the ready, the Sheik slowly strode down behind the
two lines of beautiful prostrated women.

She heard him go behind her. She caught her breath
and blushed as she realised what she would be displaying to her
Master through the cut away between the legs of her harem trousers. Oh the shame! Oh the excitement! She heard Mauve catch
her breath, too.

Suddenly she shuddered as she felt Baza's podgy little
fingers reach forward to her exposed beauty lips, and part them -
parting them for the Master!

Then she felt a slender bejewelled finger enter her.
Against her will she found herself gripping it in a secret display
of utter submissiveness and desire.

She heard the Sheik laugh cruelly. She heard herself
give a little moan as he removed his finger and moved on down
the line. Moments later she heard a similar moan from Mauve,
and then from other women, too. She felt overcome with jealousy.

The Sheik came round to the front of the low platform
and nodded to Zalu, who was standing to one side of the two
lines of still prostrate women. Zalu uncoiled the whip tucked
into his cummerbund and cracked it loudly. A little shiver went
through the women, but Amanda saw that none of them moved .

Then the whip cracked a second time, and this time, moving as one, the women all knelt up straight, put their hands on the top of their heads, and looked straight ahead. Their breasts were now well displayed, and with their knees widely parted so. too, were their bellies.

A sharp tap of Baza's whip on the inside of her thighs made Amanda part her knees, too. Would she ever learn all these complicated harem drills? What discipline! And all enforced by these horrible black eunuchs. She shivered.

As she kept her eyes fixed ahead, she saw, out of the corner of her eyes, the Sheik coming down the front of the platform reaching forward with that bejewelled hand to feel a breast or to caressingly stroke a soft cheek - a gesture that was answered by a quick flash of well made-up eyes.

She saw him pause in front of Magenta and put his hand onto her greatly swollen belly. He turned and looked enquiringly at Zalu, following him down the line.

"Seven months, Your Excellency," he murmured proudly in Arabic so that Magenta would not understand. "The twins are holding very nicely. She realises now what's happening, but can't understand how and doesn't know yet that it's twins."

The Sheik nodded approvingly. The mixture of a swollen belly and manacled wrists and ankles was very erotic.

"Good little Magenta," he said encouragingly in English. "Now thrust out your tummy for your Master."

Blushing Magenta did as she told.

"Is she ready to belly dance, yet?" he asked Zalu in Arabic.

"She and Mauve are beginning to get quite good, Your Excellency - for Englishwomen," replied Zalu.

"Then I want to see them perform in front of me," ordered the Sheik. He patted Magenta affectionately, as a man might pat an obedient little dog. "Good little girl," he murmured, and moved on down the line, leaving Magenta smiling like a cat that's swallowed the cream. As Zalu had repeatedly said to her, she was a lucky girl for being in her state. It was wonderful being the centre of so much attention.

145

And now her handsome Master had actually spoken to her and told she was a good little girl. The fact that she was in her thirties was irrelevant. Here in the harem she was just a little girl again - a happy little girl, too.

Then the Sheik came up onto the platform for a closer look at the women in her second row. Amanda could feel her heart beating with excitement. He stopped at Mauve and felt her breasts and smiled. But he walked straight past Amanda without a word! She felt utterly humiliated. Her lover, her adored handsome lover had ignored her. She hated him!

Then he turned, looked her in the eye and winked! Yes, she thought, her mind in a turmoil, her Master had actually winked at her, winked in a conspiratorial way! Oh!

But then the young Sheik turned to Zalu.

"When is that one going to have my crest tattooed on her belly?" Amanda was shocked to hear him ask in English in a harsh tone of voice.

"I shall be doing her myself, this morning, Your Highness," came the reply. "Good! I don't want her having any idea that she's now anything special," Amanda was chagrined to hear her erstwhile lover say, "I want her to feel she's just one of my indentured servant concubines now."

"Of course , Your Highness, of course - and she will be permanently marked as such within the hour."

She Sheik nodded, turned on his heel and went back towards the balcony, leaving Amanda feeling utterly subjugated - as he intended.

Zalu's whip cracked again, twice and with the second crack the women all prostrated themselves again, their noses and foreheads touching the carpet.

There was the noise of a door shutting. The Master had left the harem.

There was an intake of breath from the prostrated women as they anxiously waited for Zalu to announce the chosen ones, the ones who would share their Master's bed for his siesta.

"Mauve and Magenta!" Zalu called out, first in Arabic

146

and then in his heavily accented English.

3 - 8 PLEASURE AND FRUSTRATION Siesta Time.

In the half darkness of the harem dormitory, a dozen pretty young women lay on their backs on roll up mattresses.

The girls were naked, and their harem clothes, caps and slippers lay neatly folded at the foot of each mattress. There were no sheets, just a simple blanket on which their hands lay innocently. The mattresses were in rows each several feet apart, except for one doubled mattress on which two girls lay, chained together by the neck: the twins Crimson.

Quietly patrolling up and down the rows was the diminutive figure of Baza, his little whip in his hand. How proud he felt at having been entrusted by Zalu with such an important task: to make sure that each young woman kept her hands on show above her blanket. He was responsible for guarding the honour of the Master!

Indeed, the responsibility for ensuring the continuing purity of the Master's women lay, he knew, on his shoulders. Given half a chance they would be desperately trying to play with themselves, squeezing little fingers through the laces to get at their beauty buds - and deceiving the Master. Such behaviour was anathema to the black eunuchs and it was his responsibility today to ensure that none took place during the siesta.

But there was more to it than preserving the honour of the Master. Any such behaviour, he knew, would also undermine the work of Zalu and his colleagues in keeping the women frustrated, and so desperate to catch the Master's eye - and when they did, to please him so much that the Master would remember them and choose them again.

Moreover, when the Master was pleased with the desperate efforts of the chosen women, he would send Zalu a little financial reward to be distributed amongst the black eunuchs as a sign of his appreciation.

Baza knew only too well that the women were seriously

tempted to be impure today. Indeed there was again, as during the parade, the distinctive scent of aroused womanhood. The return of the Master had excited all their hopes. But it had also made the feeling of frustration amongst those not chosen at the parade all the stronger.

Baza also knew that the women would all be looking up at the large lit up portrait of the Master hanging on the wall, facing the lines of mattresses. It was rather like a photograph that Amanda had seen earlier, but this time the Master was stripped to the waist, disclosing his slim muscular torso, and in the background was a large sumptuously draped bed.

Nor, this time was he looking down, with an arrogant air, at a line of prostrated women in the harem. Instead he was looking down at two naked women, kneeling at his feet with their backs to the artist, their hands raised in a gesture of abject submission. The Master himself was pointing, with his whip, to the bed.

By the side of the portrait a red light was flashing. It indicated to the jealously watching women down in the dormitory, that the Master was busy amusing himself with his chosen concubines.

As Baza well knew, the combination of the lit up portrait and the flashing red light, would not only, as it was intended to do, arouse the women in the dormitory, but also drive them half mad with jealousy and frustration. It would ensure that all they would be thinking of was what was going on in the Master's bedroom, and of their own desperate disappointment at not having been chosen to be there.

These were feelings that Amanda was sharing in full measure, aggravated, indeed, by thoughts that when she had said goodbye to the Master that morning, she had been looking forward to spending the siesta in his arms.

Instead, here she was, lying on her back, her mind again in a turmoil of arousal, frustration, jealousy and disappointment - just like that of the other women.

Moreover, she could not get out of her mind that now emblazoned on her tummy was the Sheik's crest and below it, and on the inside of her wrist, the Arabic numerals of her registered number as an indentured servant. They made her feel like a branded animal - the personal possession of her Master.

Now, like the other concubines, she, a grown woman, a married woman, was having to show to a horrible little black boy that her hands were being kept above her blanket. It was all unbelievably degrading. But oh how she longed to slip a hand down, discreetly and give herself a little relief, before her beauty lips were ringed and laced up tight - as Zalu had said would shortly be done to her.

At home, even highly sensuous as she was, she had not thought about sex the whole time. There always been so many other things on her mind to worry about. And when she did it was often, in her imagination, not only with her husband, but with other men she had seen in the flesh or on the television, or had read about.

Here, however, as she had already realised, the harem system and the sensuous atmosphere, would ensure that she, like the other women, would spend all day, and all night, fantasising and dreaming about nothing else - and always about the manhood, and hands, of one man, one man only, those of the Master. Moreover, she would never forget, ever, how he had saved her from what had seemed a quite awful fate.

But soon her thoughts inevitably returned to wondering jealously about just what was going on upstairs in the Master's bedroom. In fact, she would have been surprised ... The young Sheik was dozing as he lay on his back in his large bed, his eyes closed and his hands on the pillow under his head. Oh, yes, these Englishwomen made excellent concubines and the fact that they were not used to having to concentrating on pleasing a man, made it all the more pleasurable, mentally as well as physically.

On either side of him, facing him, hidden under the silken sheets, lay two very pretty Englishwomen. They were naked except for their manacles and their pert little coloured caps of the appropriate colour. They also, however, now wore white gloves like those worn by a serving girl. It would never do for these mere concubines to touch their Master's body with their bare hands, and he gloves served as a reminder to an indentured servant of her status.

But the gloves were not resented by the women. On the contrary, they felt that they quite rightly emphasised how the station of the Master was indeed so much above theirs as mere indentured concubines. Just as enclosed orders of nuns existed only to adore and worship the Maker, so they now felt they only existed to pleasure and adore their saviour, their Master.

But there was more to it, Mauve and Magenta had learnt. Just as nuns might dedicate their virginity to their Saviour, so they were expected to dedicate their purity to their saviour. But whereas the atmosphere of a nunnery helped nuns to maintain their vows, the sensuous feelings aroused by the harem, made the concubines constantly long for relief.

Magenta, as Samantha was now called, found herself loving being brought to him every morning by Zalu to show off proudly her swelling belly. Just as a devoted nun might dedicate an act of contrition to her Master, so she mentally had dedicated her expectant state to her Master.

Meanwhile, Mauve like all the other girls, clutched her very pretty and life-like little doll and, still half unaware of her true state, dreamed of, and feared, a real maternity. Both women, however, longed to for the much sought-after status of a milk-maid.

Both were very conscious that their Master, the man who had saved them from the horrors of the prison, was also the man who could send them back there at any time, if he was disappointed with their performance.

Their performance! The very idea made them both remember the roles that Zalu had so embarrassingly made them practice over and over again with a rubber, life-size, blown up figure of a man.

Eagerly, their manacles chinking, Magenta cupped the Master's testicles with one hand and licked his powerful half erect manhood, whilst Mauve gently squeezed his nipples, sending little frissons of delight running up and down his body. Then she kissed and licked his body, the precious body of her Master. Giving her

Master pleasure was very exciting, but even so Mauve longed for a little forbidden relief for herself.

Louise, now Mauve, glanced up at her Master's handsome face. He seemed to be asleep. It was now or never!

Her hand quietly slipped down between her legs. Her chain mail breeding belt had been removed by Zalu to allow her Maser proper access to her body, and her laces had been loosened.

Gently, she parted her beauty lips and found her beauty bud. She started to tickle it. Little electric shocks of desire ran through her body.

In the harem the women were, of course, only supposed to have pleasure from the feeling of being penetrated by their Master's dominating manhood - and certainly not from themselves. Mauve adored feeling her master's wonderful manhood inside her, and indeed thinking about it now absorbed most of their waking moments - and their sleeping ones, too. But it was so frustrating not being allowed to come. Oh she longed for a little self relief that would be under her own control for once - and the fact that it was prohibited would make it all the more exciting.

As she played with herself, she could feel her own arousal becoming stronger and stronger. Relief was at last at hand.

Suddenly her young Master, stretched out a hand and pressed a bell. He was awake! Instantly she dropped her hand - like a naughty girl caught with her hand in the sweets jar. But it was too late. Baza came running in.

"This one's been playing with herself," drawled the young Master languidly, pointing to an embarrassed and fearful Louise. "Take her out and give her six and then bring her back."

Baza snapped a lead onto the ring at the front of Louise's collar and jerked out of the bed. Stumbling, she followed the young boy out of the room and into an annex. He left the door open. Silently he pointed to a cushion on the floor.

Biting her lips, Louse knelt down and then put her head to the floor raising her buttocks. Oh, what a fool she had been!

With a sudden swish of his little whip, which was clearly

151

audible to the listening young Master next door, Baza gave her the first stroke, making her cry out with pain.

"Say it!" he ordered.

Blushing, Louise hesitated. She did, she knew, feel that she had been unfaithful to her Master, but was too embarrassed to say so.

The whip came down again.

"Say it!"

This time the degrading words came tumbling out. She may have had to learn them by heart in the harem, with Zalu standing over her with his dog whip, but they were still heartfelt. "My beloved Master is my whole life ... Without him I am nothing ... I must never seek relief without permission ... To do so is to be unfaithful to my beloved Master ... I deserve to be thrashed for attempted unfaithfulness ... Please beat me ... Please let me kiss the whip that is to punish me."

"Louder!" Down came the whip again. "Let the Master hear you!"

"My beloved Master ..." screamed Louise this time. Then she kissed the whip that the horrible little boy was holding out to her.

"Down!" ordered the boy.

Blushing with humiliation, Louise again lowered her face to the floor and raised her buttocks for the whip. Three more times, now with a measured gap between each stroke, the whip came down.

"Jump up!"

Baza now led the weeping Louise back to her young Master's bed. Not a word was said, but Louise resumed her attentions even more assiduously. She was his utter slave now. The handsome young Sheik again lay back in his bed, his hands behind his neck, as he felt the tongues and fingers of Mauve and Magenta arousing him below the bedclothes. They were getting really very good! Zalu had trained them well. But now he must start training Royal Blue to work with her fellow Englishwomen

Yes, he decided, the feeling of three little soft English tongues, each driven, by fear of Zalu's cane, to please him the most, would indeed be arousing,

So, too, would the thoughts that two of them had been respectable married women and the other a formerly well paid career girl; and that two of them, perhaps, indeed, soon all three, were being made to undergo the pangs and worries of an enforced motherhood - to provide for his future pleasure.

4 - 1 ABANDONED IN NORTH AFRICA

The rather large stern faced Arab woman, dressed in a long caftan, sat down behind her big desk. She motioned to Kurt to sit down in a large comfortable chair. Olivia was left standing, twisting her hands awkwardly.

The large woman smiled at Kurt and then, looking at Olivia, started to speak to him in voluble French which Olivia had difficulty in following.

"She's certainly a pretty little creature. We've never had an English lady here before. I expect she'll be very popular with the clients. They'll enjoy a proud young Englishwoman."

Olivia was angry at the way the woman was talking about her, in front of her, as if she were a child. Had she mentioned clients? It was a little worrying. Thank goodness that she would only be here for a week or so.

As the woman rattled on, Olivia thought back to her first meeting with Kurt. It had been nearly two months ago, when she had been on holiday in the South of France, when she had time on her hands, a struggling actress between jobs. Oh yes, she had enjoyed being seduced by Kurt...

Her father, a retired Army officer, had recently died leaving all his not inconsiderable estate to her step-mother whom she loathed - and who loathed her. She was longing, she had told Kurt, simply longing, to get away for a time from England with all its sad memories.

Kurt was Austrian and very understanding. He seemed to live an exciting life, constantly travelling. Idly she had wondered whether her future might lie with him. But he himself always seemed so busy and she had begun to wondered if he was beginning to tire of her.

Then suddenly he had telephoned, saying that he was coming to London for a meeting with his business partner and would like to introduce her to him.

This 'business partner' had turned out to be a very handsome young Arab Sheik, with dark bedroom eyes. She never learnt his name, but Kurt had later said that he came from one of the oil states in the Middle East. She could see from the cut of his suit, his silk tie and his chauffeur driven Rolls that he was rich. Probably very rich indeed. There had a been a strange aura of power and ruthlessness about him that she had found fascinating and strangely disturbing.

She been surprised that that such a rich and handsome man seemed to be alone. She had expected him to be squiring some famous beauty. She had even hoped that she might see more of him herself, for he was obviously taken by her. She was certainly very disappointed when he said that he had only come to London for the day and that he was leaving that evening - in his private jet, of course!

He hoped to see her again before long, he said, winking at Kurt.

Some hope, she thought sadly. Kurt invited her to join him on an interesting trip abroad and she quickly forgot all about the young Sheik. She had accepted with alacrity, even though he had been a little vague about just where they would be going. It was to be a surprise! She was simply to meet him in Rome in two days time, where they would get visas and go on.

How exciting it sounded! Kurt certainly led an interesting life and knew some fascinating people!

So now none of her friends and relations in London had any idea she was now in this mysterious North Africa.

Olivia had been thrilled to be with Kurt again. She had also been thrilled by the real Arab atmosphere and the very different culture - so different from the Western way of life and dreary old London. And the people seemed so different too: the veiled women and the stern looking robed men.

They had been so happy together. How she loved him for bringing her to such an exciting and beautiful place. How jealous her girl friends would be when she told them all about it.

Then suddenly, after making several telephone calls,

Kurt had said that he had to go off alone on a business for a week or so. As he would be staying with Arab friends he could not take her with him. Nor could he leave her, a lone woman, alone in this part of the world - not even in their respectable hotel.

Her heart had sunk, Must she now go back to London, so soon, and start looking for a job, a new part?

She had therefore cheered up enormously when he told her that he had arranged for her to stay with a older woman who ran an expensive school for the daughters of wealthy Arabs. She would be quite safe there and well looked after. With the fundamentalists insisting on women being educated separately from men, or even not all, there was a need for a discreet school like this one.

"But I'm twenty five," she had protested with a laugh, "not exactly school girl age!"

"Oh, don't worry," he had reassured her, "there are older students there too. It's rather like a convent in Europe - and at least you won't be lonely whilst I'm away."

Then he had taken her to a villa, high above the city. It was surrounded by high walls with armed guards at the gates. "Security is very important for the families of wealthy Arabs," he had explained. Olivia had felt rather relieved she was going to be so well guarded whilst her lover was away.

The villa was built in Arab style with arabesque stone tracery or iron work, and wooden grilles, over all the windows. From the outside nothing could be seen of the inside, and clearly no one could get in or out, except through the big, iron studied, front door. This had been opened by a large black servant wearing a uniform of big baggy red trousers gathered at the knee, a turban and little jacket. He looked Olivia up and down and then, ignoring her, turned to Kurt whom he greeted like an old friend.

"Madame is awaiting you," he said in heavily accented French.

The front door closed behind them, and they were in a small hall facing another large door. There was a grille in this door behind which another black face appeared and said something in Arabic to the first Negro. Then the second door was opened. Yes, thought Olivia, security was certainly very tight here. Was it, she asked herself with a laugh, aimed only at keeping out undesirables, but also at keeping the schoolgirls in!

The two black servants had now ushered them into what Olivia imagined was the study of the headmistress, Madame - she never did learn her name, she was just Madame to everyone.

The woman had greeted Kurt effusively, whilst at the same time looking Olivia up and down, just as the black servant had done. The woman was now speaking to Kurt in Arabic, whilst still gesturing to Olivia. What on earth were they discussing, Olivia wondered. The cost of her stay? What she was going to do whilst Kurt was away?

Then the woman turned to Olivia. "Give me your handbag, my child," she said in French, speaking slowly so that Olivia could not fail to understand.

Olivia was furious at being called a child by this Arab woman. She looked at Kurt who nodded reassuringly. Silently, she reluctantly handed over her bag. The woman opened it and quickly took out her passport, her airline ticket, her credit cards and her cheque book. She put them away in a drawer of her desk.

"But -" Olivia started to protest.

"You will not need any of these here, my child."

Olivia blushed at being treated like a little girl. Then she saw that the woman was taking out her address book and even her pen.

"But I want those to write to friends in England," she cried out. "I've so much to tell them!"

"Girls are not allowed to write letters here without permission, my child. And you must learn to obey the rules, just like the other girls."

Olivia stated to protest again, but the woman ignored her and turned to Kurt saying something in Arabic. She gave an unpleasant laugh.

Olivia saw Kurt pull some papers, written in Arabic, out of his inside pocket and hand them over to the woman. Startled, she saw her signature on them. They were the so-called contract of employment that he had asked her to sign in Rome in order, he had said, for her to get a visa to come here. As a lone, unmarried, Western woman, he had explained, she would not be allowed into this country with it's strict fundamentalist laws, unless she was a secretary, travelling with her employer.

Thinking it all rather a joke, for she could not, of course, understand a word of what was written, she had willingly signed. Anything to be going off with him on this exciting trip!

But why was he now giving the contract to this rather terrifying woman? Just for safekeeping? Before she could ask, the woman had locked the papers away, and handed a brief case to Kurt. Kurt opened it. She saw it was contained several piles of American hundred dollar bills which Kurt cursorily counted.

Then, with an airy wave of his hand, Kurt quickly left the room. Hurt at her lover leaving her in such a casual way, she turned to run after him, to say goodbye properly, to kiss him and to say that loved him and would be impatiently waiting for his return.

But the two burly Negroes standing by the door barred her way...

4 - 2 OLIVIA LEARNS SHE IS TO BE A WHORE

"Now, child, hurry up and take off all those European clothes. You won't be needing them here."

"What!" cried Olivia, turning back from the door and glancing at nervously at the two big Negroes guarding it.

"And your underclothes, too!" said the large woman, in a harsh tone. "Hurry up, my girl, I've got more important things to do than waste time on a young girl like you - even if you are going to earn me a lot of money,"

"Earn you money?" cried Olivia. "Oh, you mean the money that Kurt is paying you for looking after me until he returns." Then she remembered the attach case full of hundred dollar notes that this woman had given to him. Mystified, she added: "But what was all that money you gave to Kurt?"

"Never you mind," said the woman angrily. "You just

do as you're told. Now take off your clothes. At once, do you hear?"

Olivia saw that the woman's face was hard and expressionless. "Hurry up!" she said.

Olivia pointed to the two black men. "But I'm not going to undress in front of them!"

"Huh! They've seen plenty of other naked white women, and stark naked at that - just as you're now going to be."

She nodded to the two blacks.

For such large men, they moved surprisingly quickly - as if they were used to such things. One seized her arms and held them behind her back. The other started to unbutton her dress.

"No! No!" she protested, as she struggled helplessly in the hands of the two burly black men, but soon her dress was lying on the floor and then her slip. Her little lacy bra was now quickly snatched off. She felt something being fastened round her wrists behind her back. There was a metallic click.

The black men let her go. She was now naked except for her very pretty panties. Horrified and blushing, she tried to cover her breasts with her hands, only to find they were handcuffed behind her back.

"Let me go!" she screamed. "How dare you treat me like this. Kurt will be furious when he hears about it!"

"Kurt!" laughed the woman. Then she disdainfully picked up Olivia's dress and bra and threw them into a bin.

"But that's a very valuable dress!" cried Olivia.

"Well, you won't need it here - nor ever again," said the woman grimly. She flung open the suitcase that Olivia had brought with her, and emptied the contents into the same bin. "You'll not see them again either!" The woman had a cruel laugh. "I do not allow my girls to wear European clothes. Here they must forget about Europe and Western ideas about women's rights. Nor," she added, pointing at Olivia, "do I allow them to wear panties."

She gestured to the Negroes again.

Again they gripped her, and then ripped off her panties, which joined the the rest of Olivia's clothes - in the bin.

"Nor do I allow them to argue with me. You're here to

do what you're told and the sooner you learn that the better. Meanwhile I think a little silence from you would be in order."

Again she signalled to the two black servants. Deftly they thrust a leather gag into Olivia's mouth and fastened it with a buckle at the back of her neck. She struggled to spit it out, but it was impossible.

Olivia was now feeling really frightened. Clearly Kurt had tricked her - but what for? What was this so-called school?

There was a knock on the door. A tall good looking young Negress entered. She was wearing a long white uniform like a hospitals nurse, except that she was holding a black whip, coiled up in her hand. It reminded Olivia of the whips carried by white overseers in pictures of the old black slave plantations in America or the West Indies.

The Negress gave a contemptuous glance at the cowering and naked young Englishwoman. Later Olivia would learn that the she despised white women.

"This is Mafta, my assistant, and your overseer," said the Arab woman to the cringing Olivia. "You will call her Mademoiselle Mafta. I am the Directress, and you'll call me Madame. Now come here and stand up straight."

Olivia hesitated. The Arab woman gestured to the watching Negroes. Olivia found herself being frog-marched up to the desk. The Arab woman looked her now naked body up and down. She was evidently pleased with what she saw.

Olivia then saw her pull several photographs out of an envelope that had been in a drawer - photos of her that Kurt had taken a month before on a secluded beach in France! She had been wearing only a bikini, and as a joke had agreed to let her lover take photos of her topless and, finally, naked.

Kurt had not handed the envelope to the Directress. Indeed the envelope had French stamps on it, so Kurt must have posted it to her before he came here. Perhaps weeks ago? Perhaps before he had even suggested she should join him on this trip? But why? My God!

Suddenly she realised that, in any case, it would have been long before he had announced that he had to go away for a

160

week and would be leaving her here at this strange school. So, sending her here must have been planned weeks ago! But again, why?

She would have learnt some the answers to some of the questions racing round her mind, had she been able to understand what the Directress and the young Negress were now saying in Arabic. She tried to interrupt them, to scream for an explanation, but thanks to her gag she could only make a little whinnying noise.

"So Kurt didn't let us down!" the Arab woman was saying. "She's certainly just as good in the flesh as she looked in the photos he sent me. No wonder a certain very rich Sheik was so taken by her when he went to see her in London!"

"Will you keep her for long?" asked the Negress overseer.

"Long enough to make her very grateful to the Sheik for having rescued her!"

"And how's he going to do that?"

The Directress whispered something into her assistant's ear.

"Oh!" said the Negress. "Well!"

"In the meanwhile, she'll be our star attraction here! We'll break her properly and start her training. The Sheik will be even more keen to buy her if he finds she's been taught a trick or two, and there'll be all the more demand for her if he does change his mind."

"And a little training will make sure she's on her best behaviour when he comes to inspect her," laughed the Negress, licking her lips. "A cultured Englishwoman who's been trained as a brothel girl! He'll pay the earth for her!"

"Indeed! And she's already signed the usual contract of indenture. So I've already had her registered with the police as an indentured servant and paid the annual license fee. By law, of course, even in this house, when displayed before a client, a girl must display this year's tax disc, attached to the person, to show that she's a properly registered whore. The stricter we are with Christian girls, the happier the fundamentalists are. But I don't want any trouble with the police, so make sure that the disc is properly attached to this one's collar. I don't want her snatching it off to hide her shame when she realises its significance."

The Directress turned to Olivia and spoke in French again. "Now, child, go with Mafta and do as she says. She's in charge of you now and I don't want to hear any complaints from her when she brings you back this evening for your first meeting with something I keep in that cupboard."

"Oh!" cried Olivia under her gag, frightened at what the Directress might mean. She longed to cry out that she hadn't any clothes on and that her wrists were tied.

As if anticipating her concern, the Directress handed the young Negress a ribbon from which hung a short length of pretty blue material. The young Negress fastened the ribbon round Olivia's slender waist. The piece of material now hung down in front, barely hiding her intimacies.

"This little modesty flap will be your school uniform here," the Directress laughed cruelly. "And your wrists will be released as soon as you've been properly collared and manacled."

Properly collared and manacled! - Olivia could hardly believe what she had heard!

4 - 3 OLIVIA IS PREPARED

Muzzled and with her hands handcuffed behind her back, Olivia stumbled along, stark naked, behind the tall young Negress.

The Negress led her into a large room. There were bars on the windows, and an animal-like smell. Round the room were some twenty alcoves. Some were carpeted and contained brightly coloured cushions, a small comfortable mattress, soft pillows and even sheets, pictures and books. Others were quite bare with only the hard wooden floor.

But were they really alcoves? They looked more like cages, for each was closed, not by a door, but by a barred gate. It went right across the front of the alcove. Clearly there was no privacy at all.

Olivia shivered as she saw that walking up and down in front of the cages was a large Negro dressed like the black guards who had so recently stripped her. Seeing the young Negress enter, he called out an order.

Olivia gasped as in each cage, a woman obediently jumped up with a clinking of chains. Each stood respectfully at attention in front of the Negro guard, gripping the bars of her cage with arms bent on either side of her face - evidently a well rehearsed position of respect for the young Negress.

The women's wrists were manacled and joined by a length of what looked to be a heavy chain, that they held taut under their chins. Like Olivia they were naked except for the little blue modesty flap, as the Directress had so derisively called it, that hung down over their intimacies. Their breasts were thrust through the bars of their cages. They eyed Olivia silently as she passed.

Most of the women were European, some dark haired like Olivia herself; some were dramatically blond, two were oriental, delicate little creatures, perhaps from China or Thailand. There were no Arab girls.

All were exceptionally beautiful. All, Olivia saw with a shock, had Arabic numerals neatly tattooed on their chins. Olivia had seen Arab women in the streets tattooed on the chin with various designs or dots, apparently to enhance their beauty in the eyes of Arab men - or perhaps as a sign of submission. But on a white woman it just looked degrading - especially as, looking down, she saw that the numbers were also neatly tattooed on each woman's belly just above her now hairless mound.

Indeed she could not help noticing that all the women's body hair down there had been removed - giving them all a quite shocking look, like that of a little girl.

She was even more shocked when she saw that each woman had a bright stainless steel collar round her neck, from which hung an official looking tax disc similar to the one she had seen the Directress give to the Negress.

The Negress stopped by an empty cage. It was quite bare.

"This yours. This your new home," she said in broken French.

From behind Olivia's muzzle came a moan of horror.

Fastened onto the bars of the cage was a blackboard with Arabic writing. But written in Roman letters was also the word 'Naima'. "That your new name. You are now registered as indentured servant 'Naima Ionescu', from Romania. Miss Olivia Hamilton no longer exist. She just disappeared. Anyone look through register for that name, not find it."

"Oh no!" Olivia tried to cry out.

"Only wealthy Arab gentlemen come here. Rich older men. No European men. Arab men pay much for white ladies kept like slaves, like women in harem. Only very best women here. Only respectable ladies - now registered whores, just like you. And all money go to Directress, to me and to black guards. None go to white whores."

Only wealthy Arab gentlemen come here! Olivia's heart had given gave a little jump. The only wealthy Arab gentleman she had ever met was Kurt's business partner, that handsome young Sheik. But he was not an old man.

"Now you listen carefully, white woman," the Negress was saying. "For each each ten thousand dollars you earn for Directress and me, your overseer and trainer, you allowed one item for your little home: a carpet, a mattress, a book, a blanket. So you try harder and harder to catch rich Arab men's eye! And if in any week you earn us less than two thousand dollars you lose two items and have to start again. Understand?"

Appalled at what she was hearing, Olivia nodded dumbly.

"And every week, girl who earns us least money is given to black guards to enjoy. They six big men. You saw two in Directress's office and now another one here. They very cruel. They very angry with girl for not earning more money for them. Girls not like being given to them. They take girl, rape her, one after the other and then beat her, over an over again. Girls soon learn to do anything to please Arab clients rather than be given to black guards."

The Negress stopped to let her words sink in. Olivia was listening, horrified. My God! It just couldn't be true that she was in such a terrible place.

"This week," went the young Negress, with a horrible laugh, "Negro guards have pretty French girl. She think she too grand to bother to attract clients. Now I hear her screaming all night. She'll never make that mistake again! And black guards enjoy even more having hated English woman to play with, and to beat. You scream all night, too. You soon learn not to sit back and do nothing. You soon desperate to earn money for Directress and me - and for black guards."

Again she paused.

"And if client ever not fully pleased with you, then you will have another little meeting with Directress's friend - the one she calls her Persuader. You due to meet him tonight. I think you not want to meet him again! He very good at persuading lazy little white girls never to be lazy again when with client. You soon learn what in store for you, too, unless every one of your clients really pleased with you."

Once again a little gasp was heard from behind Olivia's muzzle. Her worst fears had now been confirmed. She really was in a brothel, a luxury brothel offering white women to rich Arabs - and one in which the girls were kept terrorised. She had been brought up to loathe Arab men. Woos her father had called them.

Olivia looked ruefully at the bare little cage that would be her future home - and then at the well furnished one next door. A buxom blond of her own age smiled back at her. Had they deliberately put her next to this obviously successful tart to make her realise all the more that she, too, could have many creature comforts, provided she overcome her revulsion for elderly Arab men - and worked hard to please them?

"Soon I put you into cage. Girls stay in cages all day until clients come in evening. But first we do certain things to you."

The Negress lead Olivia into what seemed to be a beauty parlour. She motioned Olivia to sit down in front of a strange looking clamp. An Arab, dressed in a white robe, entered the room. Amanda cowered back, horrified at being naked in his presence. He seized her head, put it into the clamp, and turned a wheel. Instantly her head was held quite rigid, with her chin thrust forward.

The Negress handed him the metal tax disc that showed Olivia's registration number as an indentured servant - or whore, as the Negress said. He wrote down the numbers.

He now picked up an instrument with a long lead. Olivia tried to protest behind her muzzle as she felt a pricking feeling as the needle darted in and out of her skin. Carefully the man began to tattoo the Arabic numbers onto her chin.

Then he carefully fitted a flexible stainless steel collar round her neck. It closed with a click. She saw that the collar had Arabic writing engraved on the side and a little crest.

A strong looking ring hung from the front of the collar. The man prised open the ends and then passed them through a hole in the disc. Then, with an electrical instrument, he brazed together the ends of the ring. The disc would now remain permanently attached to the collar until it was filed off to be replaced by a new tax disc in a year's time.

Horrified, Olivia looked in the mirror. The tattooed numbers on her chin would mark her for ever. The collar and disc made her feel like an animal. But worse was to follow.

The Negress pushed her down onto a a gynaecological couch and fastened her down with a strap over her belly. With her wrists still handcuffed behind her back, she was quite helpless. Her ankles were put into raised and widely parted stirrups. She was wide open. Horrified she saw the Arab sit down at the foot of the bed, between her raised and parted legs.

Then the really long work began - the beginning of the removal of all her body hair from her mound and beauty lips, initially by wax and then more permanently by electrolysis and special ointments. Soon she was as smooth and hairless as a little girl, but it would take several such sessions before it was considered permanent.

Then carefully the man tattooed the same Arabic numbers as on her chin, down on her hairless mound.

Her ankles were now raised even higher. She felt the man's fingers on her rear orifice. She wanted to scream out in protest. She felt herself being greased. Raising her head awkwardly, she looked down between her legs and over her now hairless beauty lips. and saw that the man was holding something large and made of plastic - like a sort of plug with a flat base and groove running round it. It had a flat base with a ring on it.

She wanted to scream out again as she felt him slowly drive it up inside her, stretching her enormously, until just the flat base and the ring were visible. Desperately she tried to expel it, but to no avail. Her own sphincter muscles were gripping it by the groove.

Then a chain was passed round her waist and fastened with a little padlock in the small of her back. A rubber cord was attached to the front of the chain. She felt the cord being led down between her beauty lips, threaded through the ring and taken up to the padlock. She heard a click. The horrible big plug was now firmly locked in place.

Finally, the Arab unlocked her handcuffs and replaced them with manacles linked by a heavy two foot chain. The manacles, which fitted tightly round her wrists, were closed by lead pellets. which he squeezed with special instrument. They were now riveted round her wrists.

Olivia again looked in the mirror. Quite apart from the marking son her chin, the tattooed numbers on her now hairless mound stood out prominently, as did her beauty lips, now parted by the rubber cord. All this and her chained wrists combined to give her a highly erotic look.

The Negress took her back to the room with the line of cage-like alcoves. The horrible thing up her rear made her walk awkwardly. It felt huge. She longed to take it out but. of course, the rubber cord held it tightly in place.

The Negress unlocked a small sliding gate in the bars across Olivia's bare cage and slid it to one side.

"Get in!" she ordered, and thrust Olivia inside, before sliding the gate shut and re-fastening it. Then, reaching through the bars, she unfastened Olivia's gag muzzle.

"Please, Mademoiselle, can I have a drink of water," Olivia begged.

Contemptuously, the Negress pointed to a large round projection in the wall of the cage. It was shaped, Olivia was shocked to see, like a very masculine manhood. "For water," she said, "you must learn to suck and lick from that."

The Negress then pointed to a a hollowed channel running across the floor of the cage. "And for liquid wastes, you must learn to use the gutter." The channel run under the bars and Olivia saw, to her embarrassment, that any liquids would be led into a detachable bottle.

"More solid wastes," went on the Negress in a cold matter of fact voice, "you must learn to drop into the first bowl - when your plug is removed, of course."

She pointed to a bowl, painted red and half filled with scented rose water. and then to a similar blue bowl alongside it. "Then you must use your chained hands to wash from the blue bowl without spilling any of the water. The sooner you start practising squatting and washing the better!" She laughed cruelly. "That's one of the reasons we keep you white girls naked in your cages."

Olivia listened to her with a mixture of dismay and disgust. To be made to behave like a caged animal in a circus, and by an arrogant black girl, was almost too much.

Now feeling desperately thirsty after all that she had gone through, Olivia turned to the strange artificial manhood. Bending down she took it into her mouth and began to suck and lick. Slowly she learned to coax a little water out of it. It took nearly ten minute to quench her thirst - ten minutes of exercising what would in future, though she did then realise it, be some of her most important parts of her body: her mouth and her tongue.

Finally, emotionally exhausted by all that had happened, Olivia curled up naked on the hard wooden floor of her cage, her humiliating tax disc hanging from her collar and her heavy wrist manacles lying by her side. Soon she was fast asleep. She was woken by the sudden noise of the little gate, in the bars across her cage, suddenly sliding back. Indeed the similar little gates in all the other gates had also been slid back, by remote control.

She heard the harsh voice of the Negress.

"All you little Christian dogs - out! At once!"

Olivia saw a score of naked young women quickly crawl out of their cages and line up in front of their young lady overseer.

Suddenly the Negress cracked her whip. "You! Naima! Out!"

Scared, Olivia quickly crawled out her cage, too, and joined the line of other white women. The Negress came down the line, shouting at each woman in turn: "You Goldfish Bowl! ... You Display Room!"

Olivia had no idea what the Negress was talking about. Then when she reached Olivia, the Negress threw a simple caftan at her. "You! Naima! Put on caftan."

The caftan had special buttons on the shoulders so that a girl with chained hands could still put it on. Grateful to have something to cover her nakedness, Olivia pulled it on over her head.

"Now, Naima. You go with black guard back to Directress's office. But this time you knock on door and wait until told to go in. Now move!"

Olivia heard the whip crack just behind her.

"Run!" shouted the Negress.

4 - 4 THE BASTINADO.

A few minutes later, a very scared Olivia knocked on the same door through which, earlier, she had been politely ushered with Kurt.

So much seemed to have happened since then. Then she had been smartly dressed in her best dress, shoes and stockings. Now she was standing barefoot and naked under a simple caftan. And the awful thing up her bottom was stretching her terribly.

She heard the Directress's voice telling her to wait.

Frightened, she did so. Who on earth was this 'Persuader', whom she was to meet?

Suddenly the door opened. The same two black guards stood in the doorway. They grabbed her and dragged her up in front of the seated Directress.

"Yes! the tattooed number on the chin looks very nice. Very erotic. Now let's see the belly."

The black guards unbuttoned the shoulder straps of the caftan. It fell to her hips. One of the guards pulled her chained wrists back over her head and clamped a large hand over her mouth. The other pushed her now exposed belly forwards towards the Arab woman.

Olivia could feel herself blushing with shame.

"Yes! Very good! But me have a better look at the hair removal."

The second black man pulled the caftan down to her knees, and kicked her legs apart. The first Negro pushed her down to make her bend her knees. Never had Olivia felt so degraded.

"Hum! You've got very pretty little pink lips, and the mound is lovely and smooth. Just how rich Arab gentlemen will like to see a stuck-up Englishwoman. Soon we'll have you like that permanently... Now we've got to get you ready for your first client in a few day's time. You're going to love that! And I'm glad to see that Mafta has already started to stretch you behind. You'll find that many clients will be particularly interested in you there, and I know you'll want to offer it to them."

"Oh, no!" Olivia tried to scream behind the Negro's big hand, shaking her head furiously.

The Directress laughed. "Oh, you'll soon find yourself desperate to offer it to your clients, once you've met my friend, the Persuader."

The black men thrust her towards what seemed to be an old fashioned stocks, like a pillory, in the centre of the room. She wondered what on earth it could be for. They pushed her down onto her back and fastened the chain of her wrist manacles, above her head, to a ring in the floor. Then they lifted up her ankles and put them into two semi-circular holes in the stocks. They lowered the matching top of the stocks. Olivia's feet were now held close together.

Olivia saw the Directress go to a cupboard behind her desk. She opened it. A solitary silver tipped cane with a curved handle was hanging there: the Directress's friend - the Persuader.

"No!" screamed Olivia. "No!"

"Oh yes!" replied the Arab woman, swishing the cane through the air. "This is what makes my girls so keen to please my clients - no matter how old, fat or ugly they may be."

"No! Please no!" screamed Olivia again.

"Yes, my child, it is fear of this that will turn a nice respectable Englishwoman like you into a really eager whore, desperate to earn large sums of money for me. For that's what you're going to be doing here!"

"Oh, no!" sobbed Olivia.

"Yes, you're going to earn me a little fortune - and you'd damn well better after what I paid Kurt for you. Do you know what I'm going to charge for your services - for the use of your body? For making an arrogant young Englishwoman demean herself by offering her mouth, her hands, her beauty lips and her rear orifice to some rich old Arab? Five hundred dollars! That's what I'm going to charge for you! It's a lot of money and the clients are going to expect a lot from you for that. And, you just remember, if anyone of them should ever feel that he hasn't had his full money's worth, then you'll be sent down here again for another meeting with my friend here."

Again she swished the cane through the air. Olivia was trembling with fear and sheer horror.

"And that means that you've got to have attracted twenty clients before you can even get a thin little blanket for your cage - and another twenty before you'll have a strip of carpet or a pillow, or a mattress."

The Directress paused to let her words sink in.

"Think of that - catching the eye of twenty clients so that they chose you, and then making sure that they don't complain about your efforts to please them, before you even earn a little blanket to keep warm in at night! Twenty clients! And an-

171

other twenty before you get another blanket. How are you going to attract them to choose you and not the other pretty girls?"

Olivia gave a little moan of despair.

"And don't forget - that it means if you ever have less than four clients in a week, then you will lose both blankets and have to start earning them all over again. And if you've no blankets or other possessions to be forfeited, then it's just back for another visit to my friend. the Persuader. So to be safe you need to be chosen once every night, and preferably twice."

Again the Arab woman paused.

"But just remember that this is a very high class brothel - clients come by appointment only. Only very rich old men can afford to come here and only a few make an appointment each evening - and when they do they expect to be offered a large choice of girls, all very beautiful, all looking eager to please. So, each night, several girls will not be chosen. You'll soon be desperate to make sure that you're not amongst them - and that when you are chosen that the man is really pleased. Do you understand girl? Do you?"

She swished the cane through the air again, before bringing it down hard onto her desk with a crash that made Olivia cry out in terror.

"Yes, Madam! Yes!"

"Well, it's not just an ordinary caning on your bottom that you get from the Persuader. I don't like my girls to be marked. No, what you'll be getting is the Bastinado, and that's what you're going to get now. And, you're going to remember this for the rest of your life, my girl. A girl never forgets the first time she gets the Bastinado!"

She paused for effect, pleased to see that the girl's eyes were out on stalks. Oh yes, she thought, this girl will soon be begging the Sheik to put her into his harem!

"Ten strokes of the Bastinado!" she went on. "On the soles of your feet. Like this!"

A second later and the room was filled by a terrible scream. Never in all her life had Olivia felt anything like it. She writhed desperately but the stocks held the soles of her feet, nicely

172

exposed to the cane.

"Nine to go, my child! Just think about it! Nine more!"

"Oh my God! No! No, please! I'll do anything you want. But no more, please!"

"Oh no, you're going to have you full ten strokes - and some are going to come from those Negroes! Just look at their muscular shoulders! Just imagine the pain they'll be giving you. Much more than me!"

She brought the case down again against the soles of Olivia's feet. Then when the screams had subsided, she went on: "Like the other girls here, you'll never forget my friend, the Persuader. Like them, you'll constantly dream about him - and wake up in the middle of the night, screaming."

Again the cane fell. The screams seemed louder than ever.

"And you'll do anything, won't you my girl, absolutely anything to avoid meeting him again. Won't you? ... Well?"

"Yes! Yes!" screamed Olivia.

"He gets so lonely in that cupboard. But I don't think it'll belong before you're back here to meet him again."

Seconds later the room was again filled with Olivia's screams. Just then the door opened and the Negress came in.

"She does seem to be making a fuss!" she laughed, speaking in Arabic. "Perhaps we should offer this as a special little extra for our clients! ... Can I have a go now?"

"Yes, give her a a couple of strokes, and then we'll let the guards each have a couple too."

"Now you just listen to me, Naima," said the Negress, switching to her broken French. "You answer me back, just once, or you give me any dumb insolence, and you will be sent straight back here, getting Bastinado again. Like this!"

If anything the pain inflicted by the young Negress was even greater than from the Directress herself. When Olivia had quietened down again, the Negress went on: "And if I ever see one little spot from your wastes on the floor of you cage, then this is what you get."

A minute later she was hammering home her lesson on

173

hygiene.

"So, Naima, where you drop liquid wastes?"

"Into the special gutter, Mademoiselle," Olivia screamed.

"And solid wastes?"

"Into the bowl with the rose water, Mademoiselle!"

"And how you do that without spilling?" The harsh and degrading interrogation seemed endless, but it was having a powerful mental effect on Olivia. The Negress knew that this the best way to break the spirit of a well educated and fastidious white woman.

"I'll squat very carefully over it without touching it, Mademoiselle," cried Olivia embarrassed beyond belief.

"And how you clean yourself?"

"Using my fingers and the water in the other rose bowl, Mademoiselle."

"Yes, and you not spill any or you meet Persuader again."

"Yes, Mademoiselle, I'll try very hard, I promise," sobbed Olivia, completely broken now.

Satisfied, the Negress threw the cane to the nearest of the black guards, who was English speaking. He caught the cane deftly and stood over Olivia menacingly.

"You gonna fear us guards, child," he said. You give us one word of lip and you get this!

The pain inflicted by the Directress, or even by the Negress, had been nothing as compared to that delivered by the black guards, who took several minutes to deliver their four strokes.

"Now get out! Back to your cage!" shouted the Directress as the black guards released Olivia's wrist and ankles. She turned to the Negress. "Make sure her training starts tomorrow!"

4 - 5 TRAINED AS A WHORE

Olivia lay curled up on the hard floor of the cage-like alcove, weeping disconsolately. The pain in her feet was still awful.

The Directress was right, she would never, ever, forget her first encounter with the Bastinado. Yes, she would indeed do anything, absolutely anything, rather than have another such beating. No client must ever complain about her lack of enthusiasm to please him. She would use her experience as an actress to act the part of the best little whore in the whole brothel!

She could hear another woman weeping for her mother, and another calling for her boy friend. Boy friend! Well, she certainly wouldn't be weeping for Kurt!

Oh, how hard and cold the floor was! Clearly she must try hard to earn herself a mattress - and some blankets, and then some sheets, and pillows, and pillow cases, and a carpet, and a make-up table, and a light, and some books, and... the list of essentials seemed endless. And yet, each would have to be earned by being chosen by twenty horrible. ugly, repulsive, old Arabs. Twenty! And then, as the dreadful plug up her backside kept reminding her, pleasing them by offering herself in the most ignoble and degrading way imaginable.

Was there really no way out, no escape? Angrily she shook the bars across the front of her cage. Angrily, she shook the chain linking her manacled wrists. Angrily, she tore ineffectually at the disc hanging from her collar, the disc that proclaimed her a registered whore, a registered indentured servant.

Angrily she looked down at the registered number tattooed on her mound, and then, in the mirror, at the same number tattooed, unbelievably, on her chin.

She could perhaps, she thought, live with the tattooed numbers on her tummy, if she ever escaped, but not those on her chin. They might be rather erotic in private, but certainly not in public! They were just too awful!

Indeed, how could she ever escape? Even if she did somehow manage to get out of this well guarded building, she would be instantly recognised as a registered whore and returned to the tender mercies of the Directress and her quite terrifying Bastinado. Indeed, the Bastinado would be awaiting her!

But anyway, she had no money, no passport, no airline

ticket, no pen, no ... She had no alternative, she realised, but to settle down and become a really good whore, a really good investment for the Directress. 'Swim!' ordered the big Negro.

He was dressed in bright red pantaloons, with a blue sash round his waist and a big matching turban. His muscular torso was naked except for a small waistcoat. The sumptuousness of his dress was intended to highlight their own nakedness to the women in his charge, just as the jet blackness of his skin was intended to highlight to clients the whiteness of the skins of the women being displayed for them to choose.

Obediently, the four girls began to swim round the round glass bowl that stood in the middle of the covered patio. Tintacks on he bottom of the bowl kept them swimming. It was awkward for them with their manacled hands, but Olivia had soon learnt to swim in a rather humiliating dog-paddle.

Her body, she realised, like those of the other girls, would be well displayed to a client seated on a sofa at the bottom of the glass walls of the small pool - rather like a gold fish in a small bowl. Indeed. the patio was actually called the Goldfish Bowl.

The black man lowered a metal grille over the bowl. It forced the women down into the bowl, coming up periodically to take a quick breath, with their heads held back, in the bare two inches between the top of the water and the grille. Nor did they dare to let their feet touch the bottom of the bowl, as like goldfish they swam around the bowl. They were stark naked, except for their collars and manacles, and made an erotic sight as their body lips opened and closed in the water with their every movement.

The big Negro gave a grunt of satisfaction and drew across two curtains that now hid the bowl. Then, playing the party of an interested client, he sat down in the comfortable chair placed at the foot of the bowl. He pressed a button and the curtains parted. He pressed another button and the bowl was lit up from below, disclosing the naked girls swimming round and round it.

He checked the clarity of the large Arabic number now painted on each girl's forehead and on her backside to allow a

176

client quickly to identify a girl that had caught his eye. He checked the strong net that he would use, after raising the grille, to fish out the chosen girl and then throw her, dripping wet, to the feet of the client, for a closer inspection.

He checked that the glistening beauty lips of each girl had been painted a different colour, and one that matched the colour painted on her hanging nipples and on the lips of her face.

He checked that the grille was low enough to keep the girls' heads below the surface and yet allowed them to suck in air periodically, opening and closing their mouths, as he had taught them to do, like real goldfish - but now in time with opening and closing their beauty lips.

One girl was clearly pregnant, which made her a particular favourite with discerning clients, and the object of much jealousy from the other girls. The Directress made a point of always having at least one girl in an interesting condition. Such a girl might have been avoided by men back in her own country in Europe, but here, Middle Eastern men had no so such qualms. On the contrary they regarded it as the natural condition for a girl, and a prettily curved belly was much admired.

He rang a bell. It would be heard by the girls, even by those whose heads were under the surface of the bowl. Immediately the girls took it in turn, as he had taught the to do, to stand up in the deep bowl with their legs apart, whilst the others dived down between them, their long hair flowing back prettily in the water. He was pleased to see that the new girl, Naima, had quickly picked up the display routine.

Satisfied, he rang the bell again. Obediently the girls came up to surface for a gulp of air and then dived down in pairs to play with each others' bodies. It was an erotic scene that rarely failed to make a client decide on paying for a pair of the performing girls.

He saw that Naima was now playing her role properly, letting her partner play with her hardening nipples whilst she tickled her friend's beauty bud. At first she had been horrified to learn what she was expected to do, but the mere mention of the Persuader and she was as eager to do it as the other girls.

It would never do, of course, for a girl to reach a climax, but their increasing need to surface to take a couple of quick breaths made sure that no such breach of discipline was possible.

Idly the Negro imagined he was a client and wondered which of the naked little white bodies he would choose. He knew the answer straight away - the new English girl!

It was a pity, he thought, that she was still regarded as being under training and not yet ready to be displayed to the clients this evening. A client choosing her would be so eager to have her that he would certainly give him a handsome tip as he fished her out of the bowl and laid her at the client's feet, helplessly enmeshed in the net.

He glanced at his gold watch. The first clients were due to arrive soon, and it was time to fish the English girl out of the bowl and return her to her cage. She had learnt to perform well. The whip was a great teacher, and so was fear of the Directress's Bastinado! The red light blinked.

It was the signal that in real life would warn the girls that a client was looking at them through the one way mirror. This time, however, it was just a practice run for Olivia's benefit.

"Dance!" ordered the black guard, switching on the tape that filled the room with sensuous Arab music. Pointing at Olivia, he cracked his whip menacingly.

Nervously, Olivia tried to follow the intricate swaying movement of the other two girls. She was, she realised, showing off her body in a provocative and blatant way. She could not help blushing. But worse was to follow.

The red light flashed again. It was the signal that the client had told the black guard that he wanted to see the girls dancing topless. The two other girls began to slip off their blouses whilst still dancing in time to the music.

The Negro angrily pointed at Olivia, and raised his whip. It really was time, he told himself, that this new English girl got over her reluctance to display herself properly. He brought his whip down gently across her back - he had orders not to mark her unnecessarily.

With a little cry, Olivia unbuttoned her blouse and held

178

it back. Her breasts hung loose, and, now freed from the tight constraint of the blouse, a little bell hung down prettily from each nipple. Olivia knew that she would have to make the bells tinkle in time to the music. It was very difficult and she would have to concentrate like mad. But she was too terrified of the whip not to do so.

A few minutes later the red flashed again. Again Olivia blushed. It was, she knew, the signal that the client now wanted to see their naked wriggling beauty lips. It was so degrading - but it would be much more so in real life with some awful leering Arab client looking at her through the one way mirror.

Her thoughts were rudely interrupted by the whip. Hastily she followed the other two girls in gracefully lifting up the specially designed separate front panel of her long swinging skirt - under which she was stark naked.

Her glistening and hairless beauty lips were now on display, but Olivia could not help shyly turning away from the mirror.

"You do that again," warned the Negro angrily, "and I recommend to Directress that you punished for lack of keenness. You then replace French girl, given to us guards for our enjoyment."

"Oh, no!" Olivia cried. Almost anything rather than that! She turned back to the mirror, and held the panel up high so that anyone looking at her would have a good view of her charming and waiting intimacies. "Client coming!" shouted one of the black guards who incessantly, by day and by night, patrolled up and down the line of well lit up, raised, cages. Their duty was not only to prevent any of the girls from playing with themselves, but also to enforce silence - for the girls were not allowed to speak, or even whisper to each other. Olivia had no idea who the other beautiful white creatures in the brothel were - or how they had ended up there.

There was, Olivia soon learnt, no privacy at all, not even when she wanted to perform her natural functions. Indeed, the guards enjoyed seeing women all performing together in their cages, to their order, to the crack of the whip - something which

Olivia, shamefacedly, had had to learn to do, too.

Now, the girls were practising, for Olivia's benefit, a special client being invited by the Directress to see the erotic sight of the girls still in their cages.

She had been put into a special black leather hood, that came over her head and down to her mouth. Over her eyes two little flaps had been fastened down blindfolding her completely. Her long hair had been pushed through a little hole in the top of the hood and hung prettily down her neck.

Unable to see anything, she jumped up and, as she had seen the other girls do on her first day in the brothel, felt for the bars of her cage on either side of her head with her manacled hands. Then she pushed her hands slightly apart so that she could feel that the chain linking them was now taut under her chin. Then she blushingly thrust her breasts through the bars.

Biting her lips, Olivia somehow managed to keep her head and hands still as, playing the part of an inspecting client, the Negro reached up to feel her breasts. Oh the shame! But, as she knew she must, she pushed here breasts forwards into the palm of his hand as if trying to attract to the attention of the client and to show her eagerness to please so that he would choose her and not her rivals for his affection.

But even worse was to follow.

"Show respect!" she heard the young Negress order, and, again like the other girls, Olivia parted her legs. Then, blushing with shame, she lifted up the blue modesty flap covering her intimacies. Her hairless mound and beauty lips were now displayed, as she pressed her belly against the bars.

But even that was not all, for the Negress reached forward and parted her beauty lips - as if showing them off to a client. She felt her finger tip on her beauty bud and, as she knew she had to do, she shamefacedly wriggled her beauty lips to and fro erotically. How awful it would be when she did this for real - for her first client. It would, she knew, be soon now.

The Negress snapped her fingers and Olivia turned round to show off her long back, her slender waist and her swelling buttocks.

The Negress curtly snapped her fingers again and, obediently, Olivia bent over and then pulled the cheeks of her buttocks with her manacled hands, to show off how her rear orifice was being kept stretched - stretched for use by a client. She had noticed how the other girls just kept a feather there, a feather that was attached to a little cork, a feather that prettily curled up behind their bottoms. Would she, too, have to grip a feathered cork - when she was considered to have been be sufficiently stretched? How awful!

Hitherto, when a client came to see the girls in their cages, a curtain had been drawn across the front of her cage, like those of the girls not in a proper condition to be on display. Kneeling in the darkness of her cage, she had heard the heavy footsteps of the Arab client and his guttural male voice speaking Arabic, as, accompanied by the black guard, he slowly went down the line. She had heard the little moans of the girls being inspected and their little giggles as they had eagerly competed against each other to be chosen.

Soon, terrifyingly soon, the curtain would no longer be drawn and she would be on display, too. Oh, my God! "Kneel!" ordered the young Negress, cracking her whip and giving the lead she was holding a jerk. It was attached to a ring on Olivia's collar

Olivia fell to her knees in front of the seated, life-size, blown-up rubber doll. It was realistically male - very realistically and Olivia bent her head and started to lick the large rubber manhood up and down whilst cupping in her hands the doll's heavy male testicles.

"Suck!" came the order, accompanied by another crack of the whip. Dutifully she took the rubber manhood into her mouth.

None of the white women in the brothel, spoke Arabic, and few of the clients would speak the various languages of the women: French, Italian, Spanish, Ukrainian, German, Romanian, Polish ... and now English!

So the girls were all taught to obey a list of Arabic words of command whose full meaning was printed on a red card handed to each client when he chose his woman - or women. It was these words that Olivia was now being taught to recognise - and obey.

"On your back" came the order and the kneeling Olivia now lay right back, and eagerly thrust out her tongue invitingly. The young Negress lifted up the blown up down doll and seated it on Olivia's face.

"Lick up!" came the order and the Negress put her hand down to check that Olivia was indeed licking the doll's rear orifice and that her tongue was also stroking the highly sensitive area between it and the large testicles.

This, the Negress knew, was a favourite order amongst the clients for Arab gentlemen much enjoyed, not only the sheer physical enjoyment, but also the feeling of power that came from a white woman having to please them in this way.

"Inside!" Hesitantly Olivia thrust the tip of her pointed tongue up and with her manacled hands parted the dolls buttocks to allow her to begin to penetrate the realistic orifice

"Buttocks!" hastily Olivia knelt with her head to the floor and her bottom raised, offering her own rear orifice.

The Negress looked at Olivia carefully. Thanks to her fear of her whip, and of the Directress's Bastinado, this once proud and stuck-up young Englishwoman was training well - as a whore. Normally a new white whore would also be trained to perform with another girl. But in view of Olivia's intended fate, it might be best, she decided, to leave this out. The list of Arabic commands the girl had been made to learn and practice, together with the rest of her training, would already be sufficiently humiliating to make this white whore jump at the chance of being rescued - even if meant entering her rescuer's harem.

"Play!" was the next order. Blushing, Olivia jumped up and stood at attention in front of the Negress, and with her manacled hands parted her beauty lips and began to play with herself. The sight of a white woman, held on a lead and having to play with herself in front of him, was also something, the Negress knew, that a client would find highly arousing.

"Do it properly Naima," warned the young Negress, raising her whip. Blushing Olivia began in earnest to tickle her

182

beauty bud. Never had she ever imagined that she would be forced to do something so private and intimate in front of a young Negress - or a rich Arab. Soon she could feel herself becoming moist with arousal.

"Stop!" It would never do to let one of the whore's actually give herself relief.

4 - 6 RESCUED!

Olivia was standing at attention in front of the Directress's desk. Behind her stood the young Negress, holding a lead fastened to her collar.

Nervously she could not help glancing at the cupboard in which was kept the Persuader. Had she been sent for because the young Negress was not pleased with her progress in training to be a whore? She had tried so hard!

"Well, my child," said the big Arab woman with a smile, "I've had good reports about you. In fact my assistant feels that you're now ready for your first client."

Her first client! Oh God!

"And," went on the Directress, "just as a girl never forgets her first lover, so too, here, a girl never forgets her first client. Terrified of getting the Bastinado for not sufficiently pleasing him, and desperate to earn a little blanket or a mattress for her cage, she puts her all into giving him pleasure. I'm sure you will too, won't you?"

"Oh yes, Madame," replied Olivia, trying to appear eager.

"Well, if you really please him, he might take you away from here."

"What?" exclaimed Olivia. To be taken away from this terrible brothel! She would do anything, put up with anything, to get away. Nothing could be so awful. Nothing could have a prospect so bleak.

"Yes, this client is a very rich and cruel old man. The other day he sent his chief black eunuch to have a look at my women from behind the one way mirror. You caught his eye and he told me that, provided you have not been used by any other clients, then his Master could be interested in buying your contract of indenture, so as to acquire you for his harem."

"Acquiring me for his harem!" cried Olivia.

"Yes. Think what a lovely life of ease and luxury you'd have there!"

"Oh Madame!" gasped Olivia excitedly. A month ago the idea of going to into the harem of an elderly and cruel Arab would have appalled her. But not now - not as a way of escaping from this terrible place. Any way, she realised, she could hardly expect to be released into the normal world - and certainly not with those numbers tattooed on her chin!

"Of course, I don't normally sell my girls' indentures, and you're an important investment for me - so I shall want very considerably more than what I paid Kurt for you. Whether this client would be willing to pay such a sum for you, will depend on how you please him when he tries you out."

"Oh!"

"So, it's up to you. You please him and assure him that you'll be an adoring and obedient concubine and perhaps he'll take you away. If not," and the Directress's voice became harsh, "it'll be the bastinado for you!"

She nodded to her assistant. "Take her away and get her ready. And don't forget to wash her out behind, too. I have a feeling that he might well try her there." Sheik Ali looked at the brightly lit glass bowl and watched as the naked Olivia performed beautifully, diving down between the other girls' legs and then briefly coming up for air, before starting to play with them. He could feel his manhood stirring as he admired her delightful little figure and very pretty face. What a splendid addition she would make to his harem!

He knew that she would only vaguely be able to see, through the glass, the figure of a man, in a long white Arab robe and Arab headdress. The bright lights lighting up the bowl would make it made it impossible for her to recognise him. He laughed quietly as he thought how she must be wondering whether he was old and fat. Even if he had been, she would, he knew, be eternally grateful to him if he bought her indentures and rescued her from what she must feel to be a truly horrific fate.

Later, looking through the one way mirror, he watched this delightful creature eagerly bare her balled breasts when the red light flashed and then displayed her hairless beauty lips when it flashed again.

What she, a a typical independent minded young Englishwoman, must have been through to demean herself in this way, he thought. But that would make her all the more desperate to be rescued! Only half listening to the Directress, Sheik Ali looked approvingly at the only cage that was not curtained off. The half hooded girl was standing up and dutifully gripping the bars of her cage, her her firm naked breasts thrust out towards him.

Also thrust out through the bars was her chin. Used as he was to seeing pretty little dots tattooed onto the chins of Arab girls, he found that the sight, on a white woman, of the neatly tattooed little Arabic numbers, that showed she was a registered indentured servant, both attractive and highly arousing. They would, of course, also play a significant role in making her beg to be taken into his harem, for how could she now show herself back in London?

"And you're sure that she doesn't know who I am and can't see me," asked the Sheik in Arabic.

"Oh yes!" laughed the Directress. "Until you peel back the fastenings over the eyeholes in her hood, she wont see a thing - and all I have told her is that a rich and cruel old Arab is interested in trying her out for his harem - if she pleases him. After the terrifying time we have given her here, she is certainly desperate to be rescued!"

Sheik Ali nodded in satisfaction. So far, so good! His plan was working out well. He'd soon have this beautiful and grateful young English woman eating out of his hand.

"Show Respect!" ordered the young Negress, who was proudly standing by the cage, a little whip in her hands.

Her cheeks blushing below the hood, Olivia reached

down with both hands and lifted up the prettily decorated modesty flap that hung down from her waist, disclosing her hairless mound. Her knees however were still pressed together, in a gesture of embarrassed shame. The Negress cracked her whip. With a little sob, the girl now parted her knees, displaying her smooth and painted beauty lips, and thrusting them forward for inspection.

Still talking to the Directress, Sheik Ali felt one breast and then the other. How delightful they would be when in milk, he thought. He looked at the flat belly pressed again the bars. It seemed to be crying out to be given a nice curve!

Perhaps this one should be next - after Mauve had delivered her progeny and come into milk. Or, perhaps, it would be more amusing to have her conceive at the same time as Royal Blue. He had got used to having two little swelling bellies in the harem at a time.

The young Negress now reached forward and parted the girl's beauty lips and invited him to feel up inside her. She was nice and tight. He touched her beauty bud and smiled as she jumped. Nothing wrong here! He continued to tickle her. She gave a little moan and began to wriggle to and fro. He felt her become wet. The little minx! Well, his black eunuchs would just have to watch her carefully!

He withdrew his hand, and the young Negress snapped her fingers. Olivia stood up straight and turned round. What a delightful sight she made with her long back, her narrow waist and her flowing hips. Rather like a a violin in shape, he thought. He could feel his manhood stirring.

The Negress snapped her fingers again and obediently Olivia bent over and, reaching back with her manacled hands, displayed her now well stretched back entrance. The Negress handed the Sheik a thin rubber glove and, applying a little grease to Olivia's rear, made a little inviting gesture with her hand.

Who would have thought that the proud young Englishwoman he had seen in London only a few weeks before, would soon be willing displaying her specially stretched rear orifice to an unknown Arab! But she had certainly been well prepared there to give pleasure. Perhaps he might well later try her out here.

"I must congratulate you," he said to the Directress, as he handed the glove back to the bowing young Negress, "on having so quickly made her so anxious to obey!"

"These white women are terrified of the cane," replied the Directress, "as doubtless your own black eunuchs will have learned, too."

"Indeed," laughed the Sheik.

"I'll have her put under the bed clothes of your bedroom," said the Directress, looking pleased and rubbing her hands. "Meanwhile, perhaps I may offer you a glass of champagne in my office!" Sheik Ali lay back in the large bed and idly glanced at the printed lists of commands that the still hooded girl had been taught to obey.

"Lick!" came the order in guttural Arabic.

The voice, thought Olivia with a little shiver, half of delight and half of fear, was firm and authoritative, like that of a man who would stand no nonsense from a young woman.

Still hooded under the bedclothes, she applied her tongue to a large and erect manhood, licking it delicately up and down. She still had not seen his face, the face of her first client, the man who was interested in buying her for his harem.

"Suck!"

Overcoming her natural revulsion, Olivia eagerly took the manhood into her mouth and with the tips of her fingers began to play with the heavy testicles of the man who she hoped would be her rescuer, her saviour! Please God, she thought, make him so pleased with my efforts that he decides to take me away with him. It might be to an unknown fate, but anything would be better than her dreadful known fate here.

"Kneel down!"

Surprised she knelt and lowered her forehead to the sheets, her manacled hands on either side, her buttocks raised. She felt him kneel behind her. Suddenly she felt something touch her well greased orifice. Oh no! She remembered her determination to please this man, come what may. Biting her lips she thrust

187

her buttocks back.

Suddenly he was inside her. She was being sodomised - for the first time in her life! Oh the pain! Oh the humiliation! But equally, oh the need to please him!

She felt his hands on her hips moving her slowly to and fro, whilst his virile manhood slid in, then nearly out again, and then further in. She felt she was being split in two. She wanted to scream out and to leap forward, but she did not dare do so - not if she wanted him to rescue her!

Slowly her body grew accustomed to being stretched. She began to find it exciting. Remembering her training she started to match his thrusts with a gripping of her muscles. She felt like a bitch being mounted by a dog.

Then she gave a little moan of disappointment as he withdrew.

"On your back!"

Hastily she turned and lay out her legs straight out and together. She felt him run her hands down her body. Oh the excitement!

"Offer yourself!"

She parted her legs and raised her belly towards him, her ravisher, her rescuer, her unknown saviour.

She felt him put a large bolster under her buttocks. She bent her knees.

Suddenly he felt him on top of her. She felt him enter her. She could not help crying out with pleasure. Going into the harem of such a wonderful and virile lover might not be too bad at all!

Suddenly she felt his hands on her hood. There was a ripping noise as he tore off the velcro fastenings over her little eye holes. She blinked in he sudden light.

There looking down at her was a man's face, a bearded man, a very masterful and masculine man. Then she saw that he was a young man, a very good looking young man! Suddenly she recognised him. It was Sheik Ali! The man she had last seen in London!

"You!" she cried with a mixture of astonishment and

delight. "You!"

By way of answer, he thrust into her again, provoking another cry of pleasure. It was time he exerted his authority.

"Yes, Olivia, it's me, your future Master," came the reply in English He gave another thrust. "Say it - your Master!"

"Oh, yes!" cried Olivia ecstatically. "My Master! My Master!"

She was rewarded by another thrilling thrust.

"Oh please ... Master ...do take me away from here. It's terrible. Please save me. I'll do anything for you, but please take me away."

"You mean you want me to buy your indentures?" said the young Sheik harshly. "You mean you are willing to become my indentured servant?"

"Yes, Master, yes. Take me and hide me away. I know that with those awful numbers tattooed on my chin I can never again be seen in public."

"So you are willing to enter to enter my harem? To become one of my white concubines?"

"Yes Master," replied Olivia fervently.

The thrill of having this beautiful young Englishwoman actually begging to enter to become his slave girl, aroused the Sheik to fever pitch.

"Keep still!" he cried. "Don't you dare climax without my permission!"

He drove in and out of the now still girl and then, with a raucous cry of intense pleasure, he erupted into her.

"I'll send my chief black eunuch to collect you," he said. The big car stopped alongside the private jet. A small black boy, Baza, got out, leading the black shouted figure of a woman. A close observer would have seen that there was a discreet little chain attached to his wrist, the other end of which disappeared into the black shroud. The boy gripped the woman's arm through the black shroud and guided her towards the aircraft as if she could not see.

The large figure of Zalu followed behind. He was smiling smugly. Another English woman in his care!

They entered the aircraft. The door was shut and the engines started. The aircraft took off.

Where am I being taken, Olivia wondered. She could see nothing through the frosted glass windows.

She would have been astonished had she known that the aircraft was simply circling the Mediterranean. Two hours later it landed again at the same airport. Olivia, still hooded and gagged would never know that the long flight had ended where it had started.

Silently, she was led out into a car by Baza and Zalu.

"We now take you to palace," announced Zalu proudly. "You start new life as one of young Master's English concubines. Your name now Beige."

5 - 1   MRS MONA MILTON AND MISS DIANA MILTON
('Pink One' and 'Pink Two')

"Has Your Excellency thought of the delights of acquiring a beautiful and respectable English mother with a pretty young daughter?" murmured Zalu.

"Well!" laughed the Sheik. Pretty, and preferably rather shy, white mothers and daughters were traditionally highly prized in harems.

"Think of the shame of the mother at having to offer her precious daughter's virginity up to your manhood, and of being taken herself in front of her daughter. Think of the embarrassment of the daughter at having to give you pleasure in front of her mother. Think of them both being trained to work together to pleasure you, their Master, in your bed, or even to put on little humiliating shows for your titillation."

Sheik Ali's eyes glistened.

"Think also, Your Excellency, of later, without their knowledge, having them both put on a course of fertility pills and then watching them being covered by the same black guard. Think of them being brought to you to parade their prettily swollen bellies to you side by side, one a mature woman, the other hardly more than a schoolgirl. Think of them both having to offer you their milk-swollen breasts and carefully stretched nipples."

"Do I take it you have a suitable mother and daughter in mind?" asked the Sheik with a smile of eager anticipation.

Silently, Zalu handed him an encrypted E-mail that he had just received from Kurt, the same Kurt who had produced Olivia, now one of the Sheik's favourite concubines.

HAVE LOCATED MARE AND FILLY. ENGLISH THOROUGHBREDS. FILLY IS MARE'S ONLY PROGENY. FILLY NOT YET COVERED. BOTH HAVE IDENTICAL FEATURES, CHESTNUT MANES AND EXCELLENT CONFORMATION,

IDEAL TEMPERAMENT FOR PRIVATE STUD. PHOTO-
GRAPHS ATTACHED IN POST. USUAL TERMS FOR PAY-
MENT AND SPECIAL DELIVERY. AVAILABLE FOR IMME-
DIATE REPEAT IMMEDIATE INSPECTION.

Zalu now handed him the photographs. They were of
two beautiful women, both topless, both blond.

Sheik Ali laughed cruelly and nodded in approval. He
rubbed his hands together. He had thought of a way to handle the
matter already, once he had inspected the goods...

Mrs Mona Milton, still recovering from the sudden
death of her husband, was 36, tall, slim and vivacious with spar-
kling blue eyes and long honey coloured hair.

Left financially insecure, her main objects in life, now,
were to find rich husbands for herself and her sixteen year old
school girl daughter, Diana. She had had to warn the girl's expensive private school that she would have to take her away.

Diana was a younger version of her mother, equally
attractive, tall and slim. Mona was determined, to protect her,
meanwhile, from unsuitable boy friends.

She taken her daughter on a month's skiing holiday in
the Alps. Although both women were naturally flirtatious, towards themselves they were rather shy. Mona had always found
it embarrassing to discuss sex with her daughter and Diana had
always been far too shy to discuss it with her mother. Sex had
become a taboo subject between them - little did they think that
this would enhance their value in the eyes of a certain potential
Arab Master.

On their holiday they met a charming and good looking young Austrian, Kurt, who immediately struck up a friend-
ship with them both. He flirted outrageously with Mona, he
danced excitingly with Diana, he kissed Mona passionately and
tested her responses by stroking her breasts, whilst with Diana
he satisfied himself of her innocence by simply holding her hands
and stroking the back of her neck. However he was careful not to
'spoil the merchandise' by going any further.

He questioned Diana laughingly about her boyfriends

and checked with her mother. He was satisfied that she was still a virgin. He persuaded them to go to the heated swimming pool and there photographed them, with a Polaroid camera, wearing tiny bikinis that scarcely hid their charms. He even took them in a private alcove and there dared them to let him photograph them topless, first kneeling up side by side and then, very strikingly, standing back to back, their hands clasped on the tops of their heads. The contrast between Mona's mature breasts and the charmingly girlish ones of Diana was clearly shown.

Kurt also discreetly checked that their disappearance would not cause any undue ruffles. There were no near relatives and Mona had sold the family house. Moreover the nuns at Diana's school were not expecting her back. They were surprised one evening soon after they had met when Kurt introduced them to a handsome, sophisticated, bearded, and evidently very rich, young man who appeared to come from the Middle East. They never got his name properly.

Mona remembered how one of her friends had married a rich Egyptian. Perhaps Diana might marry this one! He was so handsome! What a pity he was a little young for herself. Sadly, however, he had to leave the very next day, murmuring to Kurt something about a mysterious business deal being very satisfactory and to go ahead as suggested.

It was the very next day that Kurt suggested that they should cut short their skiing holiday and come and spend the weekend in his villa in the south of Spain. They need not tell anyone about the trip as the would still be returning to London on time.

It would, he explained, be a wonderful opportunity for them to see a fascinating part of the world, and he could arrange free air tickets through his business, if they would just sign a piece of paper saying that they were in his employ. It was written in Spanish and Arabic, but who cares, thought Mona as she signed and passed the pen to Diana.

Arriving at Malaga airport, Kurt took them straight off to his delightful villa in the mountains - and if it had a different name to the non-existent one that he had earlier mentioned, then in the excitement they did not notice it.

Once in the villa, Kurt pressed them to accept light refreshments of Spanish sherry and local cakes. The two women almost immediately began to feel drowsy. Within minutes they had both fallen into a deep sleep. Mona stirred and slowly came back to consciousness. She felt a shaking sensation. She tried to move but it was difficult and there was a jangling metallic noise from her hands.

Suddenly she was awake, very awake. She looked around. She was lying on straw in a small covered cage in what seemed to be the back of a truck. She was naked. Her wrists were manacled with a short length of heavy chain joining them. Another length of chain went from a metal collar round her neck and was padlocked to a ring at the barred entrance to the cage.

Next to her cage was another and in it lay Diana, also naked and chained, and still asleep. She noticed that the collar round her neck seemed to be made of flexible chromium plated links, like a metal watch strap. There was a blank plate on one side of the collar and another on the other side engraved with a crest. At the front hung a ring and at the back was a strange little bulge. How odd, she thought, but also how awful to collared like a pet dog.

"Diana!" called out Mona anxiously. "Wake up! Are you alright?"

Diana stirred in her sleep and then she, too, was suddenly wide awake, her chains clinking as she crawled towards the bars separating the two cages.

"Mummy! Mummy!" she cried reaching through the bars to touch her mother. "What's happened??"

But Mona didn't know... Suddenly the truck stopped. The heavy covers at the back were parted. Two tough looking men looked in. They were wearing Arab dress and carrying short whips. Beyond them was just empty desert-like scrub.

"Silence! You not talk or you get whip!" said one of them menacingly in heavily accented English.

Mona and Diana cowered back in their cages trying to hide their naked bodies with their manacled hands.

"We get plenty money for you two. You sell well. Plenty rich Arab men like buy you two."

Then suddenly there was the noise of several trucks screaming to a halt. There was burst of shots, of rifle fire. The two men collapsed and disappeared, apparently shot. There was a pause and the two women held their breath. Then a new face appeared between the two rear covers of the truck. It was a handsome and bearded face that somehow seemed familiar.

"Mrs Milton," came a cultured voice, with a slight Arab accent, "Allah be praised, that we found you in time."

"You're Kurt's friend!" cried Mona in astonishment as she recognised the handsome rich man, whom she had idly wondered might make a husband for her daughter. She was still cowering back and trying to hide her nakedness.

"Yes! It is I!" replied the Sheik, taking in the delightful sight of the sight of the mother and daughter's naked bodies. "I only got Kurt's message this morning - that whilst he had been drugged, you two had been abducted. I thought that I and my men might find you on this stretch of deserted road along the coast. How lucky I did! But first I must give you something to hide your nakedness."

He snapped his fingers and two shawls were thrust through the bars of the cage. Eagerly the two crawling women grabbed them and wrapped them round themselves.

"Keep these on for the rest of the journey."

"The rest of the journey?" queried Mona. "You mean you're going to leave us in these cages!"

"Yes, it's the safest thing to do," said the Sheik blandly. Keeping the two women in their cages would, of course, prevent them from seeing where they were being taken. It was important that they were as ignorant of their whereabouts as the other women in his harem.

"The gang's accomplices will see the truck and not interfere," he whispered. "We'll follow at a discreet distance. But instead of taking you to the gang's hide-out to be sold, my men will drive the truck to my palace where you can rest in comfort after your terrible experience."

"Your palace!" cried Mona, thrilled. "Oh, how can I ever thank you enough for having rescued us - and now inviting us to stay in your palace. You're our saviour!"

"Yes, our saviour!" echoed Diana, eying the Sheik with schoolgirl admiration.

"But I must arrange for Diana to go to a new school."

"Oh I am sure that Zalu will be arranging suitable lessons for her," laughed the Sheik

"Zalu" queried Mona. "Who's Zalu?"

"Oh he'll be looking after you, once you arrive at my palace."

"Oh!" said Diana in a disappointed tone. "Won't we be seeing you?"

"Oh yes, you'll be seeing me alright," laughed the Sheik mysteriously, "once you've settled down. But I shall leave it to Zalu first to show you a little of our ways!"

5 - 2 CONSUMMATION!

It was late at night, two weeks later.

Diana was lying on her little mattress on the floor, naked under the blankets, restless and unable to sleep. How she longed to put her hands under the blankets and try to reach her beauty bud, hidden away under the humiliating lacing. But, with the huge fat black man quietly patrolling up and down between the rows of mattresses, cane in hand, she did no dare to do so.

Indeed, would she ever forget that first awful interview with Zalu when they had learned the were now incarcerated in the Sheik's harem. To their acute embarrassment, he had also warned her mother and herself that from now on being caught touching themselves would be regarded as being unfaithful to their Master, and very severely punished as such.

Their Master! She raised her eyes to the picture on the wall of the tall virile looking young man standing over two kneeling young women, his whip raised. Oh, how often, had she fearfully associated herself with them. Oh, what a dreadful scene!

And how appalling that here in the artificial life of the harem, the women thought, and talked, of nothing else but of sex - sex with the Master, the only man they were allowed to see.

Then she turned to other picture, the one that like, the other concubines, she could hardly keep her eyes off. This showed the Master naked and imperiously pointing down to the ground. But what constantly caught her eye, and those of all the other women, too, was that it showed his manhood in proud erection.

She shuddered at the thought that, whether she liked it or not, this was the manhood that would soon be taking her precious virginity - an event for which she was being specially prepared.

Brought up strictly, and sent to a convent school, she had never seen a man's manhood, never mind one in erection. She blushed at the thought that this was the manhood was going to take her virginity! Indeed, she found herself thinking of little else by day and dreaming of little else by night. It seemed so big and strong! She could not help dreading being penetrated by it.

Thank Heavens that so far her mother had managed to hold out against Zalu's terrifying demand: that she beg the Sheik to take her daughter's virginity. But every day that her mother held out earned them both three strokes of Zalu's cane. It was awful.

She remembered how the little pygmy boy, Baza, had described to her the traditional harem way that the Master took a virgin - with the girl tied down helpless, so that she could not harm her Master. It all sounded quite terrifying. Diana turned over on her thin mattress stretched on the hard floor. How uncomfortably the concubines were kept, compared to the luxury in which the Master lived. She had seen his huge four poster bed with a huge mirror on the ceiling bed and a lovely thick mattress - the bed where that horrible Zalu intended that she lose her virginity.

And she had seen the eunuchs' own separate, comfortable and well furnished bedrooms. Not for them the harshness of a communal dormitory and bathroom! Nor, indeed, not for them the simple diet on which the women were kept. The black eunuchs (whatever a eunuch was!) seemed positively to revel in their delicious fattening food and their vast girths. Even the boy eunuchs, Baza and Naka, were pretty fat.

It was terribly embarrassing being supervised by a little boy like Baza, whom Zalu had made their particular overseer. It must be equally humiliating for the two expectant Englishwomen, Mauve and Magenta, to have the other little pigmy boy, Naka, in charge of them.

She had been appalled at the way Naka would proudly pat the bare swelling tummies of the two blushing women and then put his hand down over their chain mail protective pouches, to check that they were still securely and tightly locked in place, before taking them off to be paraded before the Master.

Was this to be her fate, too, she wondered anxiously, a little schoolgirl mother-to-be, with a prettily growing belly that she would have to show off to the Master each day.?

She had also been appalled at the way an experienced, huge, older black eunuch, Okra, was in charge of Mrs Amanda Seymour and Miss Olivia Hamilton, now just called Royal Blue and Beige. He was training them to perform together, before the Master, reluctantly as a matched lesbian pair.

He made them kiss, swaying and wriggling their hips to sensuous Arab music, eagerly thrusting their moist beauty lips towards each other. But frustratingly they were never allowed to let their beauty lips to touch, or to touch each other's throbbing beauty buds.

Diana was still even more appalled at the way, Baza, used his whip to make her and her mother perform their most intimate natural functions before him and to his order.

Oh those awful black eunuchs! Never would she forget her initial thrashing from Zalu, when seeing for the first time the cruel way they treated the concubines, she had rounded on them and called them, with schoolgirl frankness: "black bastards".

Before she had known what was happening, both she and her mother had been seized, their harem trousers had been pulled down and they had been made to bend over - in front of the other concubines.

198

Horrified, she had seen the enraged Zalu himself slowly roll up his sleeves. Then controlling his anger he had slowly and methodically thrashed her and mother, with alternate strokes going to each. They each had twelve strokes of his long whippy, silver tipped, cane on the bare bottom.

"Sluts!" Zalu had then screamed in his high pitched voice. "Next time either of you fail to show the utmost respect to a black eunuch, you'll both get twenty strokes!"

It was the first time she had ever been beaten. She had to sleep on her tummy for several days. Indeed, lying on the hard mattress, she could still feel the weals of that terrible caning. She was now resolved to make sure that it was also the last time she was beaten by the black eunuchs - for the pain had been terrible, as had the humiliation of being beaten in front of the other women, all aghast and watching in shocked silence.

Moreover, to see her mother being similarly beaten for something said by her daughter had also been a terrible experience. No, from now on, she would certainly treat the black eunuchs as Gods! On the other side of the dormitory, Mona was also awake.

Oh what a swine Zalu was, she was thinking, to have ordered that she and her precious Diana were to be kept apart, so that they had no opportunity to whisper or hug each other.

They were only brought together by Baza for their embarrassing sexual training together and, equally embarrassing, to perform their natural functions - together and to Baza's orders. To have to squat and spend a penny or relieve themselves. simultaneously into special bowls, half filled with rose-water, with the little pygmy boy eunuch standing over them his dog-whip raised, was all so humiliating. The little boy enjoyed making them both wait for his command to perform. And what a swine he could be with his little dog-whip!

Her eyes, too, kept turning to the picture of the manhood of the Master, the Master whom Zalu had told her, his cane raised menacingly, that she was going to have to beg to take the virginity of her daughter. Not only that but she was being trained by Baza to lick her Master from behind, thrusting her tongue into his rear orifice, as he penetrated her precious daughter.

She thought of how she had scrimped and saved to send the girl to a top class convent school and of how she had planned to marry her off so well. And now the girl's fate, like her own, was to be one of the humble concubines of an Arab Sheik.

What made it all the more poignant, was that neither her daughter nor herself had seen the Master since he had 'rescued' them on the coastal road. But, he apparently had seen plenty of them, watching them from behind one way mirrors and grilles as they had been made by Zalu to practice pleasing a man together, watching them in the harem bathroom, being washed with the other women by the black eunuchs and humiliatingly performing their natural functions to their order.

Never would she forget the shock of her first sight of the harem when, still with just their shawls to hide their own nakedness, she and her daughter had seen for the first time the English and Arab concubines dressed in different coloured, and shockingly revealingly, harem dress, huge golden rings hanging degradingly from some of their nostrils, their registered indentured numbers tattooed on their bellies, and in he case of the Englishwomen, their wrists linked by a chromium plated manacle chain.

She had learnt that, like the half English Lebanese twins, Crimson, she and her daughter were to share one harem colour and one harem name: Pink. She was to be Pink One and Diana, Pink Two.

Indeed, it had only been a matter of hours before Pink One and Two, now wearing identical pink harem dress, had been tattooed and manacled like the other Englishwomen. But, of course, they had not yet earned the degrading nose rings.

She again raised her eyes to the picture of the manhood that from now on was going to be her only permitted source of sexual pleasure. As she looked up at it yet again, she could feel her beauty lips moisten under the bed clothes, as was, of course intended by the cunning and cruel black eunuchs. Their whole object in life, she realised, was to keep the concubines aroused and excited for the Master - and totally frustrated.

She thought of how she had resisted offering her daughter's virginity to the Master, of how every day, Zalu had sent for her, of how she had to stand at Attention in front of his desk, on which lay his dreaded silver tipped cane.

"Well Pink One, are you ready yet to offer your daughter to the Master for his enjoyment? Are you ready yet to heighten his enjoyment by licking his rear orifice from behind as he takes her? Well are you? If not I shall have to give you both three strokes of the cane, daily until you are. Well, which is it to be?"

Like a Christian martyr choosing death rather than denounce his religion, she had, so far, always shaken her head and they had both then been promptly given the three strokes across their bottoms. It had become a painful and dreaded daily event.

She had initially thought that her refusal to cooperate in the degradation of her daughter would earn her a terrible thrashing, not merely three strokes. But the crafty Zalu and the other black eunuchs had merely laughed.

"Soon here in harem, you will find you really want to offer daughter to Master," Zalu had smiled cunningly. "No need to beat hard! You soon come to dread even three strokes - every day. You soon want to beg Master to take daughter."

Indeed, she very soon had come to fear those awful daily three strokes. Moreover, just as Zalu had said, already she was being brain-washed by the artificial life of the harem, consisting as it did of women whose only purpose was to give physical and mental pleasure to one man, and who were never allowed even see photographs of other men, and for whom sex with the Master was the only permitted topic of conversation.

Indeed, she may scarcely know him, but already she felt he was her Master and she his slave. Of course, she decided, it was only right and proper that she should offer her daughter's virginity to him. It would indeed be an honour for them both. Sheik Ali smiled as, seated comfortably and hidden behind the metal gauze screen, watched Zalu lead Mona and Diana up to the other side of the screen. This was the moment he had been waiting for.

Mona was dressed in her normal humiliating pink harem

dress, with its transparent silken trousers cut away in front to disclose not only the tattoos of his crest and her registered number, but also her hairless and mature beauty lips. He could see the marks of the cane on her bottom, the cane that had helped bring her to her this moment of truth.

Diana, however, was incongruously dressed in a lovely white European wedding dress. She made a perfect picture of a blushing bride, an English bride, a virgin.

Zalu whispered an order, and both women prostrated themselves in front of the screen, their foreheads touching the floor, their long blond hair flung forward, their arms outstretched in supplication.

Sheik Ali gripped the arms of his chair in excitement as he saw Pink One now raise her head and look tearfully up at the screen, a picture of submissive and subservient womanhood, English womanhood.

"My Master," came her voice, repeating the words she had been made by Zalu to learn until she was word perfect. They were words that had been used for centuries in the harems of his family when they returned with their female booty from a raid on another tribe.

"I beg my Master to allow me the honour of offering him the virginity of my only daughter for his pleasure. I beg him to allow me to provide him with further pleasure as he takes her, as I have been taught to do by you black eunuchs. I further beg him subsequently to use both me and my daughter, as he wishes, as forsaking the sight of other men, we dedicate ourselves to his service."

"Yes, Master," came the girlish voice of Diana. "Please make me a woman. I wish to offer myself to you for your enjoyment." Sheik Ali looked down at the pretty young English virgin, tied down in the traditional way on her back in his bed.

Her outstretched legs were raised and fastened to two chains hanging from the ceiling of his bed, her outstretched arms fastened to two other hanging chains. She was also gagged.

No matter how willing a girl might appear to be, and certainly Diana was scarcely willing, Zalu always recommended a virgin being properly raped like this. Not only did it make it all an event the girl would remember with fear for the rest of her life, but it also prevented her from scratching, stabbing, kicking, biting or insulting her ravisher - all things that Diana was now longing to do.

Round her waist was a very tight little corselet that pulled in her waist, leaving her breasts and tattooed mound nicely bare.

Just as she had been taught to do, and still thinking fearfully of Zalu's whip, the girl was constantly raising her beauty lips, offering them to him, in a gesture of humble subservience.

Zalu had certainly arranged for her to look an arousing sight! It was a sight that, he could see, had already affected his strongly erect and eager manhood.

Kneeling behind him on the bed was the girl's mother, already sticking out her tongue, as she had been taught she must do, as a sign of her willingness to perform her forthcoming duty.

Young Baza stood proudly to one side of the bed, his little whip at the ready. His pair of women, the pair he controlled so strictly, were now going to satisfy the Master!

The Sheik nodded to Baza, who reached forward and unlocked and eased the lacing that held closed Diana's well oiled beauty lips. Then he held the beauty lips apart. Diana gave a little anguished cry of protest from under her gag.

The Sheik leant forward, his manhood pressing at the entrance to the girl's virginity.

Baza gave Mona a sharp tap with his dog-whip and instantly the young Sheik felt the mother's hot little tongue on his rear orifice. It was a sudden feeling that made him drive his manhood up between the parted lips, until he felt it come up against the virgin membrane.

There was a another little muffled cry from Diana.

There was the noise of another stroke of the dog-whip being administered to Mona's bottom, followed by an anguished cry of: "Take her, Master! Take her!"

Then her tongue was re-applied.

It was enough.

Baza deftly unfastened the girl's gag and she screamed aloud as the Sheik's proud manhood burst through the protecting membrane.

Diana was now a woman, like her mother, and from now on both would serve him together, with a mixture of hatred and adoring servility.

5 - 3 THE ENTRAPMENT OF MISS JULIA de FREVILLE ('Pure White')

Julia de Freville was a well educated, very tall, buxom and beautiful young woman with red hair, green eyes and a Junoesque figure. She was 28 and had recently separated from her husband, Paul.

She was clever and, to get away from her friends in London and her unhappy memories of Paul, she had taken a well paid job doing international public relations for the small Shadek National Air Lines - a job that involved much travel.

On a visit back to his native country, Sheik Ali had seen Julia in the airline offices. He had found her most attractive. But it was her lack of respect for her Arab employers, and the offhand way that she spoke to them, and indeed to him, that made him determined to get this magnificent self confident and statuesque Englishwoman into his harem.

Indeed he could hardly wait to watch such a woman being made to submit to the humiliating discipline of Zalu and his assistants.

He discovered that Julia was having an affair with one of the foreign pilots of the airline, a married man. They usually met abroad but in Shadek would also meet in certain hotel, or would go for picnics in the desert - and at all these meetings would make love. It was a dangerously illicit love in a country where the penalty for adultery was death by stoning and girl friends had warned her to be careful - but, scornfully, she had paid no attention.

Sheik Al now ordered the Morals Police to watch her

carefully. Soon they had plenty of evidence against her: evidence that she, a married woman, had repeatedly committed adultery with a married man, not her husband. They reported their findings to the Sheik and he arranged for her to be arrested, on a charge of adultery, at the airport on her return from meeting her lover abroad. He also arranged for her lover to be immediately made redundant from the airline and forbidden to return to Sadek.

To avoid publicity, the Sheik had Julia taken before a secret religious court. She was sentenced to death by stoning, but told that as she was a foreigner, the sentence would be commuted to ten years penal servitude.

Furthermore, remembering his need to satisfy the fundamentalist Mullahs in North Africa about some of his women being in a state of 'Salat' or purity, the Sheik also arranged for the court to sentence her to be 'cut' - a quite normal part of the sentence on a woman found guilty of immorality.

Officially this was so that she would be less tempted, in future, to persuade innocent, God-fearing, men to sin. But the real truth was quite different.

A girl who had been cut felt nothing when she played with herself or with other women - which is what the watchful black eunuchs, supervising the women in a harem, were always on the lookout for. Instead a cut girl was now utterly dependent for pleasure on being penetrated by a man; on vaginal, rather than clitoral arousal. A cut girl therefore was more desperate than ever to catch her Master's eye - something that Sheik Ali, like his forbears, knew well. He was, therefore, greatly looking forward to having a cut English girl in his harem. Julia was not allowed to contact any of her friends or the British Consul. People enquiring about her at the airline offices were simply told that she had fallen foul of the Morals Police and had been dismissed, and given twenty four hours to leave the country. The airline did not know where she had gone to.

Indeed, Julia had just disappeared, as do many white women in the Middle East - but all the time she was being kept secretly locked up in the hospital wing of a special Moral Police prison.

Not speaking Arabic, Julia had little idea what was going on or why she she had had to undergo a strange operation. It was only when the bandages were removed that a sudden scream announced that she had discovered that, where her proud beauty bud used to be, there was now only a little scar.

To understand Sheik Ali's plan it must be understood that, in Shadek, adulterous women were not sent to a special enclosed prison as had happened to Louise, in the neighbouring state of Mifsud. Instead, they were sentenced to penal servitude - hard labour, hired out to contractors who were building roads in the desert or mountains, to work under duress in awful conditions.

The Shadek authorities, and fundamentalist Mullahs, liked this to be publicly seen - as a deterrent to women tempted to misbehave.

To prevent the women from escaping, and trying to pass themselves as free women, they were neatly tattooed on the wrist and belly with their prison numbers and on the belly, above the prison number, with the state emblem of Shadek. In Julia's case, however, Sheik Ali used his position to arrange for the number to be her future number as an indentured servant in North Africa and for his own personal and similar crest to be substituted for that of the state one on her belly.

To further identify a woman as a prisoner, a broad swathe was cut down the centre of each woman's hair, removing half of it and only leaving the short hair on each side of her head above the ears.

But this was not all, for the women were also manacled with a strong cast iron chain and a similar collar was riveted round their necks from which hung a disc inscribed in Arabic on one side, and in English on the side, mainly for the benefit of Asian prisoners and their friends or relations.

Julia was horrified to read on the disc the date of her arrest and the words: "STATE OF SHADEK. PRISONER NUMBER 6784. 10 YEARS PENAL SERVITUDE FOR ADULTERY. REWARD FOR RETURNING ALIVE TO SHADEK POLICE. PENALTY FOR HELPING TO ESCAPE: DEATH!"

Julia felt utterly degraded when all this was done to her - on top, of course as being cut. She sobbed with shame and despair as she put her hand to her head and felt the wide swathe that the clippers had left. But the prison guards had not finished with her yet, for the clippers were also applied under her arms and down between her legs 'as a protection against vermin.' A few days later, Julia together with twenty other Arab, Pakistani and Indian women, was exhibited for hire to the representatives, the labour managers, of half a dozen local Arab contractors, all of who were used to using women labourers in the remoter areas where it was expensive and difficult to maintain machinery, control male convicts, or feed animals. Women were a cheaper and more malleable option.

Moreover, provided the collar and disc were returned to the police at the end of each woman's sentence, no questions were asked as to whether she was alive or dead, or what had happened to her.

The women were made to stand in a line on a little bench with their wrists handcuffed behind them, and their feet chained wide apart to ringbolts riveted through the wood of the bench. They were all stark naked. They had all been tattooed on the belly, manacled and collared with the humiliating disc handing down in front.

Down the line came two young Negro guards with a bowl of shaving soap and a razor. The contractors watched each woman's reaction as she had, first, to bend forward to have her head shaved again. Then, not daring to move for fear of being cut, each had to thrust her intimacies forward for the stubble to be removed. Whilst one young Negro laughingly pulled out one of her beauty lips and held it taut, the other would run his razor over the now well stretched skin. Never had Julia felt so humiliated.

The contractors' representatives then came over and started to examine the line of women. They took out little notebooks and carefully wrote down the number tattooed on each belly on different pages , so as to keep their notes separated. What they were looking for was health, strength and stamina -

three essentials if they were to get their money's worth from their investment in a particular woman.

They were also looking for good child bearing hips, for inevitably the women's overseer would have his way with them. Indeed, quickly removing, and selling off, the resulting progeny was a profitable side line that did not seriously detract from the work that they would get out of a strong healthy woman, even if her belly was swollen for much of her sentence.

Julia excited considerable interest, for it was rare for a white woman to be on offer. They felt and discussed her arm and shoulder muscles as if they were considering buying an ox. They felt her large breasts and discussed in Arabic, which she could not understand, whether they would impede her capacity for heavy work, her ability to run with a heavy load on her back and suitability for breaking stones. They also discussed her breeding possibilities, how much a swollen belly would affect her work, and noting that, with her well spread hips, she should have no difficulty in dropping big half black offspring.

To her embarrassment, each man looked closely at her beauty lips, parting them and writing down with satisfaction the fact that she been cut, for women who had been so treated made better labourers.

Then, whilst the men retired to the cool of a shaded terrace and drank iced drinks, Julia and then other women were in turn made to run round the yard, in the hot sun, each carrying a heavy sack of sand on her back whilst a prison guard with a long carriage whip stood in the centre of the yard flicking her backside to keep her moving fast.

Soon Julia was panting, and almost dropping with exhaustion, but the long whip drove her on and on - until the watching men were satisfied with the demonstration of her carrying capacity, her stamina and her response to the whip. Throughout all this, Julia's feelings of shame and degradation were overwhelming. Never had she been treated in such an inhumane way. She would, she kept telling herself, do anything, absolutely anything, to avoid such treatment. And, she realised, there was worse to come.

She would have been even more distressed had she known that watching through a small grill, was the handsome young Sheik whose eye she had originally caught. He had now returned to Shadek for a one day visit to make sure that everything was going to plan.

The Sheik's eyes had lit up with satisfaction as he had watched the humiliation that was being inflicted on the woman he had decided to take into his harem - but only when she was ready to beg for it!

He smiled as he thought how he had already made certain arrangements with a road contractor friend of his, whom he could rely on to give the girl a hard time... The women were now made to line up facing the shaded terrace for their services to be sold.

As the number on each woman's belly was called out, she had to mount a little display block. The bidding started quickly and quietly like the bidding at a cattle market, for all the buyers knew by now what they were prepared to pay for each woman as she was led forward.

There was some surprise when one contractor, the friend of Sheik Ali's, went on bidding for Julia in excess of her economic value as a labourer. He was, however, secretly content that he would soon recoup his outlay and more!

Julia found herself being loaded together with two other girls that the same contractor had hired, neither of whom spoke English, into a small covered cage in the back of a truck. Her odyssey had begun and no one knew where, or who, she was - for Sheik Ali had ensured that the prison records simply showed that Prisoner 6784 was an Indian girl, name unknown, accused of being a prostitute.

5 - 4 THE DEGRADATION OF JULIA

For six hours, the truck carrying Julia and the other women, gripping the bars of their small cage, swayed across rough desert tracks until it came to a small encampment on the edge of a new road that was being built.

In the centre of the encampment was a large, low, mobile cage on wheels, like that used to transport dangerous circus animals and to house them when they were not performing in the ring. However, this cage was used to transport female prisoners from site to site, and to house them at night at the end of their hard day's work.

An armed guard inspected the truck, raised the canvas covering the cage, checked the numbers on the girls' bellies with those on the driver's delivery note and waved the truck on.

It was now late afternoon. The truck stopped and the driver removed the cage cover. Through the bars Julia saw a Negro, evidently an overseer, trotting towards them mounted on a donkey. Slung over his shoulders was modern lightweight repeating rifle. In one hand he held a short stick for encouraging the donkey and in the other a long whip for encouraging a chain gang of a dozen naked women.

The women were collared and manacled, and running along, in step, behind the donkey. Large, conical shaped, wicker baskets were strapped onto their backs by straps that crossed over their breasts. Some of the women, presumably Arabs, had slightly coffee coloured skins, others brown or black. There were no white ones.

Further away, Julia saw two other chain gangs of women, also led by a Negro on a donkey approaching the encampment. Turning back to the nearest chain gang, she saw that a six foot length of light chain was fastened to the donkey's saddle and led back to the ring on the front of the collar of the first woman in the line. Other similar lengths of chain linked each of the other women's collars to rings on the backs of the collars of the women in front of her.

Horrified , she noticed, that the women chained at the front of the line all had swollen bellies. But there was no sign of any progeny.

As the overseer trotted up closer, followed by the running women, Julia saw that, like her, they all had a crest tattooed onto their bellies and below it some Arabic numerals. The swollen bellies of the leading women gave the crests a strangely distended look.

Julia watched with mounting horror as the black overseer stopped the donkey near to a iron cage standing in a sandy patch. Immediately the two leading women, both with hugely bulging bellies, quickly ran up to the donkey and, dropping to all fours, made a little dismounting block with their naked backs. Julia's horror would have been all the greater had she noticed a nearby expensive-looking four wheel drive car. The car had tinted windows all round and between the chauffeur and the spacious back, so that no one could see inside.

Inside, of course, lay back the smiling Sheik Ali, his spotless white burnouse raised as he watched the continuing degradation of Julia. Kneeling on all fours at his feet like little dogs, chained together by the neck, to reduce the risk of them trying to escape, and their wrists still manacled, were Mona and Diana whom he had brought in his private jet, under the care of Baza, to attend to his needs. They were both looking up at him, their Master, with fearful, and yet half adoring, eyes.

He felt no embarrassment at having a little black boy in charge of women when they were pleasuring him. And the boy himself obviously took great pride in the performance of the women in his care. And being a pygmy he took up so little room in the back of the car!

Baza was now holding Mona by the neck. He pushed her mouth down to the Sheik's aroused manhood. Then, as the Sheik continued to look out through the tinted window, Baza pushed Diana's head further down so that her tongue was now licking the Sheik's testicles. Shortly, he decided, he would order them to change round. The overseer now led his chain gang up to the truck. The driver handed him a delivery note which the overseer, first checking it against the number tattooed on Julia's belly, duly signed. The driver then unlocked the little cage and pulled Julia out.

The overseer seized her arm and without any more to do, quickly fastened her into the middle of his chain gang, immediately behind the expectant women. The other girls were evidently destined for the other chain gangs.

Then he nodded to the two leading women of his gang. They lifted out of the truck two heavy bins marked in Arabic: 'Pig Feed'.

The overseer then led the, now longer, chain gang to a long metal trough alongside the mobile cage. Julia saw that each woman in the chain gang, whether she was a Negress, an Indian or a Filipino, bore the same distinctive marks on her belly as herself - the Royal crest of Shadek superimposed on some Arabic numerals - though in her case, for a reason she did not understand, the crest was slightly different.

The two leading women emptied the contents of one of the bins into the trough. Startled, Julia saw that the contents were an unappetising looking porridge scattered with lumps of meat and fruit. Although she did not know it the similar contents of the other bin were destined to be the women's breakfast the following morning. Other similar bins awaited the arrival of the other two chain gangs.

Julia saw with amazement that the women were now eagerly licking their lips. Goodness, they must be desperately hungry to even contemplate eating such unappealing looking food. Indeed they had not been fed since dawn and, after their hard day's work in the quarries, they were ravenous.

"I feed my female labourers on pig meal," the contractor friend of Sheik Ali's used to boast. "And, like the pigs they are, they thrive on it!"

The overseer, stood back and gave an order. Immediately the women all rushed forward, pulling Julia with them. They knelt down and keeping their hands on the ground, started to guzzle up the food, like the pigs their owner called them.

Julia did not understand why they did not use their hands to scoop up the food. Timidly, she put her hands into porridge and pulled out a lump.

Suddenly there was a crack of a whip and Julia felt a line of fire across her naked back. She screamed in pain and turned round. Standing over her was the overseer, his whip raised ready to give her another stroke. He shouted something in Arabic and pointed to her hands in the trough and those of her neighbours carefully placed on the ground.

"No! No!" she screamed. "I'm not an animal!"

Again the overseer's whip fell with another crack across her back. This time the flexible tip went round and caught her breast. She again screamed and now held her breasts with her hands.

The overseer now leant down and pushed her face right into the middle of the sticky mess. She felt sick and tried to raise her head, but the overseer was holding her neck down in a steely grip.

Out of the corner of her eye, she saw him raise his whip for another stroke. Hastily she opened her mouth and started to guzzle and lap it all up, just like a pig. But she now kept her hands carefully on the ground.

Soon, under the whip of the overseer, the women on the chain gang were having to use their tongues to clean up the trough until it shone. Finally satisfied, the overseer poured a little water into the trough and the women all eagerly lapped up this as well. Water was precious here in the desert and the women were only watered after their feed, despite their natural thirst at the end of a day's labour under the hot sun. This was to ensure that their bodies would better digest the pig food. The watching Sheik's sensual arousal was now reaching a crescendo as he watched the once proud Julia, gobbling up the food. A pig of a Christian!

He looked down at Mona and Diana working away, bare breasted, to give him pleasure. He was rewarded with anxious little smiles from them both. How delightful it would be when both could offer him their milk!

It had been Zalu who had suggested that he took Mona and Diana with him on his flying trip back to Shadek, 'to attend to his manly needs'. However Zalu had made sure that under the women's long black shroud-like burquas, that would prevent a man from seeing anything of them, they had also been blindfolded, so that they would not see any men, nor have a glimpse of the outside world or have any idea where they were going.

Only when they were safely kneeling on the floor in the back of the Sheik's large car, had Baza removed their blindfolds and black shrouds to disclose their bare breasts to the Master.

Yes, thought the Sheik, as he saw the two women nervously looking up at him with frightened eyes, and yet obviously proud to have been chosen to give him pleasure on his trip, the harem system rarely fails, even with educated Western women.

The imposed frustration and inevitable jealousies, the helpless feeling of being kept for the personal use of one rich and powerful man, contrasting with the reassuring feeling of being under his protection, all combined to make a woman feel half in love with her Master, no matter how harshly she was treated, or how much she might miss her former freedom.

Even Mona and her daughter had found themselves jealously competing, against each other, to catch their Master's eye.

Clearly, reflected the Sheik, all six of his English concubines were half in love with their Master, and he had no doubt that Julia soon would be too, when she became the seventh. It was now the turn of the next chain gang to be fed from the trough.

Meanwhile, urged on by their overseer's whip, Julia and the rest of her chain gang crawled on their knees towards the tunnel-like barred structure that, like a cattle crush, led up to the raised mobile cage. Here he unfastened the wicker baskets on the women's backs and tossed them into a pile.

Just as a real cattle crush was designed to enable a stockman to hold an animal helpless while he examined her, so this one enabled the overseer to get a good look at each woman as she slowly crawled past him. A mirror on the far side allowed him to get a better look at the women's bodies.

A U-shaped bar could be dropped down to hold still any woman he wanted to inspect more closely, to dose, or to insert a cleansing suppository up her backside. Indeed the overseer, had a wide range of remedies for keeping his women fit and working - as well as his whip!

Julia had noticed that the overseer had stopped the heavily expectant women, as they crawled up the cattle crush, and had expertly checked their condition. She herself was still chained by the neck to the woman crawling up the crush ahead of her and to the one following her up.

She had crawled halfway along the raised crush when the overseer pulled a lever. There was a metallic crash and Julia found herself held helpless as the overseer began to examine his new charge.

Experienced hands felt her buxom breasts, through he bars of the crush, weighing each one, gauging the sensitivity of the nipples and, like the buyers at the auction, assessing the extent to which her big firm breasts might hinder her ability to run with a full load of stones on her back. He was also concerned lest they might affect her body-breaking work with a sledgehammer in the quarry, breaking up the stones, ready for laying.

He felt her arms and thigh muscles, judging how long she would take to harden up to her work. Then he parted her displayed beauty lips and grunted with satisfaction as he located the little scar, where her beauty bud used to be.

"Ah", he exclaimed aloud, "a girl that's been cut! That'll stop her wasting her energies at night, trying to play with herself. All the more energy for her work."

He would have enjoyed raping and inseminating this white woman, he thought, and she have carried her progeny well. What a pity that he had been given special instructions not to touch her, whilst keeping her hard at work. Evidently she was being kept back for something special!

He received, of course, a bonus for each live progeny that the women in his chain gang delivered. However he also received a bonus on the weight of stones that the chain gang delivered to the road each day. It was therefore a delicate matter to decide just how many of the chain gang he could fertilise without affecting the high work load that the contractor expected him to ensure that the women also produced. Ah, well, he would not have to make a decision about the white woman!

Perhaps he would slake his lust tonight on one of the pretty Indian girls in the chain gang. With a little sigh, he pulled back the lever, releasing Julia to continue crawling up to join her silent companions in the cage.

Soon Julia, too, was kneeling in it, gripping the bars of the cage with her manacled hands, and peering out onto the bleak landscape. She saw the luxurious looking car with its tinted windows. Who, she wondered, was inside. Her new owner? The ministrations of Mona and Diana were having their effect on the Sheik. These and the words of the overseer as he discovered that Julia had been cut, combined with the sight of her gripping the bars of the cage, brought the Sheik to the edge of an exciting climax.

Suddenly, with a hoarse cry, he exploded into Diana's soft little mouth, whilst Mona's tongue continued to lick away further down. He did not even bother to look down at them, so exciting did he find Julia's first humiliating lesson in how female convicts in Shadek were treated.

Satisfied, Sheik Ali now ordered Baza to put Mona and Diana back into the special kennels in the rear of the car and told his chauffeur to get out the small sack that he had brought. Immediately the women in the cage became excited, like caged animals sensing a special feed.

It was indeed a special treat that Sheik Ali had brought them to celebrate Julia's arrival in their cage, and which the chauffeur now proceed to empty into the cage, through the bars of the roof, onto the eager women below: half eaten lamb chops, the remnants of a feast he had given after noon prayers that morning to his retainers.

The bones might not look very appetising, but as Julia watched with dismayed, the women greedily snatched and fought each other, for the biggest ones. This was a rare treat for them. Being normally kept lean and hungry, they greatly enjoyed this unexpected bonus.

As Julia herself would soon discover after she had been fed on nothing but pig meal for a few weeks, to lie in the cage happily chewing on a bone, with bits of meat still attached to it, was the height of bliss.

Sheik Ali, of course, had no particular desire to have Julia degraded, erotically stimulating though he found the sight.

What he wanted to check out was that her treatment was going to sufficiently appalling to make her beg to enter his harem and to lose her freedom, as his indentured servant, as a way of escaping from it all.

Looking at the women chewing their bones, he now felt satisfied that all he had to do was to let matters progress normally for few weeks and this lovely Englishwoman would willingly fall into his hands like a ripe apple.

Still hidden himself behind the tinted windows, he instructed his chauffeur to drive to the airport where his private plane was waiting to fly him back to North Africa.

Perhaps, he thought, he might while away the flight by having Baza bring Mona and Diana, soon to renew their harem names of Pink One and Two, to pleasure him again. How right Zalu had been proved! It really was delightful imposing his will on a beautiful English mother and daughter, whilst carrying out the entrapment of the beautiful Julia. Meanwhile Julia's first night in the small mobile cage was an awful experience.

The mysterious car carrying the Sheik and his attendant women had scarcely driven off before first the second chain gang and then the third one all crawled up into the overcrowded cage.

It soon got dark and Julia found herself looking up at the stars through the bars that formed the roof of their low cage that kept them crawling on their knees.

In the cage there were now three dozen women of different races, all stark naked, and chained together by the neck to form three separate and rival chain gangs, each with its own black overseer anxious to out-do the others, both in the weight of stones delivered to the road by his women and in the number of half black progeny safely delivered to the contractor.

Julia saw that several women in each chain gang seemed due to deliver shortly. Hardly any of them seemed to speak a word of English and they appeared astonished to see a chained white woman in their midst. Their black overseers had retired to their comfortable caravan and Julia could hear the noise of music and raucous male laughter. There was also the smell of delicious cooking.

All this served to emphasise her own animal-like status, deprived of all the normal things that distinguish women from female animals: clothes, combs, mirrors, good cooked food, shoes, freedom to move about and do what they want and, perhaps psychologically, most important of all, the ability to perform their natural functions privately, secretly and discreetly.

A heavy monsoon shower suddenly poured down on the women through the open bars of the cage roof. Eagerly, the women used the water to clean themselves, for they were only hosed down once a day, when they left the cage to work.

Like the other women, Julia was soon soaked and, when the shower suddenly stopped, the water evaporated off their skins in the warm air like steam rising from well exercised horses. But the straw was now soaking wet, too.

After a time the door to the overseers' caravan opened and the overseers came out smoking, making Julia long for a cigarette. One of them switched on a light over the cage - the night security light intended to enable a patrolling night watchmen to check that the women were all lying down on the backs and not playing with themselves.

Suddenly Julia heard her overseer call out a number in Arabic. The other two overseers also called out numbers. Immediately three girls came forward to the front of the cage, dragging their next door neighbours on their chain gangs with them. They pressed their tummies against the bars of the cage, displaying their tattooed belly numbers. With a torch each overseer checked the number and satisfied patted the girl's belly. Each girl then turned round on her knees, and surrounded by the rest of her chain, pressed her buttocks against the bars.

"Head down onto the straw," one of the overseers ordered.

"Pull buttocks apart!" ordered another.

Then, once again to Julia's horror, they lifted up their simple burnouses and pushed their manhoods up between the bars of the cage towards the girls' proffered beauty lips.

"Keep head down!" warned Julia own overseer as he

218

pushed his hand through the bars and gripped his girl by the back of her neck, thrusting her further down and holding her still.

Then, as Julia watched open mouthed, he and his companions, slowly penetrated the subserviently kneeling girls, their necks gripped by their overseers, their heads thrust down onto the wet straw.

Slowly and deliberately, laughingly calling out to each other as they did so, the overseers took their pleasure.

5 - 5 JULIA BEGS THE SHEIK TO TAKE HER INTO HIS HAREM

It was a month later and Julia and the rest of the chain gang were running behind the overseer's donkey.

They had just left the quarry, where they had had to smash large rocks into smaller stones, using sledgehammers, and then throw the stones over their shoulders into the long wicker hampers strapped to their backs. Now, for the umpteenth time that day, they were being taken to the new road where they would have to empty their baskets, before running back to the quarry, to start all over again.

It was a back breaking task and Julia was staggering under the weight of her load, as she strained to keep in step with the woman chained in front of her.

My God, she was thinking, another ten years of this! She would do anything, accept anything, to get away from this terrible life. Moreover, she had seen the way the overseer, kept eying her body. Was she, like so many of the other women in the chain gang, destined to be covered by him, like an animal?

As they approached the road, she noticed the same large four wheel drive vehicle that she had seen on her first day. She could hear its air conditioning running. Who, she wondered, blushing at her nakedness, was inside. Sheik Ali watched the naked Julia running up towards them. She was looking fit and bronzed. His friend, the contractor, had assured that she had been treated just as harshly as the other women, but that she had not been

219

touched by the overseer.

He felt soft little tongues, mixed with a feeling of cool metal, on his manhood. He glanced down. Amanda Seymour and Olivia Hamilton, chained together by the neck, were kneeling on the floor of the large car. Like Mona and Diana, a month before, they were naked to the waist. They were leaning forward to give him pleasure, their tongues erotically thrust through their big brass nose rings.

The Sheik smiled with satisfaction as he saw the gleam of their shiny wrist and ankle manacles, mixing with their equally gleaming nose rings. Oh, the pride of ownership!

On the seat alongside him was a little dog whip, left for him by Okra to use if the girls did not please him sufficiently whilst their trainer sat in the front alongside the chauffeur unable to see what was going on behind.

Sheik Ali had been quite happy to have the little, young, Baza in attendance on him whilst their charges pleased him, but not the hugely fat and older Okra. But he had to admit that Okra had done a good job in training these two sophisticated women to work together - something that would have horrified them before they entered his harem. Suddenly Sheik Ali flung open the door and stepped out into the bright sunlight. The heat hit him like a furnace after the air-conditioned cool of the car.

Quickly Okra went into the back and, with his muscular arms, held the two now abandoned women by the neck, their heads down on the floor. Zalu, he knew, would never forgive him if the caught a glimpse of a man, other than the Master, on this short trip away from the harem.

The Sheik strode across to where the chain gang were approaching. Seeing the immaculate dressed Arab with the royal strip of gold in his thin black cloak, the overseer stopped his donkey, as if expecting Sheik Ali. Then he dismounted and made a deep obeisance. Nervously the women in the chain gang fell to their knees behind him.

"Your Highness!" he murmured respectfully.

The young Sheik strode down the line of kneeling women, each woman dropping to all four as he passed. Suddenly he stopped. At his feet was a white woman, her naked body tanned by the sun.

"Good Heavens, Miss de Freville," he said in English, "what on earth are you doing here. This is terrible - a white woman treated like an animal - in a chain gang."

With a gasp of astonishment at hearing herself addressed in English, Julia raised her head from the sand. There standing in front of her was the handsome young Sheik she had seen a couple of months before in the airline office. His pristine Arab dress contrasted embarrassingly with her own nakedness.

"Oh, Sir," cried Julia, totally overcome and unable to find words. It was the first time that anyone had spoken to her in English since she had been locked into the chain gang.

Sheik Ali turned to the overseer and blithely asked what Julia was being punished for and how long was her sentence. The overseer pointed to the disc hanging from her collar on which was written in Arabic: "Ten Years for Adultery."

"Miss de Freville," said the Sheik in a compassionate tone of voice. "I can't bear to leave you here like this. And I understand that you have another ten years penal servitude to serve."

"Oh, please, Sir, please help me! Please take me away from here. I will do anything. I just can't stand any more of it! Please help me!"

Sheik Ali smiled as he looked down at the English-woman grovelling at his feet.

He again turned to the overseer and spoke to him again in Arabic. Then he turned back to Julia.

"Of course I would like to help you, but your offence is taken very seriously here. Moreover the contractor has paid a substantial sum to have the use of your services for the next ten years. I'm afraid that I can't interfere with the due process of the law."

"Oh, please, Sir, please save me," cried Julia. "I would be for ever in your debt. There must be something you can do!"

Sheik Ali stroked his beard as if deep in thought. Then he shook his head.

"No, I'm afraid there is nothing anyone can do. You must just serve out your sentence. Unless, of course ... but then you would not want to do that!"

"Do what?" cried Julia. "I will do anything to get away from this terrible chain gang."

"Well, Miss de Freville, I suppose I might be able to buy out the contractor and then use my influence to persuade the authorities to have you transferred to my service."

"Oh! How wonderful!" cried Julia.

"But I would still remain responsible for you during the rest of your sentence. They would want to be sure that you could not escape or run away back to Europe.

"Oh no, I wouldn't do any such thing!"

"You say that now, but how could they sure that you would keep your word? No, they would want my assurance that I was going to keep you safely locked up in my harem."

"Your harem!" exclaimed Julia. Visions of a comfortable and luxurious life suddenly raced through her mind. To be in the harem of this handsome young man would be wonderful as compared to her life here breaking stones as a convict.

"Yes," said the Sheik. "Of course, the authorities would insist on you signing papers to become my indentured servant - virtually a slave. But obviously you, a married Englishwoman, wouldn't want to do that! No, I'm afraid there's nothing I can do. You must just concentrate of keeping alive and surviving the next ten years."

He turned on his heel and made as if to return to his car.

"No! No! Don't go" screamed Julia. "I'll sign anything. I'll go into your harem. I'll be your slave. But please save me, please."

The Sheik turned back. "Are you really serious Miss de Freville?"

"Yes! Yes!"

"Well in that case I suppose I could set things in motion".

"Oh, please hurry. All that could take months and

months. I can't stand another day here!"

The Sheik turned to the overseer and quietly slipped him an official looking document.

"Well," he said to Julia, "you're in luck. The overseer's got a set of indentures here. If you sign these now, then I could register them today and arrange for the contractor to release you. Then I'll send my servants here to collect you and take you to my palace in North Africa."

"North Africa! Right away from here! Oh, how wonderful!" cried Julia. "Ill sign anything, now!"

The Sheik smiled. It had really all worked out very well. Zalu was waiting at the airport with his plane. He would come here later, take delivery of Julia, dress her in a black shroud so that she looked just like any other anonymous Arab woman, and then give her something to make her sleep.

The Sheik smiled again at the thought that, when Julia awoke, she would be hundreds of miles away, safely locked up in his harem - the seventh of his English concubines. Like the others, she would not know where she was, nor even just who her Master was.

And the best thing about it all was that, unknown to her, she was already permanently marked with his crest and her registered number as his indentured servant - now his indentured concubine!

It was all very clever and neat!

"Oh, my Saviour!" cried Julia. "How can I ever thank you enough for rescuing me!"

A tremendous feeling of power and of pride of ownership swept through Sheik Ali. For the second time that morning he was sitting unseen in his office looking through a wooden grille before which Zalu, cane in hand, was parading his harem of beautiful women.

He really enjoyed having his women paraded before him, even when it was not to for choosing women for his bed. It was as exciting as watching them in the harem through the various grilles, one-way mirrors and internal television screens.

First came his remaining Arab concubines. Highly satisfied with the service that Zalu was providing him from his half dozen English concubines, he had now only retained half a dozen of his best and most beautiful Arab ones.

Then came the delightful half English twins, Crimson, chained together by the neck as always.

Finally came his special pride and joy, his seven well bred English concubines. Smiling hesitantly and swaying provocatively as they ran up to The screen, each was controlled by their particular black eunuch overseer.

The Sheik's prettily tattooed crest and their registered numbers as indentured servants glistened on their bare bellies and mounds, framed by their cutaway harem trousers. Their now specially elongated nipples thrust aside their open boleros.

Then, in response to an order from their supervisors, they dropped to their knees, and with outstretched arms, their big brass nose rings and manacle chains clanking against the marble floor, flung their long blond hair forward and lowered their foreheads humbly to the floor. The young Sheik smiled approvingly as he saw a blushing Mauve and Magenta, the harem names of Louise and Samantha, being led up by a proud little Naka, dog whip in hand.

He was also holding a double dog lead, with one end fastened to the ring at the back of each of the women's collars. The Sheik's crest was prettily expanded across their now greatly stretched bellies.

It would not be long now, he reflected. Already, thanks to Zalu's clever pills, they were vying with each other to offer him their copious milk.

Then it was the turn of little Baza to bring up the blushing Mona and Diana, more simply known in the harem as Pink One and Two. Surprisingly each was carrying a life size baby doll. This was, Zalu maintained, an effective and natural way of bringing on a girl's maternal instincts and so help her conceive more easily - and Zalu had reported to the Sheik that these two, their monthly cycles having been brought into step with each other, would be ready next week to be covered, one after the other, by one of the Sheik's giant, highly virile, Dinka black guards.

They had, of course no idea what was in store for them and, hooded, would not be allowed to see the mate chosen for them.

Okra had been furious that Pink One and Two had been finally chosen to covered and not his own Royal Blue and Beige, Amanda and Olivia, whom he brought up next before the screen. However the Sheik had found the idea of first breeding simultaneously from a mother and daughter quite irresistible.

Later, of course, both covered by a white boy, he would use them to produce little girls who would be both the daughters and granddaughters of his favourite concubines!

"Don't worry," the Sheik had told the downcast Okra, who was regarding the now delighted young Baza with a mixture of scorn and jealousy, "I will tell Zalu to have your two done next - after the Pinks have safely delivered their big black half-breeds."

Okra now looked happier. He'd show those two little guttersnipes, Baza and Naka, how an experienced black eunuch brought on a couple of mothers-to-be!

"And," had added the Sheik with a laugh that brought a smile to Okra's fat face, "they'll know not anything about it, until you finally tell them - for we'll use Zalu's artificial insemination test tube technique to breed two beautiful little blond girls for my old age!"

Finally Zalu himself brought up Julia, now known as Pure White, a reference to her state of Salat or purity.

225

Zalu had solved the problem of what to do about her half shaven hair by shaving it all off - and then using a special cream to keep her head erotically shiny and bald.

The Sheik felt his manhood stir as driven on by an admonishing sharp tap on her buttocks from Zalu's cane, Julia prostrated herself before the screen and humbly lowered her head displaying his crest now beautifully also tattooed onto her smooth and hairless cranium. Indeed, as Zalu had intended, the Sheik had found the sight of this smooth and decorated cranium nodding dutifully between his thighs extremely arousing.

Perhaps, he thought, he should tell Zalu to have her registered number added there, too!

Oh the feeling of excitement that was engendered by the sight of these once free and sophisticated Englishwomen, now his property. his obedient concubines, his slaves to do with as he liked. Ten minutes later there was sudden knock on the door. Zalu entered.

"Your Highness," he said, "the delegation of Mullahs have arrived."

"Show them in," ordered the Sheik, discreetly drawing a curtain across the screen.

Three clerics, clad in black, entered. The Sheik greeted them warmly. Over coffee they explained that they had been sent by the Ulama, the local body of religious scholars, to enquire into his attitude towards the Western women that he was rumoured to keep in his harem.

Clearly they were concerned lest these women, used to what they regarded as the shocking freedom enjoyed by Western women, might form a hotbed of feminine revolt against the strict teachings of the fundamentalists regarding the treatment and control of women.

"Women are naturally licentious and promiscuous," stated one of the clerics, "and should be kept in the home or harem, away from the sight of other men."

"My sentiments entirely," smiled the young Sheik.

The Mullahs were clearly delighted when Zalu described how he prevented the Sheik's women, once in the harem, from leaving it, from seeing other men, and from having any

226

knowledge of what was going on in the outside world, the man's world.

Zalu then looked enquiringly at the Sheik who nodded approvingly. He had no objection to his women being seen by these clerics.

Zalu pulled the curtain over the screen, displaying to the clerics a scene of girlish innocence. A dozen collared women, some manacled, were all now playing naked in the pool, laughing and splashing as they threw a large rubber ball to each other.

"Ah, yes," quoted one of the clerics. "The bodies of mature women, kept with minds of children."

Zalu pointed to the swollen bellies of two of them.

"A woman's natural state!" said one of the clerics approvingly.

Tactfully, the clerics enquired about masturbating and lesbianism, and were greatly reassured to hear from Zalu of the steps he took to stamp on any such scandalous behaviour amongst the women in his charge, whether they were Arab or Western.

"And how about the imposition of the state of Salat on these potentially licentious creatures?" asked one of the Mullahs.

The Sheik clapped his hands and immediately little Baza and Naka led in a tall shrouded figure hidden in an all-enveloping black, Arab woman's, shroud. She was made to stand up, hesitatingly, on a little stool.

"You will understand that she has been blindfolded and gagged under her shroud," explained Zalu. "We do not allow His Highness's women to see or talk to other men."

The Mullahs nodded approvingly. This young Sheik certainly had the right ideas - and the money to impose them! He was an example to the whole community.

Their approval was even greater when the two black eunuch boys parted the woman's robe to disclose on her naked belly the tattooed crest of the Sheik and below it her indentured servant registration number. The jet black hands of the eunuch boys contrasted strikingly with the whiteness of the woman's exposed belly.

"And is this one a Christian woman?" asked another of the Mullah's in surprise.

227

"Indeed she is," replied the Sheik proudly. "A formerly free woman of the West."

The Mullahs exchanged more looks of approval.

"Legs apart! Knees bent!" Zalu suddenly ordered in English, giving Julia a tap on the buttocks with his cane through the shroud. The he gestured to the two boys. Immediately they parted her beauty lips, to disclose the little scar where the beauty bud should have been.

"Salat!" admiringly cried first one and then the other two Mullahs as they bent down and peered more closely. "His Highness imposes Salat even on his European women! His piety can be in no doubt!" The clerics having departed, the young Sheik turned back to look through the screen again. He again felt his manhood stir at the sight of so many beautiful creatures all so anxious to catch his eye.

Yes, he decided he wanted one - now!

But which? In view of the discussion with the clerics, it just had to be one of the Englishwomen, he decided. Oh the thrill when Mauve and Magenta kneeled down alongside him as he lay back on his bed. Four over-flowing hanging breasts, four elongated nipples. And the delicious tasting sweet milk!

Or Beige and Royal Blue shockingly trained to excite each other and himself at the same time.

Or Pink One and Two, still delightfully shy at having to please him in front of each of each other, and each quite unaware of their forthcoming maternity.

Or Pure White with her strangely affected state of Salat - a state that made it all the more exciting mentally to take her and which left her crying out to feel him inside her. Yes, he decided, it had to be her!

He reached forward and pressed a button on his desk, marked "Pure White". Whilst he was waiting for Julia to be made ready for his bed, the Sheik was turning over in his mind his next step. He had originally planned to acquire a dozen well bred English women and already he had seven - with no problems with their families or the British authorities. Nor had there been even a breath of scandal to anger his own Ruling Family or the authorities of his host country. The women had just mysteriously disappeared without trace!

As regards the women themselves, his cunning scheme to make them, each in a different way, intensely grateful for having apparently rescued them from a terrifying situation had at last enabled him to get them into his harem.

Here is the prologue of our book for next month, CHURCH OF CHAINS, by a new author *Sean O'Kane* - and our editor says "It's probably the best title we have released so far!"

PROLOGUE

Father Burton's gaze swept round the courtyard of the monastery as the girls of the new intake, the novices and the initiates were shepherded to their quarters for the night. There had been two formal punishments to administer that evening. It had rained heavily during them, but it hadn't mattered. He had surveyed the faces of the other girls during the floggings, and all of them had seemed suitably fearful as they stood; legs apart, hands behind backs and watched as the rain had plastered their scant clothing to their bodies and their hair to their faces. Apart from the occasional flick of a head to clear the hair from in front of their eyes, none had dared move a muscle while the sentences were being carried out. Of course it was forbidden for them to look away during punishments and the brothers had patrolled the ranks to make sure none did.

In fact Father Burton felt the rain had added to the spectacle. Once the girls had been chained naked to the whipping post, it had made their palely exposed flesh gleam very pleasingly. And the whips of the brothers charged with carrying out the punishments had cracked down with an interestingly wet, smacking sound, sending sprays of rain and sweat up from the helpless bodies. Also it had added to the picture of utter dejection and defeat the girls had presented as they hung in their chains when they had taken their lashes, hair matted down and the panting, moaning bodies running with water.

The public humiliation of these floggings had denied, was specifically designed to deny the girls the usual pleasure their sex had been ordained to take in being dominated by their masters. As he watched now the two victims struggled to carry the heavy whipping post back into storage, just as they had earlier sweated to carry it out. The brothers' whips played mercilessly round their thighs and calves to encourage them.

The Father felt well pleased. The work of the Church was progressing fast, all round the country, monasteries like this one were quietly being established and those who could not live by the laws espoused by the Church were being purified and redeemed. The wickedness of society was being beaten out of it in various ways. But here was where he belonged, here with these errant girls, it was the task the Patriarch himself had bestowed on him. And Father Burton knew he was equal to it.

In only a few nights' time there would be yet another new intake of girls. He strode back into the monastery, yet again he would see to it that they were purified, every trace of their previous, sinful lives expunged. He couldn't wait to move the great work on.

CHAPTER 1

WPC Paula Cheever gave herself one last critical examination in the mirror of the ladies' toilets before going on duty.

The bright red lycra dress hugged every curve of her body. Her full breasts which were naked under the thin material stood out proud and firm, the nipples thrusting into little peaks at their tips. The plunging neckline bared a daring expanse of the creamy skin at her cleavage. The skirt was short enough to leave her stocking tops invitingly visible and it clung lovingly to the neat swell of her taut buttocks. She had been allowed to grow her hair for this assignment and now it fell in gleaming black waves to her shoulders.

Pretty good Paula, she told her reflection smugly, whoever christened this 'Operation Honeypot' knew exactly what they were doing.

When she reached the Vice Squad office with its desks piled up with paperwork that needed attending to, and would be one day, and its dingy walls covered in polaroid snaps of girls who were persistent offenders she found the Chief Inspector was waiting to give them a pep talk.

The Chief Inspector was Margaret Barfield, a good looking woman in her mid-thirties and tipped to go right to the top. She was sitting on the front of the Inspector's desk, her shapely legs being secretly appraised by the men sitting on the rickety chairs that were the room's only other furniture. They were wasting their time, Paula thought, her tastes didn't run to men. And several WPC's had had their careers blighted by refusing to hit the sack with her.

As Paula entered CI Barfield gave her an ironic smile. "Well WPC Cheever, should police work ever lose its appeal, I don't think you'll lack for alternative employment," she said.

The men sniggered and Paula groaned inwardly. For one thing she was getting tired of the snide comments from the men; for another she was terrified that CI Barfield would propostion her, she had already seen her eyeing her up. But the Chief Inspector moved on briskly and everyone settled down.

She briefed a group of four officers who were on the trail of a new pimp who had recently moved into the area and they left to set up their observation point. That left Paula and the two officers who were to man the mobile unit which would back her up.

Her job was to pose as a prostitute on one of the city's streets which was regularly used by kerb crawlers. She would have a small microphone attached to her dress and when she was propositioned the man's voice would be recorded in the unmarked van parked just round the corner from her. At the crucial moment the van would pull round and he would be arrested and brought in.

"You both know the drill," the CI told the men. "Don't leave Paula out there any longer than you have to with a punter. Just get the evidence and then go in and get her; and him. And there's an added reason why that's important at the moment. Anyone ever heard of the Church of Ultimate Purification?"

They all shook their heads, and then Paula remembered a documentary she had seen some weeks before. "Aren't they some kind of fundamentalist sect that's setting out to reform society?"

"That's them," Margaret Barfield nodded seriously.

232

"They've got some pretty far out ideas and some questionable methods. Up north we're trying to infiltrate them. Amongst other things, known prostitutes are vanishing off the streets. We think they're behind it, and what's more we think they may be about to start operating down here. So you," she addressed the men, "keep a close eye on Paula."

They acknowledged their orders and left to pick up the van from the depot downstairs. The CI said she would drop Paula off at the agreed corner on her way home. It was an uncomfortable drive, Paula tried to use body language to convey to the other woman that she wasn't interested but Barfield just smiled. The bitch is biding her time, Paula thought.

It had been thought best to keep the decoy as far apart as possible from the van until the very last moment. When the van did arrive, a couple of minutes after Paula had taken up station, she would simply lean in at the driver's window as if she was negotiating with him. She would be fitted with the mike and the van would take up a discreet station and wait to see who fell into the trap.

Paula shivered a little as she climbed out of the car. Margaret Barfield leaned over before Paula could shut her door.

"You show a lot of........promise Paula," she said, managing to make the word 'promise' sound like Paula had asked her to leap into bed with her.

"When you've finished your attachment to Vice, we really must have a drink together. I like to get to know promising young officers."

Paula managed to make some non-committal reply and closed the door. The Chief Inspector's car pulled away and left her.

"Oh bloody great!" She muttered after it, "I either get felt up and laid by a creepy lesbian or stay as a PC for the rest of my career!" She knew there was no earthly point in reporting any proposition, Margaret Barfield could do no wrong in the eyes of the brass hats. Well it was a problem she would have to face in due course. She sighed and summoned up all her professionalism to concentrate on the job in hand.

233

The evening was chilly and the cold air cut through her thin clothes. How the real tarts stood it in all weathers she would never know.

She checked her watch and tried to stand in the shadows of the trees which overhung the high garden walls behind her. The van, a big, white, unmarked Transit, would be along any minute but if she could avoid being approached before it reached her, then so much the better.

The minutes passed. A couple of cars cruised by; the only traffic on this quiet street. The drivers looked hard at her, but the fact that she was standing well back from the kerb made them uncertain and they drove on. Paula wasn't concerned, she knew they would go round and round the kerb crawler's circuit. Once she had been miked up she would make it very plain that she was touting for business, then they would stop and the trap would spring.

She checked her watch again, a small frown on her face. The van didn't normally take this long. The road was very quiet, all the big old houses set back behind their stone walls seemed deserted. A small shiver of alarm went through her. She felt very much alone.

Where the hell was the van?

Suddenly the silence was broken by the sound of a vehicle turning into her road off the main street. It sounded like something larger than a car. Paula stepped out of the shadows to get a better look as the lights approached her. She watched anxiously as the vehicle made its way slowly towards where she was standing. It was only a few yards away when she breathed out a sigh of relief and hailed it.

It was a large, white, unmarked Transit.

In the vehicle depot the two Detective Constables were searching frantically for jump leads. Over the weekend the van had been parked with its lights left on and the battery was dead. By the time a set had been located and a car manoeuvred into a position from which the leads would reach the van, they realised that Paula had been out for half an hour with no back-up.

234

They drove across town as fast as the van would go but their hearts sank as they turned into the quiet road on which Paula was keeping station. Even though the street lights cast pools of shadows under overhanging trees, the road looked deserted. They drove slowly along peering into gateways and every dark corner which could be hiding her, but at the end of the road they exchanged grim glances.

The driver picked up the radio and raised the desk sergeant back
at the station.

"Operation Honeypot here Sarge. We've got a problem."

As soon as the van pulled up beside Paula, she approached the driver's door.

"About time!" she began. "Where the hell have you. .?
She got no farther.

The door was suddenly pushed open violently, hitting her with savage force and knocking her backwards off her feet. She lay on the pavement, fury and bewilderment roiling in her dazed mind. But before her head could clear a cloth was pushed firmly over her nose and mouth and held down hard. It had an overpowering smell which was somehow familiar. Chloroform? Even as she began belatedly to struggle a part of her mind wondered professionally who would be using that stuff in this day and age? A young man's face came into view above her, he was looking down with calm disinterest and it was the image of his clean-cut features, so at odds with the situation, that Paula took down into darkness with her.

And when she came round she was sitting in darkness, but it was a swaying, moving darkness. She blinked her eyes until they began to focus and tried to bring a hand down to rub them but found she couldn't. She tugged harder, what were her hands doing above her head anyway? There was a pain in her wrists as she struggled and she heard the clink of metal. She was handcuffed!

Now for the last sight of the Victorian Scrapbook, Vignettes from a Sterner Age by Stephen Rawlings, the author of Jane and Her Master

LETTER FROM YOUNG LADY TO HER BOSOM FRIEND.

Darling Pippa,

As I solemnly promised, I take up my pen to tell you more of my reception at Madame Turinger's Select Academy for Young Ladies. If I sound a trifle breathless I have good reason.

Darling, I have been put in stays!! What, you cry, did you not wear them back in England? Why yes, I did wear something that carried that appellation but, here in the Helvetian Republic, the Swiss order things quite differently. What you and I wore are as bodices for babies compared with the rigour of what now encases me.

I cut short my first letter to you, to answer a summons to Madame's room, which one does not delay to answer, or risk her wrath and her rod. Ugh. I have felt it already, and will take care to avoid it in future, at all costs, for she cuts like a razor, but that is another story.

The reason for my presence before her was to be assessed as to what special forms my 'finishing' might take. On beholding me out of my travelling clothes, she threw up her hands in horror and exclaimed, "Quel horreur! This is intolerable. How is it, ma petite, that you have been allowed to reach the age of seventeen years without your waist and figure being formed as fashion and decency require? Do you not have stays in your barbarous Angleterre?"

I will admit to you I was most taken aback by this attack, not only on myself and my figure, but on our country, and replied rather stiffly that I wore my corset continually during the day, and that no person of intelligence would insult our country by calling it barbarous.

Madame informed me that I was wrong on both counts, and that my impertinence would cost me dear, but first it was her duty to rectify immediately what she considered lacking in my training. While we awaited the arrival of her housekeeper, for whom she had immediately sent, she informed me that the pupils of her school were sent out into the world with eighteen inch waists at most, a figure that might be spanned by a strong man's hands. No young woman, she informed me, could possibly hope to make a suitably advantageous match, with a man who would support her in the highest echelons of society, which was where her clientele were destined, with a more coarse and heavy centre and, though I had been given into her hands desperately late, she intended to see to it that I did not let her or her establishment down.

At this point the housekeeper arrived, and Madame gave her certain instructions, including the need to communicate urgently with one Madame Polcvinsky, who I gathered was corsetiere to the school, and to fetch one of the training corsets that might suit my present lamentable shape. I did protest lightly again, at this reflection on my figure, but Madame silenced me with a glance, and promised to attend to what she called my forwardness, when she had attended to my figure.

And then, Darling, I had to strip before her! Really, truly, I do not exaggerate. I was made to remove my clothes until I stood before her in my stockings and my shift. Can you imagine my humiliation at having to display myself thus before two older women who were practically strangers! Moreover I had to raise my hands above my head, while the housekeeper ran a tape measure over me, and pronounced my waist to be twenty-four inches, a result that produced a snort of such derision and scorn from Madame that I could have wished the floorboards might split asunder and let me fall through into darkness night.

The training corset was applied. It fitted me tightly from below my bosom to my hips, fine canvas cloth of denime with steel bones and stout laces. From the first it gripped me like a vice, not the comforting embrace of my own stays, but a grip like a giants fist, for it was cut to press on my waist and, with the housekeeper working the lace, loop by loop, its grip increased until I thought my ribs would crack.

At this point Madame ordered her to stop.

"It does not do to make the laces too tight to start with,"

she remarked. "Leave it loose for now, but take up the slack a little before supper, and again before the girl retires."

If I could have gasped I would have done in horror. As it was the tightness around my chest and belly left me little breath for speaking but my mind raced at her words. If this was 'loose', or 'not too tight', what could she intend for later?

Dismaying as those thoughts were, they were soon driven from my head by a more immediate cause for consternation. Before she would permit me to dress again, Madame recalled me to my impetuous and impertinent remarks regarding the barbarity of England, and my rejection of her estimate of the worth of my poor figure. Without reawakening in myself the pain and humiliation of the events that followed by going into every detail, much as I know you would relish each second of my sufferings, I will tell you that I was made to lean forward from the waist at a steep angle, wish my hands clasped on the back of my neck. The fear some grip of the training corset in which I had been placed not only lifted my breasts hugely in front, but caused my derriere to project strongly behind. Madame took a horrid length of whalebone, I suspect she obtained it from the stock Madame Plocvinsky uses to fashion her corsets, and brought it down in vertical slashes, to cut me on the most prominent part of my anatomy.

Darling it hurt so, you can't imagine. Nothing Miss Cattermall did to us in the schoolroom can compare to it. And none of that lovely warm juicy feeling afterwards, either, that made us want to curl up together under the covers, and kiss each others wounds. When Madame cuts down like that it feels as if she has sliced you with a razor and, indeed, I bled a little from one, as I discovered later.

Six times she cut me, and I howled at every one, though I dared not move, for she had promised me that I would get more than 'this little dose' if I did. I wept till it was time for the housekeeper to come to my room, before supper, and tighten the lace further. I did not think it could be done, I was almost breathless as it was, but she put her foot against my back, and worked the laces even tighter.

After supper she came again. This time, after ensuring

that my belly was quite emptied into the night pot, she placed a ruler in a loop of the lace and twisted it, gaining even more purchase before she tied it off. I must wear it like this all night. My bottom aches from sitting at the writing desk, my lungs long for air. It is time to blow out the candle. Think of your poor friend, caned and corseted, with aching belly, and throbbing bot toms. You are enjoying it you beast, I know you are. Why do I love you, Your Sophie.

We hope that you have enjoyed the extracts from The Victorian Scrapbook. Eventhough this is the last time that you will see them in the bonus pages, never fear, they have been so popular that we have plans to publish even more as a complete title.

Look out for it in the Millenium!

NB: Just to reassure our loyal followers that we are not short changing you, what we are doing is increasing the length of all our future titles to 75,000 words of non-stop erotic action!

TITLES IN PRINT

Silver Moon

Silver Mink

UK £4.99 except *£5.99 --USA $8.95 except *$9.95